MISERY, MUTINY
& MENACE

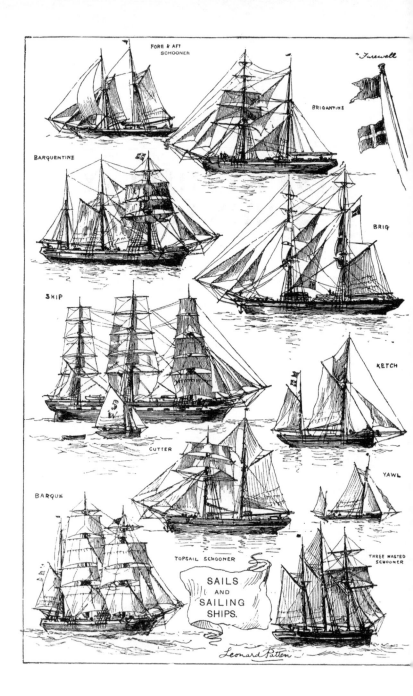

SAILS
AND
SAILING
SHIPS.

FORE & AFT SCHOONER
BRIGANTINE
"Farewell"
BARQUENTINE
BRIG
SHIP
KETCH
CUTTER
YAWL
BARQUE
TOPSAIL SCHOONER
THREE MASTED SCHOONER

Leonard Patten

MISERY, MUTINY
MENACE

Thrilling Tales of the Sea

Volume Two

GRAHAM FAIELLA

The
History
Press

First published 2019

The History Press
97 St George's Place, Cheltenham,
Gloucestershire, GL50 3QB
www.thehistorypress.co.uk

British Library Cataloguing in Publication Data.
A catalogue record for this book is available from the British Library.

ISBN 978 0 7509 9085 1

Typesetting and origination by The History Press
Printed and bound in Great Britain by TJ International Ltd.

CONTENTS

PREFACE

'... and the great shroud of the sea rolled on as it rolled five thousand years ago.' (from 'The Chase – Third Day', Ch. 135, *Moby Dick,* or *The Whale*, by Herman Melville [1819–91])

The possibilities of danger, menace and death have always been closer to the lives of salt-water seafarers than to the rest of us clay-footed commoners. And even greater in the times of the deep-sea wind-ships that in their thousands and by their tens and hundreds of thousands of seafarers sailed Melville's – Ishmael's – 'watery part of the world'.

From the shallowest edges along continental and island coasts, to the abyssal depths of the great oceans and seas, peril has always stalked the shadows of sailors who have voyaged thereabouts. Nature has sunk ships and drowned their occupants, ripped the rigging out of ships, battered ships into wrecks, knocked ships' seafaring crews senseless and cast them away upon foreign and savage shores. Calm, windless weeks and months, and the gradual diminution of food and water, have, on wind-ships at least, brought such desperate hunger that men have looked even upon their shipmates as a last shake of the dice resource for survival.

The natural perils of the sea were known and, though feared, largely accepted as hazards of their trade by those who made their lives in ships. Seamen, and passengers, could be sickened by fevers from tropical ports, assaulted by storms, maimed or killed by accident, even ripped away from the security of their vessels by mishap or storm or a fog-shrouded coast or by collision with another ship. But there was also the unnatural danger of other men: 'savages' who attacked them in foreign lands, and brutal shipmates, especially ships' officers, who inflicted lawless misery upon their bodies and minds and souls.

Discipline in a ship was one thing (and absolutely necessary for the safety of the ship and her crew). And violence and brutality amongst hard-bitten crews did oftentimes bloody noses and stain the decks of their water-borne homes. But the unmeasured malevolence and crushing cruelty that some ships' captains and *bucko* mates sometimes inflicted on ordinary sailors was of a different magnitude altogether: it was bestial, what we might today even call psychopathic. Few perpetrators were ever held to account for what was usually perceived by the landlubberly judiciary to be a necessary regime of seagoing discipline whose boundaries were ill-defined – if at all.

The sea itself held the terrors of drowning of men, most of whom deliberately never learnt to swim so that they might sink quickly, mercifully, into the black embrace of the depths. Sometimes a ship might be able to haul a man back to safety, but many more did not; in the teeth of a howling

gale or tumultuous seas, they simply could not. A man –
or men, sometimes half the crew – swept overboard had
less chance of returning alive to a ship than of escaping the
hard-knuckle assault of a brutal mate with violence spliced
into the very sinews of his vicious being.

I

DESPERATE VOYAGES

As many seamen who crewed sailing ships before the twentieth century did so out of desperation to escape lives of poverty, criminality and unremunerated idleness, as they did for the adventure of seafaring and ambition of going to sea as a career. A shore life presented to many of them the prospects of a foreshortened existence from not much in the way of any prospects at all. What they did not, could not, know at least at first, was that a seafaring life often led to the bare-knuckled fists of fate knocking them around mercilessly, trampling over them by the violence of storms or treachery or just bad luck. It blighted many, and sent as many others to Davy Jones' locker.

The strongest, or luckiest, or most resilient of sailors lived to fight another day; to struggle against the raw nature and indomitable forces of the sea and the wind and the elements, and also, not least, snarly shipmates they encountered along that way; cursed and scathed and scarred, but not, finally, undone by the indifference and sometimes pure terror of their plight. Life, somehow, won the skirmish against death, not once but a thousand times, though it left in its wake derelicts of desperation that, by the buoyancy of fortitude and courage, refused to founder.

A South Seas Cruise of Piracy, Treachery and Murder

In June 1831 the barque *America* was wrecked on a reef off the 'Loo Islands' on the Queensland coast of Australia while on passage from Hobart, Tasmania, to Batavia (Jakarta). Her castaway crew sailed in two boats 250 miles down the coast to Moreton Bay, off Brisbane, where there was at the time a penal settlement for hard-core criminals (the Moreton Bay Convict Settlement, which closed in 1835). They arrived there on 27 July 1831. The schooner *Caledonia*, under the command of Capt. George Browning, was sent from Sydney up to Moreton Bay to retrieve the *America*'s two boats. She left Sydney on 16 December 1831 and arrived at Moreton Bay on 24 December.

Prisoners from the convict settlement were used to tow the two *America* boats 40 miles from Brisbane to where the *Caledonia* lay at the mouth of the bay. The prisoners then hatched a plan to steal arms and ammunition from the pilot's house and seize the *Caledonia*. In the middle of the night eleven men rowed out to the *Caledonia* and took over the vessel. They put the *Caledonia*'s crew (except Capt. Browning) in the boat they had come in, and 'let them do the best they could with only the steer oar' to get ashore. Capt. Browning was forced into the charge of navigating the vessel to the island of Rotuma, on the outer edge of the Fiji Islands.

The leader of the pirates was John Evans ('one of the greatest villains under the sun', Capt. Browning later wrote), nominated chief mate. A man named Hastings (called 'John

Imgan' in Capt. Browning's memoirs) was second mate. On the eighth day out from Moreton Bay two of the pirates were killed and a third, under threat of also being shot, jumped overboard. The life of a fourth man was spared, on Capt. Browning's urging that no more killings take place.

Wanderings

The *Caledonia* first put into a place on the coast of New Caledonia, where Hastings was left, his first option, to be shot, being rather less desirable to him. They then sailed to Rotuma (annexed in 1881 to Fiji, but at the time a solitary island to the north of the main cluster of Fiji islands) where one of the convicts absconded, leaving six pirates and Capt. Browning on the *Caledonia*. Next stop was intended to be Wallis Island, but they bypassed it and 'steered for the Navigator's Group (Samoa Islands)', where they landed upon the island of Savaii (probably – the name was uncertain), one of the two big islands of the Samoan archipelago. Three pirates who had become allies of Capt. Browning then left the vessel which was scuttled offshore.

The three remaining pirates and Capt. Browning went ashore at Savaii where an island chief, Tongalore, took Capt. Browning to live with him and his family. A few weeks later an English whaling ship, the *Oldham*, arrived off the island. When Capt. Browning went on board to trade on Tongalore's behalf, he discovered his piratical nemesis Evans on the ship. The captain narrated the events of the 'piratical seizure of the schooner at Moreton Bay' to the *Oldham*'s master, Capt. Johnstone, who consequently clapped Evans in irons.

The *Oldham*, with Capt. Browning on board (and Evans 'in irons'), sailed for Wallis Island. There they came across an American vessel, the *Milo*, looking for crew for their passage to Sydney. Capt. Browning persuaded the *Milo*'s Capt. West to take him and Evans on board to go to Sydney. Evans jumped ship, Capt. Browning went alone, and four weeks later, in July 1832, the *Milo* arrived at Sydney.

Thus ended the six-months'-long 'cruise' and adventures of the ill-fated *Caledonia* and her brave commander Capt. George Browning – who later learned of his narrow escape from an even more awful fate of the *Oldham* at Wallis Island shortly after he left in the *Milo*:

A Tale of Adventure in the South Seas – Mutinies and Massacres

A few weeks ago we published a paragraph reporting the death in Sydney of Captain George Browning, brother of Mr. Samuel Browning, of Auckland, and brother-in-law of John Ericson, the renowned civil engineer, the inventor of the Monitor [the USS *Monitor*, 'a revolutionary armored ship with the world's first rotating gun turret,' launched 30 January 1862].

Amongst the papers of the deceased gentleman is a journal of a voyage to the South Sea Islands in the schooner *Caledonia*, belonging to Sydney. This is of very considerable interest, as showing the events and actors in those early days:

Capt. Browning's Journal of the Voyage of the Caledonia
'Sixteenth December, 1831, sailed from Sydney in the schooner *Caledonia* for the inside passage of Torres Straits, "Loo Islands," to pick up the wreck of the *America*, and proceeded to the northward, with variable winds, intending to go to Moreton Bay [off Brisbane] (at that time a penal settlement) for two boats left there

by the ship's company. On the 24th December, arrived at Moreton Bay, and communicated with the authorities. Captain Fyans, the commandant, ordered the two boats to be sent down from Brisbane to the Heads, where the vessel was lying. It took some time to bring down the boats; the boats, being so dry, they would not float.

'At that time the pilot was a free man, and his boat's crew were prisoners, generally termed convicts. There were also three soldiers stationed at the pilot's house. It took three large Government boats to tow the boats down from Brisbane, a distance of forty miles. On the third day the boats arrived, with the commandant of the settlement, about six o'clock, p.m., and it was made up amongst the convicts to try and take the vessel.

'It was known to the convicts that the pilot had arms in his house; and about 2 a.m. the men made a hole outside the house, and, tunnelling under it, came into the middle of the room without noise, and got five muskets and some sabres, besides some ammunition. When this was effected, they without delay secured the pilot boat, and, after taking all the spare oars from the other boats, they started for the vessel. It was unusually foggy that morning, and eleven men rushed on board, and told me to get the vessel underweigh as fast as I could.

'Some of the pirates that belonged to a pilot boat at Newcastle knew me there when I used to trade, and pointed me out to the others. There was a light wind blowing from the westward, and it took some time to get over the bar. During this time my crew were below, and a sort of council sat to decide what to do with them, when it was decided to put them in the pilot boat that the pirates came off in, and let them do the best they could with only the steer oar, the other oars being taken out of the boat.'

Captain Browning Given Charge

'When all my crew were in the boat, I made a spring over the stern to get into her, but the pirates got hold of me, and drew me back, telling me they had not done with me. The vessel then stood off the land. When about thirty miles away, I was asked to take charge, and select two officers from amongst the pirates. I told them I knew little about navigation for so long a voyage as they intended, which was to Rotumah, an island frequented by English sperm whalers and also American ships. The answer I received from them was they would soon teach me. After a while I told them I would do the best I could, if, in the event of being successful, they would behave well to me. They made all the promises imaginable, and said they would.

'We steered to the eastward, and in our track an island appeared to be laid down, called Sir Charles Middleton's Island. I told them if it was there we should see it, but in the old charts many reefs and islands were laid down that did not exist; and we, of course, did not see it.'

Murder

'On the eighth day after leaving Moreton Bay, the three men living in the cabin with myself called me about three o'clock in the morning, and told me something was up, and we were to get the arms ready. The arms had been taken into the cabin for safety some time before. I told them not to be rash, and do nothing rashly. One of the pirates told me not to say a word, or I should be the first to fall. He asked me whether I would stick to them, and I answered, "Yes," but begged them to do nothing rashly. He then ordered me to load my gun, which I did with a heavy charge – enough to kill two men. When I had completed that, I was told to take the helm, and the man that was there before went down below.

'It was now four o'clock, and the parties they wanted to kill were in the forecastle. From what I could make out, some of the pirates had felt dissatisfied at not sighting the island, and proposed to heave me overboard, and run the schooner on a certain course, and chance what they would fall in with. This, with some old grudges, was no doubt the origination of the mischief.

'The names of the men living in the cabin with myself were: John Evans, chief mate; John Imgan [*sic* – Hastings], second mate; and an old man as steward, called George. Evans then went forward, and called up a man, by name McDonald, and said to him, "Are you as good a man as you were last night?" McDonald answered, "Yes," and he then put a pistol to his head and shot him through the forehead, and he laid half on deck and half below.

'Another man (William Vaughan) was called up, and the second mate [Hastings] undertook to quiet him, and fired at him between the luff of the foresail and the mast. He shot two of his fingers off as he held up his hands to his head, and he fell on deck. They then got hold of him, and threw him overboard. On passing astern, he caught the reef pendant hanging in the water, which was immediately cut by the steward.'

O'Connor Overboard

'The next man they called up was John O'Connor. When he saw what was going on, he told them not to fire, as he would jump overboard, and began to strip himself. When naked, he said, "God have mercy on you all," jumped overboard, and swam in an opposite direction the vessel was steering, and never, to my knowledge, looked round. A fourth man was called up [John Smith], but, as by this time I was nearly mad, I called out that we had had enough of it, and got the first and second mates in a line with my gun, and, after some little talking, they let him off with a caution. From that hour he was one of my fast friends, and did what I could to lighten the misery I was in.

'After this business, they washed the deck, and called the other four on deck, and eventually retired into the cabin, where they drank a quantity of grog, and then knocked out the bung of the rum cask, saying it was the cause of all the mischief; so there was a chance of getting along better than before.'

At New Caledonia

'We now steered for New Caledonia, and on the sixteenth day after leaving Moreton Bay we made the land about sundown, and hove-to till the morning alongside the reef. At daylight we were looking for the entrance to Port St. Vincent, and about noon we discovered an opening in lat. 22.5 south, which we entered, and beat up. We brought up at 6 p.m. at the head in three and a-half fathoms of water. As we wanted water, we sent the boats away the next morning to look for it. During the time the boat was away, some natives came off in canoes. We would not allow them to come on board, so, after some bother with them, we thought it best, as we could not see our own boat, to fire over their heads, which drove them away.

'Not seeing our own boat coming, as it was getting late, we thought it best for the safety of the vessel to get underweigh, and stand out to sea for the night, which we did. We stood out to sea, and beat to windward all night, and next day we found ourselves much farther to windward than we expected, there being a strong current setting to the northward. Bore up for the harbour again. At 4 p.m. saw our boat pulling towards us. They had been outside looking for us. At 6 p.m. brought up at the old spot.'

Confrontation With Natives
'The following day one of the natives came on board, and, not being allowed to get into his canoe, became rather furious. I begged them to land him, which we did. We then manned the boat to get water, but found so large a number of natives that it was agreed to let them see the power we possessed. We were in the mouth of a creek, and found the natives all armed with bows and arrows. Being in a whaleboat, we sterned out into deep water, followed by the natives, and were very nearly cut off.

'We then considered what was to be done. After a consultation, it was agreed to fire at them, as we wanted water, and dare not go ashore for it. About 1,000 men had congregated to annoy us. After a few discharges, the natives all ran into the bush, and we went on board again. One old chief stood his ground behind a canoe, and after some time we beckoned him to come to us, no other natives being in sight. We exchanged a tomahawk for his club, which gave him great satisfaction. We tried to make him understand that we wanted water by dipping a pannikin into saltwater and throwing it out again, after tasting it.

'On the following day we went into the boat, and pulled to the creek again, where we met the old chief with two men. We also saw some more natives not far off, and we told the old chief to send them away, which he did. We then formed a line to the watering-place, all armed, and with the three natives, we got four casks of water. We paid the old chief for his assistance, and went on board.

'That night the second mate [Hastings], who had been away in the boat the night we went outside, told the rest of the boat's crew he would destroy any of us if he saw us again; and when this was told to Evans, the first mate, he decided to let him have the option of being shot or landed on the island. He preferred the latter, and the next morning was landed with a bag of bread and a pistol without a cock to it.'

At Rotumah

'The next day we started, and made sail for Rotumah, four men out of the eleven that took us being accounted for, eight being left with myself. We had a long passage to Rotumah, having no chart. We had to take the latitude and longitude out of the Epitome [navigation manual], and make a sort of outline chart. The weather being rainy and thick, my position was fearful. However, I told them one evening that it was likely we should see the land in the morning, which most fortunately we did, as my observations told me that I would not be safe much longer.

'All hands were so overjoyed at the sight of land that I thought they would have eaten me, the chief mate (Evans) saying I ought to be an admiral. He was one of the greatest villains under the sun.

'About 10 a.m. we anchored in the usual place, and a man called Emerey (a Yankee) that was living there, came on board (I was put out of sight when any stranger came on board), and had a conversation with the pirates, and some of the men went on shore, leaving two armed men to look after me. At 4 p.m. a ship was seen in the offing, steering for the island, when the men on shore came on board in a great hurry to get underweigh and go to sea. They had seen an old convict on shore that told them not to trust me, and that dead men told no tales. Consequently I found what I had to trust to. The name of this vagabond was John Ready.

'During the run at night I had taken the bearings of the ship, and run right for her. About 8 p.m. one of the men shouted out that the vessel was close to us. I was at the helm, and thought it likely the ship would run over us, and I might escape by jumping into the water; but the man forward gave the alarm too soon, and we passed on. The name of the ship I afterwards found was the *Warrens*, Captain Bliss.'

Samoa

'The next place I was told to go to was Wallis Island, and I started for it; but, noticing a difference in the behaviour of the men in the cabin, I thought I would miss this place. About 18 or 20 hours out of the 24 I was at the helm, as none of the pirates could steer at all, or very little, so I had a large share of the helm.

'About five days after leaving Rotumah, where one of the men ["a man called Harry"] had run away from the boat, making five altogether, and six and myself left, it came on to blow very hard from the northward. We ran as long as we were able, but the sea rose so terribly that we were obliged to heave the vessel to. We lay very uneasily for some hours, shipping much water, when the pirates got frightened, and asked me if nothing could be done. I told them we should all go to the devil together, but, after much persuasion, I altered the sails so that she was very easy; so much so that when the weather became finer they told me I did it purposely, and threatened me accordingly.

'I passed Wallis Island at night, and said the current was running very strongly. I steered for the Navigator's Group [Samoan Islands], and six days after passing Wallis Island we saw very high land. Shortly after two more islands were sighted. [The island landfall they made and eventually landed upon was probably Savaii, the largest of the Samoan Islands.]

'I felt very bad on seeing the land, knowing that the pirates could steer for the shore as well as I could. I omitted to state that Evans had insisted on my learning him how to keep the vessel's way. The only thought that struck me was to say that all the natives were cannibals, which did for a time. Shortly we had a visit from some white men that lived on the islands, who told us the natives were friendly, and that several English whalers came there during the year.'

Allies

'As the provisions began to run short, and no chance of getting a fresh stock, it was decided by the pirates to scuttle the vessel, and go on shore. It appears that I had some three friends among the pirates. Their names were William Hogg, Thomas Watson, and John Smith. These men took the first opportunity to leave the vessel, and left me with the three in the cabin. (On the 20th of Feb. she [the *Caledonia*] made Davi [Savaii], where John Smith was landed, together with the three Rotumah women [picked up at that island]. Watson and Hogg also, acting under the dread of personal violence from Evans and the rest, got into a canoe, went on shore, and remained behind.)

'When I understood they intended scuttling the vessel, I begged hard of them to leave me the vessel, and for them to go on shore; but they said I should be miserable by myself, and it would be better for me to go on shore.'

Scuttling The Vessel

'A great deal of secrecy was practised now among them, and one of them, in leaving for the shore, told me to try and save my life, and not beg for the vessel, as they intended to go ashore without me. I expected something of the kind would happen from their altered conduct, and the night previous to sinking the vessel was one of great anxiety to me. They had taken everything off the deck that I could defend myself with, even to the cook's axe, and left nothing for me but the tiller, which I took out to see if I could handle it. I watched very anxiously the men that were down in the cabin, making up my mind to be on the alert with the tiller as soon as I heard or saw any firearms brought out, but nothing transpired during the night.

'At daylight it was resolved to commence to sink the vessel. The boat was launched, and one of the men went down with a crowbar to make a hole; and after some time working he asked me to come down to assist him. I went willingly to see what sort of a hole it was, so that I might plug it up if left by them by myself. During the morning the wind was right, and three men would have been ample to have pulled on shore; but just as the vessel was half-full of water the breeze became very strong, and they called me out of the hold to make four in the boat, and we pulled for the shore.'

It wasn't clear at this point whether the boat with Capt. Browning, the head pirate Evans and his brethren went ashore at Savaii, or made the rather long pull in the boat almost 400 miles to the south to put ashore at the Tongan island of Tofua: '... and about 12 o'clock on the following day the vessel was scuttled, and the whole party got into the boat, and stood in for Toofoa [Tofua], where Mr. Browning and a man named Thomas Massey were taken by one chief, and Evans and Smith by another', as one report observed.

Later remarks ('We sailed for Wallis Island, and made it three days after leaving Samoa') suggested that the *Caledonia* was more likely scuttled off Savaii or a nearby Samoan island, and the men befriended by Samoans ('I must say that the treatment I got from the chief, his wife, and people was of the kindest, and Tongalore might well be called the Samoan gentleman'), rather than much further south in the Tongan group:

'About noon, when we had lost sight of the vessel, a large canoe came alongside, and the chief jumped out of the canoe, and got hold of the boat. Evans presented a musket at him, and I said if he was hurt every man of us would be killed directly on landing. He asked me what I would do to send him away, and I took a cutlass, and struck him across the fingers with it. He looked savagely at me, and went into his canoe again, and pulled for the shore.

'The canoe went much faster than our boat. We pulled for the shore, and, after a long pull of about 18 miles, landed in the mouth of a small creek. Immediately the boat got on shore, we were lifted on the shoulders of the natives, and carried up to the town with the crew in her. When they put down the boat, I saw the same chief I had struck sitting on a large stone by himself. When we got out of the boat, he beckoned me to come to him. I thought my time had come at last, as the first thing he showed me was his injured finger.

'After looking at me for a long time, he rubbed his nose against mine. I had my gun in my hand, intending to shoot some of them if anything was intended to be done to me in the shape of harm; but, after the rubbing of noses, I dropped the gun, and felt quite satisfied.

'In a short time I felt perfectly at home, being taken away from the rest of the pirates, and I lived with the chief, whose name was Tongalore, and his wife, Vatalla, who treated me on all occasions with the greatest kindness. They had only one daughter, a little girl of about 12 years old. In fact, the chief was one of the greatest warriors of the group, being married to the chief of Monono's daughter, the head chief of the Navigator's Islands. I was housed with the chief, and spent the time happily enough until one of the chiefs at Sautipitare came over and stole the boat we landed in. Tongalore got quite furious when made acquainted with the fact, and was obliged to be held down until his passion cooled.'

A Tense Exchange
'The chief of Sautipitare was the man whom the men that were my friends, who landed the day before the vessel was sunk, came ashore to, and thought that they had a right to the boat as well as ourselves. The white man then came up to me, and said that now I should be revenged on the men that remained in the cabin with me at sea; and all I had to do was to hold up my hand, and every one of the others would have been shot, as the three men had taken the guns from their chief for the purpose.

'I had great difficulty in making them reasonable, saying to them, "If the natives saw us murder one another, they would kill the survivors, finding us such bloodthirsty fellows." They at last seemed to understand me, and desisted, saying to the other pirates it would only be for a short time that I was amongst them, and then they would carry out their revenge. With this they went away with their chief home.

'About a week afterwards I was employed making ball cartridges and cleaning up and repairing some old guns that had been bought from the whalers for pigs. This was for the purpose of going to war with the same natives that stole the boat. The whole of the natives in the town went into a fortified camp, and the day was fixed to fight it out, which is the usual way of giving notice there.

'We had been in camp for a few days when I got a note from one of the opposite party, asking me not to fire on them in action, as they knew I was a good shot. I returned for answer that I had been very well treated by Tongalore, and I felt it my duty to fight for him, although much against my will, as those parties had shown such good feeling towards me. Shortly afterwards some news of peace arrived, and they returned the boat with many pigs to adjust the matter. I gained a good deal of popularity by this affair, although not firing a shot. I afterwards heard from the whites that peace had been made in consequence of the three men telling the chief that I should kill them all before any of them could get a shot at me, and they declined fighting.'

An English Whaler

'A few weeks afterwards the *Oldham*, an English whaler, came off the island, and Tongalore asked me to go on board to trade for him. I did so, and found Evans, the chief mate, on board as well. He, it appears, had got some liquor, and was very talkative. A white man, by name "Monono Tom," was on board also as trading master.

'Tom, being an escaped convict, was soon aware of Evans. He came to me when Evans was below bargaining with the captain for a pair of pocket pistols, and said, "I think matters were not right in the schooner you commanded." I said he was right, and told him all the particulars. He wanted to kill Evans with a cooper's hammer. I afterwards related to Captain Johnstone the piratical seizure of the schooner at Moreton Bay. In consequence Evans was put in irons on board the *Oldham*.

'After this I did not go on shore, and Tongalore came off to the whaler, when "Monono Tom" explained to him the circumstances of the taking and destruction of the schooner. He then brought two large canoes off loaded with native provisions to take me to Sydney, saying it would be hard if the parties in Sydney did not give me enough to return to Samoa, which I promised to do.

'I must say that the treatment I got from the chief, his wife, and people was of the kindest, and Tongalore might well be called the Samoan gentleman.'

Wallis Island

'I intended to go on board the first Sydney whaler we fell in with. We sailed for Wallis Island, and made it three days after leaving Samoa. When we got there we found several English whalers and American ships lying in the harbour. There had been a great revolution at Wallis Island. A half-caste named George Minini had come there with a body of Sandwich Islanders [Hawaiians], and put up a king of his own. This lasted for a few months, when one of the old King's men shot George Minini, and the old Government was reinstated, and matters went on as before. This had taken place a short time before we arrived in the barque *Oldham*.

'While there I was much annoyed at the behaviour of the *Oldham*'s crew and officers. In fact, there was too much grog used by every person on board. An American barque (the *Milo*, Captain West), was bound for Sydney to get a crew, as she was shorthanded, some of her crew being landed at Wallis Island for mutiny. I spoke to Captain West about a passage to Sydney for myself and Evans, and he agreed to take us. He was getting wood and water in at the time.'

Sydney Bound

'After three days I went on board the *Milo*, and found, on looking for Evans on board the *Oldham*, that he was nowhere to be found, so we sailed without him. I found that the *Oldham* would be the last vessel left in the harbour, and I strongly advised Captain Johnstone to get his arms in order, as some Samoan men had told me that the natives would take the ship when left by herself in consequence of her ill-treatment of the natives on shore. The greater part of the crew laughed at my caution, and I left them.

'The passage to Sydney in the *Milo* occupied four weeks, with the usual westerly winter gales. On the passage I got very ill with fever, and I am much indebted to Captain West for his kindness and attention to me, which enabled me to get well again. On arrival in Sydney Governor Bourke allowed Captain West to sell [whale] oil from his ship to pay expenses without charging him the duty of £36 10s per tun, which was the duty in the colony at the time.'

Massacre at Wallis Island

'It was fortunate that the *Milo* was bound to Sydney, as I found that the natives of Wallis Island, the day after we left, boarded the *Oldham*, and killed the whole of her crew of 36 men, and also 36 white men living on shore, as the natives said it would not do to let any of them live to tell the tale. Only one poor boy, by name Craven Nicholson, was saved. He was cut down, and fell down the cabin companion into a flour cask that partially stopped the blood from a deep gash in his head, and some two days afterwards he was taken by a girl, the daughter of King William, a chief of consequence, who claimed him as her own.' (*The New Zealand Herald*, 3 September 1887)

The Oldham Massacre

The British sixteen-gun sloop-of-war HMS *Zebra* was at Keppel Island (Niuatoputapu), in the Tonga islands, in May 1832, when her commander, Capt. Macmurdo, heard about the *Oldham*'s problems at Wallis Island to the northwest. On 14 May *Zebra* 'departed without delay', arriving at Wallis six days later. A boarding party from *Zebra* went on to the *Oldham*. A group of thirteen natives came off from shore, boarded the *Oldham*, and revealed that the islanders had massacred all the crew of the *Oldham* apart from the boy mentioned, Craven Nicholson. One of *Zebra*'s crew, Thomas Williams, was tomahawked and killed by the islanders who came on board the *Oldham* 'when there was an exchange of hostilities'.

With the help of a mate from a British vessel sunk there, *Zebra* was piloted through the reef into the lagoon of Wallis Island where they found the *Oldham* on fire 'which it was not possible to extinguish'. On 26 May, 'a communication was opened with Lavalore, the principal chief of the island'. The following day Lavalore and a party of attendants 'went on board *Zebra* with the only *Oldham* survivor Craven Nicholson'. They all sat down together to a feast.

'The king [Lavalore], as much out of curiosity probably as good humour, tried to eat with a knife and fork, to the great danger of his eyes, nose, and face, with which they were continually coming in contact.'

Capt. Macmurdo and some of his officers returned the visit to the island king the following day, and to find water and fresh provisions for the *Zebra*. After partaking of a ceremonial *kava*, Capt. Macmurdo demanded that Lavalore return all the articles the natives had stolen from the *Oldham*. He eventually recovered two chronometers, three whale-boats, arms and ammunition, and 'everything which had belonged to the *Oldham* worth carrying away'.

Attack of Retribution

In talks with Lavalore, it was revealed that the massacre of the *Oldham* crew was rooted in revenge. Five or six years before, a man named George Minimi, 'whose father was an American, his mother being a native of one of the Sandwich Islands [Hawaii], where he was born', arrived at Wallis with 'a number of adventurers'. He essentially took over the island and 'assumed the part of a despotic sovereign ... [and] violated the laws and customs of the islanders ... His last act of violence (about November 1831) was to invade the king's village, and carry off or destroy all the live and dead stock belonging to the villagers'. He also threatened the king's life.

The villagers, in consequence, rebelled, 'and in the midst of his [Minimi's] fancied security, his life paid the forfeit of his crimes. His followers were nearly to a man cut to pieces, and his property distributed over the island'. The *Oldham* arrived soon after, 'and the captain and crew commenced the same lawless and unjustifiable line of conduct'. It was therefore no surprise 'that the islanders had recourse to so severe a retaliation'.

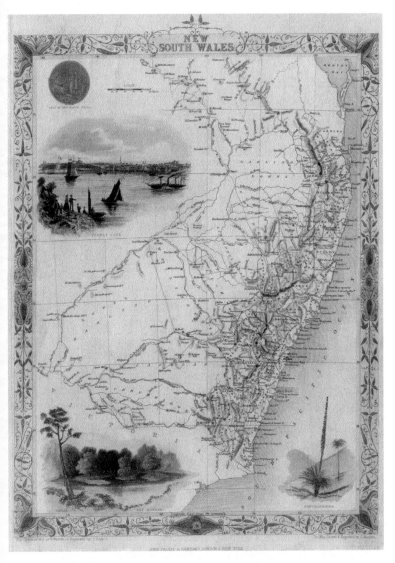

The coast of New South Wales – Moreton Bay is at top right.
(John Tallis, 1851)

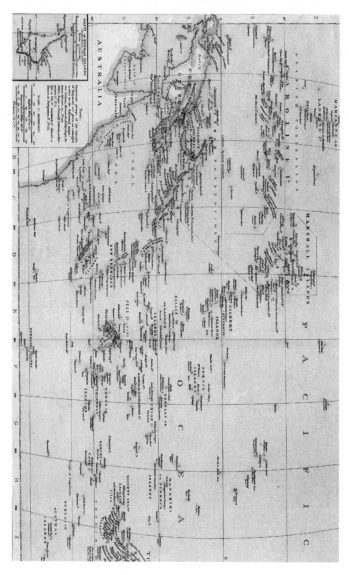

Map of Polynesia, *c.* 1900.

Lavalore denied any part in the attack; he blamed one of his chiefs, Tuccoroa, 'who was killed by the *Zebra*'s people, when the *Oldham* was first boarded by them'. In giving back *Oldham*'s properties to the *Zebra*, Lavalore 'fully expected that Tuccoroa's friends and relatives, who were the principal holders of this property, would kill him as soon as we [*Zebra*] left the island, which we did on the 3rd of June'.

Eingeborne der Insel Rotuma ('A group of Rotuma islanders'), *c.* 1830.

Ile Rotouma – *Indigenes appelant un navire étranger* ('Rotuma Island natives signalling a ship offshore'). (Firmin Didot for Domeny Rienzi 'Oceanie', Paris, 1834)

Kamp der schipbreukelingen ('Castaways' campsite') at Wallis Island. (*De Aarde en Haar Volken* ('*The World and Its People*'), 1886)

The *Frank N. Thayer* – Mutiny, Murders and Incendiarism

Towards the end of 1885 the American ship *Frank N. Thayer*, 1,600 tons, took on a cargo of hemp at Manila. Her master, Capt. Clark, was accompanied in the cabin by his wife and child. The number of souls on board totalled twenty-four. In the first few days of January 1886, the *Thayer* was 700 miles south-south-east of the island of St Helena, running up the South Atlantic on her return voyage from Manila to New York, having rounded the Cape of Good Hope, when two 'Manila men' amongst the crew mutinied and killed five crew members (the two mates, the carpenter, and two seamen). Eventually the other crew succeeded in re-taking control of the ship by wounding the two mutineers who both jumped overboard, though not before one of them set fire to the ship. Capt. Clarke and sixteen others abandoned the burnt and sinking *Thayer* in the ship's boat. They arrived at St Helena after five days of 'suffering all privation':

Mutiny, Murders, and Incendiarism on an American Ship

Accounts have been received of a terrible mutiny on board the American ship *Frank N. Thayer*. The outbreak was of a desperate character. The bloodthirsty conduct of the mutineers and the cowardice of the crew of the vessel are almost without parallel in the history of sea tragedies. The *Frank N. Thayer* was an American ship of 1,600 tons, which on the night of Saturday, the 2nd of January, was sailing with a fair breeze about 700 miles to the south-east of St. Helena, on her way from Manila, with a cargo of hemp for New York, when the mutiny broke out.

There were 24 persons on board at the time, including Captain Clarke, his wife, and child. The following is the captain's account of the mutiny:

'On Saturday, the 2nd of January, in lat. 25deg. S., long. 0.25deg. W., about midnight, two of the crew (Manila men), suddenly surprised the first and second mates while conversing on the booby hatch. Before the mates could answer they were both stabbed; the first mate ran forward to the forecastle, and died next morning at 5 a.m. The second mate ran into the cabin, and with a terrible cry to me, "Captain Clarke, Captain Clarke," dropped dead there.

'The mutineers then came to attack me (as I was aroused by the second mate) and coming out of the cabin to see what was going on, I was stabbed all over the head. The man at the wheel might have saved me had he given alarm, but he was afraid to. I managed, however, to strike the mutineer, and knock him down, but from loss of blood could not follow up the advantage thus gained; the mutineer then arose, and, with another deep stab at me, ran out of the cabin, leaving me, as he thought, dead. The mutineers then barricaded the cabin, with my wife and child and a Chinese steward inside. My wife saved my life by quick attendance to my wounds.

'After this, the mutineers ran along the deck, saying the captain and mates were killed, and they were in charge; meanwhile, cutting and stabbing right and left, wounding four seamen who managed to get to the fore-castle. The mutineers then stabbed the carpenter, threw him overboard, and ransacked his chest for plunder. The seaman who was hiding in the bathroom peeped through an opening in the cabin, and saw the mutineers murder the man Maloney at the wheel and throw him overboard.

They next dragged a seaman named Antonio out of the carpenter's shop, and murdered him near the main hatch, and threw him overboard. They then went forward and battened the forecastle with 12 men inside – namely, four men dangerously wounded, first mate dying, and seven other seamen who, it must be presumed, stayed there through sheer fright.'

Mutineers in Control … Temporarily
'Thus, at 4 a.m. on Sunday, the mutineers had the whole vessel under their control, and having dragged the Chinese cook from the coal locker, they made him cook for them, threatening his life. They then tried all day Sunday to enter the cabin. My wounds having been dressed by my wife, I had strength enough to keep the murderers off with my revolver. I wounded one mutineer in the foot. I also armed the steward and seaman who had hidden in the bathroom with revolvers, and gave orders to fire as soon as a chance offered.

'On Sunday afternoon the cook (Chinese) watched his opportunity, and handed an axe through the forecastle window to the seamen. On Monday morning at half-past nine a mutineer was wounded by a shot from the cabin. I then chopped my way out, and the mutineer jumped overboard. At the same time the men broke out of the forecastle and one man came down from the rigging, having been there since Saturday night. The other mutineer had then been between decks for 15 or 20 minutes setting fire to the ship. A party of men then went below to hunt the remaining mutineer (the vessel being on fire). One of the crew, Henry Wilson, succeeded in wounding him in the shoulder, and the mutineer, taking advantage of the smoke and fire, escaped by the after hatch and jumped overboard.

'All efforts were then made to subdue the flames. The fire was fought for four hours with no success. At 8 a.m. on Monday two boats were got out, and one capsized. The wounded men and provisions, and the captain's wife and child were placed in the remaining boat, then the captain and ten men, making 17 souls. The boat remained near the vessel all night, and started for St. Helena at 10.30 a.m. On Tuesday morning the vessel was a mere wreck, with main deck and three masts gone.

'For a boat's mast we lashed three oars together; for sail we used blankets. We arrived at St. Helena harbour at midnight on Sunday, the 10th of January, after suffering all privation, being in an open boat for a week, with five men dangerously wounded on board, 17 souls all told. I am entirely unable to give any opinion as to the cause of the mutiny, except that it was a diabolical plot for rapine and murder, and presume that if they had killed all, as they evidently intended to do, they would, if picked up, pretend to be innocent men, and the only survivors of a dreadful mutiny that had occurred on board.' (*The Argus* [Melbourne], 22 March 1886)

It later emerged that Capt. Clarke's (and the chief mate's) tyrannical behaviour, particularly towards the two muti-neers, might have sparked the mutiny, the destruction of the *Thayer* and the killing of the five crew members. Seven of the crew who arrived at Boston, Massachusetts, in April 1886, 'gave detailed accounts of their brutal treatment' and stated that:

Captain Clarke and Mate Holmes were very abusive, and that was the undoubted cause of the mutiny. It was a common thing to hear the noise of beating and clubbing of sailors in the night, and this accounts for no notice being taken of the mutiny in which two men only were concerned until they had secured possession of the ship, which they held for more than twenty-four hours. The two Manilla men who committed the murders were frequently beaten, and it was the outrageous tyranny inflicted on them which led to their mutiny. (*Daily Alta California* [San Francisco], 11 April 1886)

The Disastrous Voyage of the *Roanoke*

On 22 August 1892 Arthur Sewall & Co., a great Yankee shipbuilder of Bath, Maine, launched the *Roanoke*. At 3,539 tons she was the largest wooden-built square-rigger of her day (and second biggest ever after the Bath-built *Wyoming*, 200 tons larger, in 1909). Her master was Capt. Joe Hamilton who 'had a known drinking problem', which was reflected in some observations on the ship by 'The Red Record' that detailed instances of cruelty on American vessels. She might also have been jinxed even before the start of her voyaging life from New York:

The first person to die aboard *Roanoke* was a ship's boy who fell into the hold at New York. His father, a small-town photographer from Ansonia, Connecticut, was told that he had been injured, and only learned the sad truth when he arrived at the ship. The Sewalls covered the $111.25 funeral expenses. (*Live Yankees: The Sewalls And Their Ships*, W.H. Bunting)

Roanoke's third voyage began on 20 June 1895, under Capt. Hamilton, from New York bound round the Horn for San

Francisco. It was to be a passage littered with injury and death by hard weather, hard luck, and misadventure, though the ship herself arrived at her destination largely unscathed. Capt. Hamilton's record of the voyage was as compactly sparse and terse as any ship's log. Observations by some of the crew were, unsurprisingly, somewhat more colourful.

Disasters And Deaths – Sixteen of the Crew of the American Ship Roanoke *Were Disabled – Battered Rounding the Horn – Two Sailors Fell From Aloft and Were Killed and One Was Lost Overboard*

Death and disaster seem to have followed the American ship *Roanoke* from the moment she left New York on June 20, 1895. The following is the captain's short but graphic description of the voyage:

From Capt. Hamilton's Log
'Sailed from New York June 20, 1895.

'June 29, G.W. Dobbins, a native of the United States, fell from the mizzen royal yard [usually the highest yard on any mast] and was killed instantly.

'Was forty days to the equator. Got the southeast trades in 5 N. and lost them in 18 S., and from there to 44 S. had very hard gales and heavy seas.

'August 26, latitude 42 S., shipped a heavy sea which disabled eight of the watch on deck.

'August 28, Oscar Spennet, a native of Finland, fell from foretopsail yard to the deck and was killed.

'August 28, B.G. Palm, a native of Denmark, fell from the foretopsail yard overboard and was lost.

'August 29, kept the ship off for Montevideo, having but eight men on deck. Could not fetch that port, so kept on for Rio de Janeiro. Arrived at Rio September 16 and put sixteen of the crew in the hospital, and sailed again October 28.

'Had strong easterly gales to 40 south. From thence to Cape Horn had variable winds and fine weather. Was thirty days from 50 to 50 [i.e. rounding Cape Horn, from 50° S in the Atlantic to 50° S in the Pacific]. Had strong westerly gales west of Cape Horn. Got the southeast trades in 33 south and 96 west and had them strong and carried them to 3 north.

'Was nineteen days from 50 south 80 west to the equator. Crossed the equator in the Pacific January 4 in 117 west. Got the northeast trades in 3.10 north and carried them to 22 north 128 west. From there to the Farallon Rocks [coming up to San Francisco Bay] had southerly winds and fine weather, with a very heavy swell from the southwest. Sighted Farallon Rocks January 21, 87 days from Rio and 213 days from New York.'

Quarantine

When the *Roanoke* was reported there was a flutter in the quarantine office, and Dr. Chalmers at once notified the Board of Health. The vessel was known to have been in Rio de Janeiro, and in that port both yellow fever and smallpox were epidemic. Dr. Williamson responded to the quarantine officer's call, and together they visited the ship. Not a single case of sickness was found on board, and in spite of the troublous times and the storms she had passed through the vessel looked more like a yacht than the biggest American merchantman afloat.

Captain Hamilton reported that while he lay in Rio de Janeiro there had been six deaths from yellow fever and 141 from smallpox, but as the vessel had been eighty-seven days on the way here and there was no sign of disease aboard, it was decided to allow her to enter.'

Harry Jones' Account

'From the day we left New York until we reached Rio de Janeiro we had nothing but hard luck,' said Harry Jones, one of the original crew, yesterday. 'When Dobbins fell, from the mizzen-royal a few days after we were at sea all the old-timers said the ship was going to have bad luck. For a couple of months, however, there was nothing to bear out the assertion, and then by all that's glorious if it did not come on us in a heap.

'It was along in August and the ship was making heavy weather of it. We were under snug canvas, but wave after wave was breaking aboard, and the watch on deck had hard work of it dodging the water as it swept from stem to stern. Suddenly a heavier one than usual came rolling along, and just as the warning cry came from aft it broke aboard, and the entire starboard watch was washed into the scuppers. When the watch below had been called and the disabled men cared for it was found that only three out of the eight were able to get around. Even those three had to take to their bunks next day, and they had to be left behind at Rio.'

Fall from Aloft

'Our troubles seem to have only just begun, however, as two days later Spennet and Palm were lost from the foretopsail yard. Spennet fell to the deck and was killed instantly, while Palm fell overboard and was never seen again. After that we ran into a succession of gales, and when we did finally reach Rio de Janeiro sixteen of the men had to be sent to the hospital. A more battered, disconsolate looking set of men I never saw leave a ship. The captain and the American Consul did everything possible for them, and they will reach home all right.

'It was the most disastrous and hardest voyage I ever made round the Horn, and I don't want another one like it. Strange to say the ship was damaged very little, but the crew made up for her escape.' (*San Francisco Call*, 24 January 1896)

'Aloft in a Gale'. (*Harper's Weekly*, 20 December 1873)

The *Craigmullen*'s Deathly 'Voyage'

The British barque *Craigmullen*, 760 tons, with a crew of twenty-five (including the master, Capt. Loades, two mates, and three apprentices), sailed from Liverpool in July 1894 for Port Natal (now Durban), in the then colony of Natal, now part of South Africa, to discharge cargo. From there she sailed to Java, Bangkok and Singapore. At her last port she took on a cargo of rice to deliver across the Pacific to Callao, Peru. She left Singapore at the end of June 1895 on a passage that would normally take two or three months. Subsequent events, however, were decidedly not normal.

Craigmullen's 'voyage' was actually a prolonged and death-littered drift across the Pacific that starved most of her crew. The less than a handful of survivors who arrived at the other side of the Pacific almost ten months later in March 1896 were reduced to skeletal shadows of their former selves from the privations, exhaustion, despair and terror of that ill-starred odyssey:

The Ship That Disappeared – Adrift for Ten Months

Strange indeed is the tragic story of the British barque *Craigmullen*, which sailed from Singapore in 1895 and mysteriously vanished. Nearly a year later she reappeared under dramatic circumstances, with three unconscious men on board in place of a crew of twenty-five.

The full narrative of her dreadful voyage is set forth for the first time by Captain E. [Edmund] G. Mann, who was the *Craigmullen*'s chief mate, one of the only two survivors of the ill-starred ship's company.

Capt. Mann's Story

'The *Craigmullen* was a barque of about seven hundred and sixty tons register, belonging to Liverpool. She carried a crew of twenty-five men. Leaving Liverpool in the middle of July [1894], we first went to Port Natal [Durban], and discharged our cargo. From there we sailed to Java, and thence to Bangkok and Singapore to load rice for Callao, Peru. To shorten the passage as much as possible, the captain decided to go south from Singapore, through the Straits of Sunda [between Sumatra and Java], depending upon the north-east monsoon to give us a shove along in the Pacific.

'Baffling winds [i.e. winds from all directions] met us almost from the start, first from the south, then south-east, and back to south and south-west. Finally, after six weeks' battering about, we were compelled to swing round and sail to the northward. Then the skipper decided upon the other extreme. Instead of trying to work the ship through the islands, he conceived the idea of running right up the Borneo coast, the whole length of the China Sea, and through the Bashi Channel [between Y'Ami Island of the northern Philippines and the southernmost tip of Taiwan].'

'Supernatural Calm'

'Under the circumstances this was a serious blow. On two occasions I overheard talk among the men of compelling the captain to put in somewhere. For already we were on short allowance. However, all talk of putting back came to an end with the dying out of the wind as we reached the latitude of the Bashi Channel. A dead, breathless calm, such as can only be met with in a tropical sea, succeeded the few days of spirited wind. And there we lay, lifeless as a log upon the water, which had the appearance of molten lead.

'Day succeeded day; week succeeded week; month succeeded month, and still the wind came not. Each morning the sun would rise out of the sea in the east, burn a path across the brazen sky, and sink in the west in endless, unchanging monotony. Oh, it was maddening – terrible! Sometimes we would furl the sails in the very hopelessness of despair. At other days we would have the boats out, and try, weakened as we were, to tow the ship anywhere, away from that accursed spot. By this time the food and water were doled out to us in just sufficient quantities to keep us alive. I wonder some of us did not go mad with thirst, hunger, or terror at this supernatural calm.'

Death and Stagnation

'Then the men began to fall sick. Too weak to help themselves, they lay down in corners, and passed into a sort of coma. The first to die was our youngest apprentice, a boy of fifteen, and one who, by his kindness of disposition, had endeared himself to all of us. It was Christmas morning, I remember, when he died – Christmas, of all days in the year, and what a Christmas!

'The captain was the next to go; he died raving. After that not a week passed without one man dying. Sometimes they went with quite a fluttering of the heart and a sigh; at others, shrieking in maniac fury and cursing with foam-flecked lips. I buried them all in the same grave – beneath the oily surface of that leaden sea.

'Words are too poor to picture the dreadful loneliness and deathlike stillness of our surroundings. Stagnation was everywhere – the sky was dead, the sea was dead, the very atmosphere seemed lifeless. Not even a bird came near us to give us an inkling that somewhere – Heaven only knew where – there was life and movement. But for the daily passage of the brazen sun through the heavens, scorching our starving bodies till the skin hung on our emaciated frames like dried-up parchment, we should have thought the world had ceased to revolve on its axis.

'From horizon to horizon the surface of the sea was thickly coated with some oily-looking substance that broke like glass when anything dropped into it. Animalculæ of every description abounded, and marine vegetation grew to the length of some inches around our water-line.

'For *one hundred days* this mysterious calm lasted – a hundred days of unspeakable horror and living death. Only once in all this time did we see a steamer's smoke, far off on the eastern horizon. When we beheld that smudge of vapour, it was pitiful to see those of our crew who were yet able to get about. Clambering with frantic shouts into the rigging, these poor, starving wretches called and beckoned with imploring hands and words. But the vessel passed on, and they descended and cowered in the scuppers, wild-eyed and chattering, cursing heaven and earth in their hopeless anguish.

'Why I did not go mad during this terrible time I cannot tell; how I kept my strength and health is another mystery. The captain was dead, and the weight of all these horrors was upon my shoulders. It was I who tended the sick, and, with the help of the second mate, buried the dead. It was I who doled out the meagre allowance of water, I who began boiling the rice in our holds when the last scrap of our own food had been shared out.'

Change of Weather

'But everything comes to an end, and so did that uncanny calm. It was the afternoon of the hundredth day that the coming change of weather made itself manifest.

'The first indication of what followed was given us by the barometer. I could plainly see the mercury falling. Then the sky darkened. A long, rolling swell, momentarily growing, rushed away from the eastward, and in it we rolled and wallowed. Heavens! How we rolled! Presently the sun was shut out, while overhead hung a pall of thick motionless clouds, seeming to rest on the mastheads of the ship.

'A typhoon was close at hand; we knew it. Our sailors' instinct caused us simultaneously to gaze aloft. Almost every sail was set, yet we could do nothing, for our crew were past work. What mattered it? If the masts went by the board when the wind came it did not matter to us now. If the ship turned turtle – well, we should be out of our sufferings all the sooner.'

Typhoon!

'Out of the blackness burst a vivid, piercing flash of light, seemingly composed of thousands of forked tongues. We waited for the crash to follow, but none came. Another blinding flash, this time from the west, forked out of the smoky blackness, wriggled down the wire backstays and vanished in the sea. Next came the thunder, bursting right overhead, shaking the ship till it felt as though she were splitting in two. Peal after peal rang out, and the air was filled with arrows of light, and with them came the rain. A moment more and the storm burst upon us in fiendish fury.

'Shrieking and howling, it struck us like an iron wall, tearing up the sea as it came into a tempestuous, whirling field of foam and spoondrift. Over went the ship till I made sure we would capsize; then, blending with the roar and rattle of the thunder, I heard the sharper cracking of breaking wood and steel, and the masts went overboard, broken off by the tops.'

Aftermath

'I need not describe the terrible time that followed. Suffice it to say that when the typhoon had passed, and I was able to get about, I found the *Craigmullen* a hopeless wreck. Deck-houses, boats, everything movable had been washed away. The masts and yards had been broken clear of the restraining rigging, luckily without hurting us, and had drifted away.

'In one way only had the elements been kind to us. The sea had broken in the top of a water-tank, which stood abaft the apprentices' house, without washing it overboard, and in the heavy rains it became filled with fresh water.

'Two more of our crew had died during the gale. I found them, poor wretches, huddled up under the break of the forecastle, where – probably too weak to help themselves – they had lain throughout the dreadful turmoil. We were now reduced to fourteen men all told; abject specimens of starving humanity whose clothes literally hung upon their skeleton forms, and whose wild, staring eyes showed the terror through which they had passed, and fear of the lingering death awaiting them.

'A little while longer and the inevitable happened – scurvy, followed quickly by a slow, virulent fever, and the men began to die more rapidly. I used every available drop of medicine in vain efforts to fight this dread sickness. Soon my stock was finished, and one and all of us sat down to await the fast-approaching end.'

The 'Vague Hope of Rescue' ...

'As each dreary, hopeless day dawned I, now almost too weak to walk, crept out on deck and gazed with fast-dimming sight round the horizon, in a vague hope of rescue. Afterwards I visited my patients, giving to those who could eat a handful of uncooked rice; to those who could drink a pannikin of rain-water. Those who had passed away the second mate and I dragged to the bulwarks and, with infinite labour and many rests, committed to the deep.

'So it went on until no one was left but three starving wretches out of a crew of twenty-five, waiting for the end. We lost all count of time. We scarcely ever spoke to each other; our moody thoughts were our companions, and our tortured minds dwelt on the ghosts of the past. Sometimes I found myself alone, lying on the poop, and I dreamt strange dreams of home and friends. These visions became more frequent, more incoherent, till at last I sank into oblivion.'

... and Resurrection

'The earliest recollection I have after this was a sound of voices. Before my eyes, dimmed and hazy, vague forms seemed to flit. The sun beat down upon my upturned face, the breeze blew in my hair.

'"It's salvage, right enough," said someone. "He is dead, and there is no one else here."

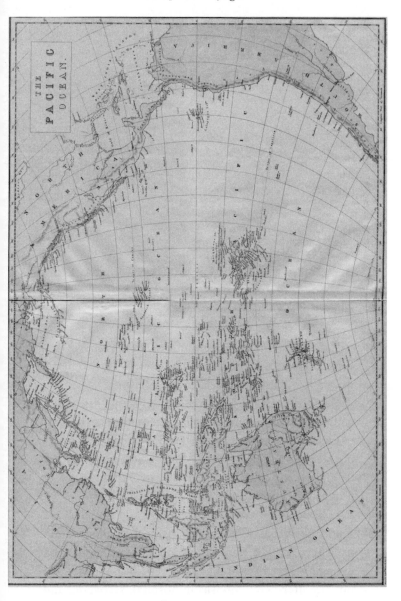

The Pacific Ocean. (*Blackie & Son*, 1883)

Ship in a storm.

'I stirred, trying to frame words to tell the speaker that I lived. Then I again became unconscious. When next I woke I found myself in bed, and in a hospital.

'We had drifted right across the Pacific, dismasted and derelict, to within three hundred miles north-west of Callao. Here we were sighted and picked up by a coasting steamer belonging to the Pacific Steam Navigation Company, and towed into port – strange to say, the very port to which we were bound!

'The second mate, the sailmaker and myself were found, all unconscious, yet still with a spark of life left in us. The sailmaker, poor fellow, died immediately upon eating his first mouthful of food. The second mate and myself, after many months in hospital, recovered and were sent home. As a reward for my services – that is,

A Gleam Of Hope – Drawn by S. Read. (*The Illustrated London News* Christmas number, December 15, 1875)

for being alive and thus saving the owners and under-writers some thousands of pounds – I was presented with a sextant.

'We had left Singapore in the month of May [*sic* – June], 1895; we were picked up in the month of March, 1896. We had been ten [*sic* – nine] months on that terrible passage – ten months lost to the world – the horrors of which I shall never forget.'(*Marlborough Express* [Blenheim, Marlborough, New Zealand], 21 September 1908; *Wide World Magazine*, August 1942)

2

WRECKED!

The seabeds, coasts and reefs of the world are littered with the skeletons of ships wrecked thereupon since time immemorial, each the result of a calamity of tempest, human error, or any vast number of phenomena that could strike a vessel, and its crew, into submission, defeat and destruction. Wrecks themselves might tell mute tales of how or why or where they came to be so. But survivors of wrecks tell tales of a personal narrative of fear and terror, and, finally, of hope and redemption from the chaos.

The *Reliance*: A Survivor's Story

Early in April 1868 a brig, the *Reliance*, out of Rockhampton, Queensland, struck upon one of three atolls, the Indispensable Reefs, in the Coral Sea south of Rennell Island in the Solomon Islands group. The crew and master, Capt. Horsman (or possibly 'Austin'), took to the brig's two

Posted At Lloyd's As Missing: Wrecked At Sea. (*The Illustrated London News*, 30 September 1911)

boats, a longboat and a whaleboat, abandoning the *Reliance* to their fate as castaways.

Curiously, or more likely deliberately, some reports about the wreck never mentioned that the *Reliance* carried a human cargo of Pacific Islands labourers – described pejoratively then as *kanakas* – which a survivor, William Benson, included in his narrative, below. *The Brisbane Courier* of 16 January 1869, *The Sydney Morning Herald* of 19 January 1869, and *The Sydney Mail* of 23 January 1869 also published reports of the wreck of the *Reliance* headlined 'In Quest of Kanakas'.

But *The Mercury*, of Hobart, Tasmania, published an earlier report by 'Captain Austin, owner and captain' of the vessel, on 19 August 1868, which said that the *Reliance*'s cargo 'consisted of ten tons cocoanut oil, one ton tortoiseshell, three tons pearl-shell, and a quantity of other shells and curiosities, and she was from the South Sea Islands bound for Sydney'. No mention of Pacific Islanders. Perhaps the other 'curiosities' were the *kanakas* mentioned elsewhere – but not by 'Captain Austin' in *The Mercury* because they were, perhaps, illicitly procured. Perhaps …

Castaways

Whatever the truth of the matter, the islanders took no further part in the narrative; they either drowned or drifted away on a raft, or made land somewhere. The two *Reliance* boats and crew stayed by the wreck for a few days, then headed west for Rossel Island in the Louisiade Archipelago to the south of New Guinea. After straggling around the islands thereabouts, skirmishing with the natives, and losing the whaleboat and her four crew in stormy weather, the longboat castaways (including Capt. Horsman) made it across to the Torres Straits at the northern tip of the York Peninsula. From there they hop-scotched southward down the Queensland coast along the Great Barrier Reef. By the end of May 1868 they were amongst the Claremont Isles, halfway down the York Peninsula. There they encountered and were rescued by the captain of a bêche-de-mer fishing schooner who eventually took them back to Sydney.

As for the whaleboat castaways, commanded by the *Reliance*'s mate, which disappeared in the squalls amongst the New Guinea islands, 'no word ever came, nor was any trace ever found, of the boat and crew of which the mate [who "had been married a little over twelve months, and his wife and one child are at present in Rockhampton"] sailed into the bay for shelter that threatening night':

Story of a Survivor from the Wreck of the Reliance

From a survivor of the wreck of the *Reliance*, lost on Indispensable Reef, on the 2nd April last [1868], we (*Rockhampton Bulletin*) learn the following particulars:

The survivor is a seaman, named William Benson, at present employed on board the schooner *Clara*, which leaves for Sydney to-day. The *Reliance*, Captain Horsman, sailed from Rockhampton [Queensland] for the Islands [i.e. Solomon Islands and thereabouts], for the purpose of securing about 200 Kanakas [originally the Hawaiian word for 'man', *kanaka* became the pejorative slang for any Pacific islander]. The vessel had 76 on board when she took the reef, about 4 a.m. on the date named above.

Castaways

The Kanakas rushed for the boats, two in number, but the captain, mates, and crew were beforehand with them, and under the captain's orders got away from the vessel; the only thing in the shape of provisions they had with them were 28 lbs. of bread [hard ship's biscuits] and a coffee-tin full of water; they managed also to secure possession of the firearms and ammunition that were on board.

On leaving the wreck they beat about within six miles of her for four days; during that time the Kanakas appeared to do nothing towards getting away from the wreck. Towards the end of the fourth day, those in the boats descried a raft bearing about fourteen of the niggers leaving the vessel. The raft drifted in a N.W. direction; the boats followed in their track, but night came on, and by the next day they lost sight of them. They were afraid to go back to the wreck lest the Kanakas might set upon them and kill them.

The captain decided on putting to sea, and the first land they made was Cape Deliverance [at the south point of Rossel Island in the Louisiade Archipelago], at New Guinea. The men went ashore for water, and to Benson and another fell the lot of remaining by the boats. The natives approached the men ashore, and, yabbering, passed their hands over the limbs and bodies of the men, selecting the stoutest. They failed to procure water, and the savages, after some palaver, made a rush for the boats. The men tumbled in pel-mel, and Benson, who had been previously in the mate's boat, now found himself in the captain's. They put off from the shore as fast as they could, but not before the steward received a spear in the leg.

There were then in the captain's boat – the captain, the second mate, his brother-in-law, Brown, and the steward (a Portuguese); while the party of the mate (Miles) consisted of himself, George McGregor (seaman), John Coventry (seaman), and another seaman named Harry.

The crew were now nine days out and had no water, the bread had run out within the four days after the vessel struck, and the men, to relieve intense thirst, cut up bullets of lead and chewed them. After quitting New Guinea they attempted to land on several of the smaller islands, but at every point they were met by the savage islanders, and obliged to keep off. They, however, succeeded in touching one of the smaller islands, and had barely time to cut a few sugar-canes, which were subsequently cut up into small pieces, and served out most sparingly.

Not being able to effect a landing, they resolved to put to sea; but it came on to blow, and towards evening the mate and captain determined to run for shelter under one of the islands; this was the seventeenth day from the wreck. The captain was in the long boat, and the mate in the other, which possessed more speed than the long boat.

The captain ran under the shelter of two small islands, and anchored; while the mate ran for a bay in a large island. The long boat being heavy and leaky, watch was kept; and about half-past 6 on the morning of the 18th, Benson, while on watch, saw two large war canoes full of savages, about forty in each, coming towards them from the very bay into which the mate and crew had gone the previous night for shelter. The remainder of the party were aroused and the boat freed from her anchor, and escape attempted. They set the sails, and plied with all their feeble strength at the oars. The natives pursued, and for an hour and a half were gaining upon them, but the breeze freshened a little, and for a time longer the natives did not make much closer to them. The breeze increased, and the savages, after continuing the chase for four hours, gave it up.

To the Queensland Coast

Every other island they came near they were driven away from, and they had nothing before them but to stand across Torres Straits. They were then in a most deplorable condition – weak for want of food, almost mad with thirst, emaciated, and covered with boils, which had broken out upon them a few days after they left the wreck. (*Empire* [Sydney, Australia], 23 January 1869)

From this point somewhere at the eastern end of Torres Straits, the castaways headed south, skirting the Cape York Peninsula and Great Barrier Reef, towards their intended destination of Cape Cleveland, near Townsville on the Queensland coast:

On crossing the Straits they sighted one of the Clermont Group [Claremont Isles, half way up the York Peninsula], a low sandy island with no water, but the men found plenty of oysters, which formed very welcome food after the great privations they had endured.

When they had been from thirty to thirty-five days out, they were picked up by the *Maid of Riverton*, schooner, which was fishing for bêche-de-mer, and after remaining on board for two and a half months, until the vessel had finished her cruise, they were brought to Cleveland Bay [Townsville], and subsequently found their way to Sydney, where the steward entered the hospital, and had the fragment of the spear taken from his leg.

The Rescue

The *Reliance* survivors in the longboat (the whaleboat having disappeared in squally conditions around the Louisiade Islands) were rescued after twenty-seven days (not 'from thirty to thirty-five days') since abandoning the wreck. Another version of their desperate voyage was narrated by another seaman who described how they came to be picked up by the *Maid of Riverton*:

On the afternoon of the 29th [May] we made all ready to start for the mainland, for we were almost famished, and getting sicker every day. If we had landed on the mainland we should have delivered ourselves to instantaneous death, as we learned afterwards, and were providentially delivered. As we were starting at 9 p.m., saw a schooner standing towards the island, which proved to be the *Maid of Riverton*, Captain Fraser. He kindly received us all on board, and told me that it would be two months before he went to Sydney, as he was loading beche de mer.

We very gladly accepted the offer, and stayed on board; having been 27 days in open boats, and four days without anything to eat or drink; coming a distance of 1,100 miles in boats 15 feet long by 5¼ feet beam. By the time we got on board we were nearly done up. (*The Colonist* [Nelson, New Zealand], 4 September 1868)

Wreck of the *Hilda* off St Malo

The tidal races off the French Breton coast and around the Channel Islands, together with numerous rocks and reefs, fog, stormy weather and strong currents make the navigation of vessels in that area at the very least a risky, and at worst a potentially treacherous, business. Testament to those perils were two steamship wrecks and consequent great loss of life around the turn of the century, by, in 1899, the *Stella*, and, in 1905, the *Hilda*.

In March 1899 the London and South Western Railway Company's cross-Channel steamship the *Stella* foundered in fog when she wrecked on the Casquet Rocks off Alderney, one of the Channel Islands. One hundred and twelve people drowned; 115 persons were saved. In November 1905 another of the same company's vessels, the *Hilda*, struck the rocks off the Breton port of St Malo with even greater loss of life, and far fewer survivors.

The Hilda Wreck

The *Hilda*, 378 reg. tons, 235.6' long, left Southampton at 10 p.m. on the night of Friday 17 November 1905 'bound to St. Malo with about 109 passengers ... manned by a crew of twenty-eight persons all told (including the pilot), and under the command of Mr William Gregory'. Fog had delayed her scheduled sailing time of 8.15 p.m. and also obliged her to anchor off Yarmouth, Isle of Wight, until 6 a.m. the following morning (Saturday, 18 November).

Late that Saturday evening, at around 11 p.m. in strong easterly winds and buffeted by heavy seas and a thick snow-storm, the *Hilda* struck rocks about 3 miles off St Malo. Just twelve minutes later, 'there was a crash and the *Hilda* broke in two, at the same time, heeling over to such an extent as to put those who were clinging to the eyes of the rigging into the water, and causing the loss of most of the others' (from the Court of Inquiry in February 1906). The chief mate fell off the rigging later in the night as he told the only survivor from the crew, James Grinter, AB, 'All gone, not a soul left to tell the tale!'

But Grinter did survive. He and five Breton onion sellers were rescued the following morning by the steamship *Ada*, another London and South Western Railway Company vessel, which the bad weather had forced to remain at St Malo overnight. As she left for Southampton at 9.30 a.m. on Sunday, 19 November, she discovered the tragic scenes of the wrecked *Hilda*. 'The chief mate, a fireman, and two Bretons were found dead in the rigging.'

Wreck of the *Hilda* – After Twelve Hours of Frost And Tempest: The Rescue Of Survivors of the *Hilda* from the Rigging by The *Ada*'s Boat. (*The Illustrated London News*, 25 November 1905)

The official Court of Inquiry recorded that the *Hilda* left Southampton with about 109 passengers and 28 crew, totalling 137 souls. AB Grinter was the sole survivor from amongst the crew. The five Breton onion sellers also survived, so that the total loss of life was about 131:

Hilda *Wreck Victims 128 – Loss of Life in Steamship Disaster Greater than the First Reports Indicated – Only Six Survivors*

London, Nov. 20. – One hundred and twenty-eight persons lost their lives in the wreck of the London and South Western Railway Company's steamer *Hilda* off the northern coast of France Saturday night [18 November], according to an official estimate given out to-night by the officials of the company. This roll includes twenty-one saloon [first class] passengers, eighty French onion and potato sellers and twenty-seven of the crew.

St. Malo, France, Nov. 20. – Realization of the full extent of the disaster to the Cross Channel steamship *Hilda* came to the people of St. Malo as reports of the finding of bodies were received from different points along the nearby coast. In all more than sixty bodies have been washed up, including that of Captain Gregory, the commander of the wrecked ship, which now lies in the hospital here, and as fast as other bodies arrive they will be placed in a room prepared for their reception.

Survivors

James Gunter [*sic* – Grinter], the only seaman saved from the wreck, says there was no panic on board. Attempts were made to lower the boats, but the rough sea rendered it impossible. Gunter clung to the fittings of the topmast with nine others below him, including the chief mate and three Bretons, who died of exposure during the night.

The *Hilda* struck at 10 o'clock on Sunday [*sic* – Saturday] night. She was going very slowly at the time. Rockets were sent up, but there was no response. Seven minutes later the ship broke amidships and her decks were

Les Naufragés de L' *Hilda*, Au Lever Du Jour (Shipwrecked Castaways of the *Hilda*, At Daybreak). (*L'Illustration*, 25 November 1905)

swept bare, with the exception of the few survivors who clung to the mast. They were rescued by the steamship *Ada* at 10 o'clock this morning [Sunday, 19 November], after having endured twelve hours of agony.

LE NAUFRAGE DU VAPEUR " HILDA "

C'est un des sinistres maritimes les plus effroyables qui se soient produits en ces dernières années, que ce naufrage du steamer *Hilda*, de la Compagnie anglaise *South Western*, qui, dans la nuit de samedi à dimanche dernier, est venu se fracasser sur les rochers des Portes, à proximité du phare du Jardin, à l'entrée de la rade de Saint-Malo, en engloutissant une centaine de victimes.

Dimanche matin, un autre vapeur, l'*Ada*, qui partait de Saint-Malo pour Jersey, apercevait, émergeant des flots, comme il sortait des poses, un mât auquel étaient cramponnés dix naufragés, toute une grappe prête à s'égrener. Plusieurs étaient morts, mais leurs membres raidis les retenaient au gréement. Six seulement vivaient encore, cinq marchands d'oignons de la côte bretonne et un matelot anglais, exténués, défaillants de froid, de misère et de fatigue. Une chaloupe de l'*Ada*, avec l'aide d'un bateau pilote, put les recueillir et les ramener à Saint-Malo. Ce sont les seuls survivants de la catastrophe.

Le chauffeur anglais Grinter.

Les marchands d'oignons : en haut, Paul-Marie, Le Penn, Olivier Careff; en bas, Louis Rozec Tanguy-Laot, Jean-Louis Mouster.

Les Six Survivants du Naufrage, Qui Ont Été Recueillis dans la Mature de L' *Hilda* (The Six Survivors of the Shipwreck, Rescued From The *Hilda*'s Rigging). (*L'Illustration*, 25 November 1905)

In response to the captain's appeal, when he found it would be useless to attempt to launch the boats, all the women and children mustered on the main hatch and the stewardesses fixed life belts around each of them, the French onion sellers assisting in the work. Everybody was very quiet.

Gunter says there were about twenty persons in the rigging when the vessel foundered. He describes pathetically how the men gradually dropped off, exhausted by the terrible cold, and says the roar of the elements was awful. As the men fell off they ejaculated: 'We have had enough of this. It does not matter how we die. Good-by.'

Gunter himself fought against a strong inclination to sleep and says that at the time of his rescue he cared little what became of him.

Paris, Nov. 20.– Special reports received here of the wreck of the steamship *Hilda* give a graphic description of the disaster. Owing to the rough sea, together with a

Naufrage Du Steamer *Hilda* Devant Saint-Malo - Le sauvetage des survivants (Wreck of the Steamer *Hilda* Off Saint-Malo – Rescue of the survivors). (*Le Petit Journal*, 3 December 1905)

thick snowstorm, the captain of the *Hilda* probably took the buoy light of the rocks for St. Malo lighthouse. He gave signals which were not seen by harbor employees, and then the steamship proceeded slowly toward the light. When the *Hilda* struck the rocks, her boilers exploded and she was cut in two, giving the passengers no time to save themselves.

Seven bodies wearing life belts were stranded off the village of St. Cast yesterday evening. The coast near St. Malo is covered with wreckage and the carcasses of cattle. Two-thirds of the *Hilda*'s passengers were French farmers returning to France with heavy sums of gold for the yearly harvest of potatoes. The others were English families who were going to spend the winter at Dinard.

Bodies

The wreck lies on the beach three miles off St. Malo, showing only her mainmast and forecastle. A correspondent of the *Matin* [newspaper] went to the scene on a Government steamship, which picked up five bodies which were entangled in the rigging of the *Hilda*. The bodies presented a dreadful spectacle, the arms and legs twisted in all directions and the hands torn by desperate struggling. (*San Francisco Call*, 21 November 1905)

The *San Rafael* Survivors – 'Escape from a Watery Grave'

The 1,200 ton British ship *San Rafael* (sometimes spelled *Raphael*), Capt. McAdam, sailed from Liverpool in October 1875 with a cargo of coal for the main Chilean port of Valparaiso. In the first few days of January 1876, off Cape Horn, she burned and was abandoned. Three boats got away: one with the captain, his wife and seven sailors; the second with the first officer Mr Kilgour and six sailors; and the third with five sailors.

In April 1876 Fuegian Indians reported to Capt. Willis of the yawl *Allen Gardner*, of the South American Missionary Society based at Ushuaia in Tierra del Fuego, that they had discovered nine bodies at a remote spot on Hoste Island to the north-west of Cape Horn. On 18 May a party from the Missionary Society led by the Rev. T. Bridges discovered 'nine dead bodies much decomposed, one of them being that of a woman, evidently the captain's wife': the remains of the occupants of the first boat from the *San Rafael*, who had starved to death.

Until that discovery, there had been no news of the fate of the *San Rafael*'s Capt. McAdams, his wife and the seven crew. The occupants of the other two boats, however, were rescued at sea by the British ship *Yorkshire* three months before, at the end of January, having suffered extreme privations and hardships from being twenty-seven days adrift in those frigid seas off 'Cape Stiff'. The story of their rescue was told by 'a lady passenger' sailing in the *Yorkshire*:

Burning of the St. Raphael

The *Sydney Morning Herald* of the 20th inst [i.e. 20 July 1876] publishes the following extract from a letter from a lady passenger by the ship *Yorkshire*, from Melbourne, bound to London, respecting the saving of the ship [*sic* – castaways from the ship] *St. Raphael*, burnt at sea:

'And now I am going to tell you the sad story of the shipwrecked crew that we were fortunate enough to pick up and save on the 31st January, when we rounded the Horn. Their ship, the *St. Raphael*, was burnt at sea, and when we found them it was twenty-seven days since they had left her. Early in the morning the Captain of the *Yorkshire* was signalling the *John Duthie*, when he noticed something on the horizon.

'On taking the glass he saw at once that it was a boat; so we began to heave-to. The *John Duthie* began to do the same, but when they saw that we were doing it they sailed on. Whether they saw the boat of course we do not know, but at all events they might have waited to see what was the matter or if they could lend any assistance.

'I then heard that there was a boat coming to the ship, and, standing at the cuddy door saw the men being helped over the main deck. They looked fearful, such poor wretched creatures, their arms all covered with frost boils, their teeth chattering, and shaking all over as if they had the ague. There were six sailors and the first mate, Mr. Kilgour.

'Just as they came on board we heard the second boat was coming to us, with five men in her.* They were got on board safely. The men were so weak that they fell back into the boat as they were trying to get on the ship. Their feet were all frost bitten. One poor fellow's sufferings were dreadful. The doctor had to amputate both his great toes. He was ill for a long time, but you now see him shuffling along the deck. They suffered much when circulation was returning. It was one of the saddest sights I ever saw.

---

* At the end of December 1875 the *San Rafael* was being assaulted by heavy weather off the pitch of the Horn. On Sunday 1 January 1876 smoke was discovered from a smouldering fire in her cargo of coal. The next day a plume of flame shot up 6oft in the air from one of the hatches: the coal was on fire from spontaneous combustion. Capt. McAdam decided to steer for the Falkland Islands, 1,200 miles to the north-east, to make repairs and, in the meantime, try to contain or extinguish the fire by pumping water on it. But by Tuesday 3 January the fire was still gaining hold. The order was given to abandon ship in the boats: a long-boat, a pinnace, a gig, and a 17ft-long dinghy. The gig was immediately stove and sank. Twelve men got away in the pinnace and the dinghy (but just *eleven* survivors were rescued by the *Yorkshire*); the captain, his wife and seven other men (those who died and were discovered on Hoste Island) occupied the biggest boat, the long-boat.

'The poor fellows wept like children directly they came on board, and "God bless you all" was their first exclamation. They all lived, and are now on a fair way to recovery, but the doctor says they will all be rheumatic. They say their feet feel quite dead, and it is now two months since they were picked up.'

The Fatal Voyage

'It was 25 days since they had abandoned their ship. She was a larger one than ours, bound for Valparaiso with a cargo of coal. They had most tempestuous weather, and, of course, they had to round the Horn, where the winds are nearly [always] contrary. So they had been out a good deal over 100 days. The vessel took fire when they were near the Horn; spontaneous combustion. The hatches blew up. They discovered the fire three days before they left the ship, and made all necessary arrangements.

'The captain and his wife were in the long-boat with his officers, and they had all the provisions, charts, and compasses put in her, intending to keep together. The captain, who used to drink, became so disagreeable that the first and second mates, who each had charge of the other boats, agreed to part from him. He then gave them as much provisions as he deemed sufficient, but keeping the lion's share for himself. They had only enough to allow each man two ounces of preserved meat a day.

'They landed on some of those rocks off the Horn, and agreed that when on land they would touch none of the provisions, but keep themselves alive on what they could get ashore. The only thing they could get was mussels, but they had enough fresh water and plenty of boxes of matches; but with the fearful cold their feet were in such a state that they could hardly crawl on the rocks, so those who were not so bad gathered for the rest. But you may fancy the amount of mussels it would take to make sufficient food for a meal.

'They used to cruise about, and had hoisted a red shirt for a sail. They saw several ships, but were not seen. They had been back to the island twice, and when we picked them up had been cruising about two days. Mr. Kilgour told us it was as much as he could do to get the men into the boats again. They did not seem to care for life. They had almost given up hope when we saw them.'

'Spartan Courage'

'Of course, we do not know whether the longboat has been picked up. They had determined not to put back upon the island again, and if they saw one boat in danger to turn their backs, as neither of the boats was big enough to take them all. They showed Spartan courage about refraining from the food when they were almost starving. They had sufficient left when we took them on board to have lasted them three days longer.

'Just think what it must have been to be twenty-seven days off Cape Horn in those fearful waves (it blew a hurricane for seven days, when they were obliged to remain on the land); the careful rowing it required – for if they had once let a wave get over the boat they would have gone over in a second. When they came alongside, both the boats were half full of water; they had both been hurt in lowering over the side of the *San Raphael*.

'The day after they were rescued there was a dreadful storm and sea, in which neither of the boats could have lived, so they had a most marvellous escape from a watery grave.' (*Nelson Evening Mail* [New Zealand], 3 August 1876)

Castaways

After the three boats cut away from the doomed ship, the captain's long-boat became separated from the other two in a snow squall. They were never seen again, until their remains were found on Hoste Island three months later. The overwhelming fear of the twelve other castaways was that the captain's boat 'had aboard the great bulk of the provisions'.

The two boats and twelve men landed with great difficulty in a small cove on the coast of Tierra del Fuego where they camped and shared a meagre meal divided amongst them from a 4lb tin of Australian mutton, and half a hard ship's biscuit per man from two 50lb bags. A few days later, on Saturday 7 January, it was decided to put to sea again to try their luck in being picked up by a passing ship. Provisions then consisted of two bags of biscuit, twelve 4lb tins of mutton, and about 8 gallons of fresh water, together with a 28lb case of tobacco (but only one pipe to share amongst them).

The two small boats weathered fierce gales. 'Every man was cold and numb, and with every bone aching acutely; but curiously enough, instead of despairing our nervousness had in a great measure worn off, and, like old soldiers, we were getting accustomed to staring death in the face' (from 'Twenty-Seven Days in an Open Boat', by Capt. James Richards, *World Wide Magazine*, September–October 1899; Richards had been third officer in the *San Rafael*). Rations were half a biscuit per man, and half a tin of mutton equally divided – 'between 2oz and 3oz of meat' – per day.

On Wednesday 18 January a sail was sighted, a 'large barque, about five miles distant, standing in towards the land, close-hauled on the port-tack'. Labouring at their oars they pulled so close to the vessel that they could see the helmsman, no more than half a mile away. But she did not see them, and 'On she went, silent and spectre-like – the twelve castaways craning their necks in the direction of the rapidly disappearing ship'.

By Saturday 21 January they were down to the last scrap of their provisions, 'This was our last meal, and everyone knew it'. A few days later the cook died. They buried him at sea on Wednesday 25 January. Their numbers were now reduced to eleven – although the letter from the lady on the *Yorkshire* (above) stated that twelve men were rescued.

Towards the end of January:

> We presented, indeed, a terrible sight – we were surely the most pitiable objects. Haggard, unkempt, wild, hungry-looking fellows, with a blood-shot, famished, fierce look in the eyes, that was horrible to see … Fortunately all hands were British, and it is but common justice to say that from first to last they, one and all, behaved remarkably well. Throughout the whole of this terrible ordeal every order was obeyed to the very last and to the best of the men's ability.

Salvation

The eleven survivors of the *San Rafael* salvaged from the sea by the *Yorkshire* had been cast away from their burned ship for 30 days, 'and of these twenty-seven had been spent in an open boat, and the last eight of these had been spent totally without food'. The apprentice lad's legs were so gangrenous that they (or possibly just his toes) had to be amputated by the *Yorkshire*'s doctor. The others were so badly maimed by their ordeal that 'the best of us were over three weeks before we could leave our berths'.

'Twenty-Seven Days in an Open Boat', by Capt. Jas. Richards, 3rd Officer of the *San Rafael* at the time she was wrecked and an occupant of the castaway boat. (*Wide World Magazine*, August–September 1899)

The *San Rafael*'s third officer James Richards returned to the sea and rose to the rank of master. As Capt. Richards, writing twenty-three years later about the dreadful month of his and his shipmates' ordeal off Cape Horn in January 1876, he observed, 'Many events have occurred since then, but none yet has happened, or is likely to happen, which can obliterate from my mind this terrible tale of the sea, in which I was one of the leading characters.'

The *Ocean Queen*: Shocking Sufferings at Sea

The North Sea and the Baltic could throw up every bit as nasty weather and vicious, short-steeped seas as the more notorious regions of Cape Horn or the Southern Ocean, particularly in winter with the added misery of icy conditions. A voyage by the brig *Ocean Queen*, from Riga, on the Baltic coast, to Hartlepool, on the north-east coast of England, in December 1866, became a disaster from which only the vessel's captain and one seaman out of the eightman crew survived, and then only just by the slenderest tendril of fate:

Shocking Sufferings at Sea

A tale of unusual sufferings at sea has been unfolded by the arrival at Arbroath [north-east coast of Scotland] last week of the Blyth brig *Ancient Promise*, Captain R.B. Stannard, from Memel [on the then Prussian coast, now Lithuania], with a cargo of flax for an Arbroath firm. The *Ancient Promise* has brought with her Captain Currie, master of the brig *Ocean Queen*, of Blyth.

Early in December last [1866] the *Ocean Queen* sailed from Riga for Hartlepool, with a crew of eight hands, and a cargo of deals [wood planks] on board. From the day of her sailing she encountered fearful weather, and about the 12th she sprang a leak. The men worked hard at the pumps and the captain steered for Danzik [now Gdansk]. The water, however, made upon them rapidly, and in consequence of the heavy seas sweeping the deck the crew had to betake themselves to the rigging for safety. The vessel was so waterlogged that she did not answer to the helm.

Disaster Strikes

About seven o'clock in the evening, the brig being half full of water, she capsized. Two of the crew – Samuel Turner, able seaman, and John Petrie, an apprentice, the latter belonging to Aberdeen – were drowned. The remainder of the crew had managed to get hold of the vessel, to which they clung. The cook, Robert Hadley, [of] Blyth, also died of exhaustion and hunger, and two days after that again another of the crew succumbed.

On the fourth day two ships, one of them Swedish, and the other supposed [believed] to be from Memel, passed close at hand, and indeed were spoken by the crew of the *Ocean Queen*, who, however, were left to their fate.

The unfortunate men were now in a deplorable condition, and had been reduced to the shocking necessity of allaying the pangs of hunger by eating parts of the bodies of their comrades who had died. To quench their thirst they sucked pieces of ice and drank sea water, the latter bringing on fever and insensibility. On the 7th day after the capsizing of the brig, the mate, Robert Oliver, of Blyth, died, and a young apprentice named James Hamilton died on the eighth day. Just as he died, the vessel, on the 21st December, struck the beach near the fishing village of Niddin, 45 miles from Memel.

Salvation

Of the eight of the crew who had sailed with her when she left Riga, only two were now alive – the master, Captain Currie, and a seaman named Julius Fortis, a native of the Cape de Verde Islands. Both men were in a shocking state – frost-bitten, suffering from hunger and thirst, and in a raging fever. At Niddin, the villagers showed them kindness, and sent to Memel to inform the British

Consul there of what had occurred. They were removed
to Memel for treatment.

Fortis was found to be so badly frost-bitten that both
his feet and both his hands had to be amputated. He is
still in Memel. Captain Currie had to get the sole of one
of his feet cut off, it was so much injured by the frost.
He left Memel on the 26th ult. [26 April 1867] with the
Ancient Promise, which vessel arrived at Arbroath on
Saturday [4 May].

A local newspaper report about the incident added:

It is not known how Fortis got ashore, but the Captain
had, without knowing how, got astride a plank of wood,
and was so washed upon the beach. They appear to have
lain there some hours before they were noticed by the
villagers. When the Captain first came to consciousness,
he found himself and Fortis laid upon the backs of horses,
and being conducted by some fishermen to Niddin ...
The unfortunate men suffered greatly on the journey
to Memel, which was made on horseback, and there
was no proper road. (*The Maitland Mercury and Hunter
River General Advertiser* [New South Wales, Australia],
10 August 1867)

Loss of the *China*

In December 1868 the Welsh barque *China* was on a
voyage from Quebec to Cardiff, stiff up against heavy
winter weather in the North Atlantic. On the morning
of 13 December a duet of 'tremendous seas' pooped her
(came aboard over her stern) with such forceful malice

that they swept overboard seven of the crew, including Capt. Brannan, as well as inflicting other disabling damage to the vessel.

Shipwreck on the Atlantic – Loss of the Barque China *– The Captain, Chief Mate, and Seven Men Washed Overboard – The Second Mate and Six Men Rescued after Two Weeks of Starvation – Gallant Conduct of Captain Lewand and the Crew of the Barque* W.H. Jenkins

The barque *China* sailed from Quebec, sometime in November last [1868], with a full cargo of timber, for the port of Cardiff, in Wales. The *China* was a ship of 635 tons, and was owned by Watsons & Co., a large and wealthy Cardiff firm. Her crew consisted of sixteen men, viz: Captain Brannan, a native and resident of Cardiff; chief mate John Fortune, of Shields, England; second mate – Boaz, of Cardiff, son of Captain Boaz, of the barque Eleanor, also of Cardiff; a steward, a carpenter, and eleven British and Irish sailors.

Disabled by 'a Tremendous Sea'

She had favorable winds during the early part of the voyage, but the gale was so fierce and the ship steered so wildly, that about 11 o'clock on the morning of December 13th, she was brought to the wind; and, within less than twenty minutes, a tremendous sea broke over her with such sudden fury as to snap the mizzen-mast like a pipestem, shiver the stern to fragments, smash the rudder and wheel, and sweep away both the boats and the house on deck, which served as a cabin and contained the ship's store of provisions. At the same instant, the wind tore the close-reefed maintop-sail into ribbons.

The Captain, who had just left the cabin, saw the breaker coming, and shouted to the crew to run forward for their lives; but so fearfully swift and irresistible was the fatal wave that two of the sailors – the man at the wheel and the chief mate, who was in the cabin – were swept into their ocean grave in the twinkling of an eye; and before the rest of the men could save themselves among the fore rigging, another terrible sea plunged down on the doomed barque, swept off the forecastle house, and carried the Captain and four more of the sailors after their unhappy companions.

As the cargo completely filled the hold, and the cabin and forecastle house were tossing in fragments on the sea, the only shelter left for these horror-stricken men was under a little forecastle deck, beneath which they crept as soon as they dared risk themselves on the clean-swept main deck, over which the seas were rolling mountains high.

A 'Frightful Situation'

Stowed away in this little recess, scarcely large enough to hold them, and entirely open on one side to wind and waves, they suffered the fourteen days and nights all the agonies of cold, hunger and thirst, beside the unutterable mental tortures inseparable from their frightful situation. The only provision left on the ship was a barrel of salt pork, under one of the hatches.

From this, at the imminent risk of their lives, they obtained every particle of their food, and slaked their thirst with hailstones and such precious drops as they could squeeze from ropes' ends and bits of canvas when it rained. Without a moment's sleep, without a spark of fire, or a dry thread to keep them warm, pierced by the keen gales of December, drenched anew every now and then by the seas that rolled over the deck in constant succession, and with scarcely anything to quench the thirst that the salt meat only aggravated, these men suffered misery as few mortals have ever endured; and yet it is a positive and shameful fact that during the weary days in which the wreck of the *China* pitched and tossed upon the wintry Atlantic waves, three ships passed within hailing distance, and never even tried to save the wretched remnant of her crew.

An officer on the deck of one of these vessels was seen to wave his hand, but passed on with heartless indifference!

The W.H. Jenkins' *Encounter with the Battered* China

In December, 1867, exactly twelve months before this terrible shipwreck, the *China* and the barque *W.H. Jenkins*, of Yarmouth, Nova Scotia, lay side by side in Cardiff docks. The *W.H. Jenkins* is a ship of 721 tons, commanded by Captain Henry Alexander Thomas Lewand. She left the port of Middlesbrough, in the north of England, with a cargo of iron for New York on August 20, 1868. The seventh day out she encountered a severe gale shortly after passing between the Orkney and Shetland Islands, and sprang a leak, and only succeeded in reaching Ardrossan, near Glasgow, by diligent use of the pumps, and by tying sails, soaked in tar and stuffed with oakum, under the bottom.

After thorough repairs at Ardrossan, she put to sea again, and encountered a hurricane on about the seventh day after leaving port, which threw her on her beam ends [i.e. on her side], shifted the whole of her cargo out of place, and compelled the Captain to throw about 50 tons of it overboard in order to right the barque and reach Ardrossan again. Here the cargo was restowed and secured, and the undaunted Captain put to sea the third time on the 11th of December, two days before the *China* was wrecked.

The weather was fearfully cold and boisterous, and the barque's progress westward was extremely slow, as appears from the fact that the trip to New York took 84 days, while the *Jenkins* made the same voyage last winter in 37 days.

About 11 o'clock on the morning of the 27th of December the thick mist cleared up a little, and the second mate, whose watch it was on deck, reported a vessel about seven miles to the windward. In the course of half an hour Captain Lewand made out that it was a wreck, apparently abandoned. A signal flag was immediately hoisted to ascertain if anyone was aboard, but the sharpest watch did not reveal any signs of life, and the flag was hauled down, after flying two hours.

The wind would not permit a closer approach during this time, but about 1 o'clock it veered a little to the southwest, and Captain Lewand, unwilling to leave until absolutely sure that the wreck was really abandoned, wore ship and sailed toward the *China*. When the miserable men on the wreck saw the signal flag fly from the masthead of the fourth vessel that had passed them since the fatal 13th of December they fell on their knees and thanked God.

The anguish of the bitter moment when they saw it hauled down was the keenest stroke of all, and no pen can paint their joy when the barque finally turned with the changing wind, and sailed towards them, and Captain Lewand, spying the poor fellows crawling feebly from under the forecastle deck, hailed them with, 'All right, boys; I'll take you off if it's possible!'

But how? The seas were washing every moment over the ill-fated *China*. The timber cargo projected some eight or ten feet from her crumbling stern. Everything but the flywheel of the pump, the two forward masts, and a few stanchions, was swept away, and the bare yards were swinging in every direction.

So high did the sea run that a boat lowered from davits would have been shivered like an eggshell, and it was only possible to launch the yawl by carrying it amidships. Even then it looked like tempting Providence to undertake the rescue, but four brave men volunteered for the service, and the yawl put off only to find that it was absolutely impossible to board the *China*! But the poor wretches on the deck, spurred on by hope and desperation, mustered at last strength and courage enough to climb upon the forecastle deck, crawl out on the jibboom, and slip down a cord into the water, from which they were speedily lifted into the boat.

The Rescue
The second mate was insensible [unconscious], but even he was finally let down with ropes into the yawl, and in two perilous trips all of the seven were carried to the barque. The steward seemed to have the most strength of any of them, but even he had to be hauled up the barque's side, and could only exclaim, in piteous tones, as he was lifted over the rail, 'My God, Capt. Lewand! fourteen days and nothing to eat!' And the mate died of utter debility within two hours after his rescue, notwithstanding the strenuous exertions that were made to restore him to consciousness and life.

All the men were not only as thin as skeletons, but were covered with boils, caused by exposure to the salt water,

A Gale At Sea: 'Pooped' – Drawn by Frank Brangwyn. (*The Graphic*, 25 November 1893)

and which added greatly to the other miseries of their hard lot. Every care was taken by them, and by the time the barque reached Fayal [Azores], on the 20th of January [1869], they were strong enough to walk on shore, after showering thanks upon the Captain, and, with streaming eyes, blessing him for his humanity in rescuing them.

It is probable that ere this some British bound craft has touched at Fayal, and carried them all to Cardiff, to tell as sad a story as ever was told since men began to go down to sea in ships ... (*Daily Alta California*, 5 April 1869)

3

FEVER AND SCURVY

Scurvy was the scourge of deep-sea sailing ships' crews. Vessels provisioned salt pork and beef in casks to last for six months and more, but the only fresh vegetables they took on at the start of a voyage lasted no more than a few weeks. The lack of vitamin C in sailors' diet, which caused scurvy, from the absence of fresh vegetables and fruit, was to some extent attenuated by daily dosages of lime (or lemon) juice. But if the remedial juice was of poor quality, or insufficient to last a prolonged voyage, or even absent altogether (it was first required to be provisioned in British naval and merchant ships by the Merchant Shipping Act of 1867), the dreaded disease could spread rapidly through-out a vessel's crew which might be *fed* enough but still be poorly *nourished*.

'Fever' could be any number of nasty tropical diseases that disabled or killed off sailors in their thousands, particularly those in vessels trading around the steamier ports of Asia, West Africa, South America and the Gulf of Mexico. The general blanket illness termed 'Java fever' (named for its eponymous Indonesian origin) was probably dengue or zika or yellow fever, but possibly malaria, too. Malaria, yellow fever ('yellow jack') and cholera could be picked up in any tropical port, particularly in certain seasons of the year.

The only remedy to such afflictions (if any) was recourse to the captain's exceedingly basic 'medicine' chest, his rather slender (if any) knowledge of treating such diseases (he usually just combined numbered bottled compounds according to a prescribed formula), but mainly to whatever breezes of fortune, good or ill, prevailed at the time. And usually it was of the ill – indeed, fatal – kind.

The Scurvy-Stricken *Bremen*

On 1 February 1858 the steamship *Bremen* slid down the ways at her builder's yard at Greenock, on the Clyde, the first transatlantic steamer built by her owners the North German Lloyd line. She was 2,674 tons, 333ft long, carried over 500 passengers, and had a crew of about 100. In June 1874 the *Bremen* was sold to a Liverpool shipping company, E. Bates, which converted her into a full-rigged ship. Her first voyage as a sailing ship, from Liverpool to San Francisco in 1875, 'in command of Captain Lawrence S. Leslie, an old and experienced commander', was not only particularly long for that west-bound route round Cape Horn (192 days), it was quite literally a sickeningly hard passage.

Scurvy Stricken – A Ship's Crew of Fifty Taken Down with the Loathsome Disease – Thirteen Buried at Sea – Twenty-two Sick when the Ship Arrives in Port – A Tedious Voyage of One Hundred and Twenty-one Days [sic – 192 days] from Liverpool to San Francisco

The long-expected British ship *Bremen* was telegraphed ten miles out yesterday morning, and soon afterward Captain Bingham, of the firm of Menzies, Bingham & Co., went out over the bar to meet the ship, and, on arriving on board, was informed by the Captain that the crew was down with the scurvy and assistance was needed to bring her into port. Captain Bingham at once returned to the city and ordered twenty men out to work the ship and the powerful tug *Rescue* to tow her in.

The Bremen

On the 6th of February [1875] she sailed from Liverpool for this port [San Francisco] with a cargo of coal, the Captain, three Mates, carpenter, sailmaker, carpenter's mate, three apprentices, two stowaway boys, one white ordinary seaman and thirty-six colored seamen. She was well provisioned in every respect and sailed with every prospect of a fair passage. On the 12th of February, six days after leaving port, the first case of sickness was reported to the Captain, the invalid being Charles Parry, one of the colored crew, who came aft and complained of a bad chest and throat. The Captain examined him and found that his lungs were completely gone, and gave him a dose of cough pills, which he was unable to swallow. Parry grew worse until February 21st, when he told the Captain that he was feeling easier, but was satisfied he was going to die. Two days afterward Parry fainted in the arms of two of his shipmates. The Captain was sent for, and on the Captain's reaching the forecastle Parry's life was extinct. From this time on sickness continued to increase among the crew, although the Captain commenced to serve out lime juice on February 14th.

At midnight, on March 13th, the mate came below and reported to the Captain that the colored crew refused to do duty; that the ring-leaders were Black and Scott, and Scott had threatened to cut the second mate's lip off. The Captain armed himself and went on deck, determined to restore discipline at all hazards. He found one watch in open revolt, and another of eighteen men standing by, ready to join the others. The ring-leaders, Black and Scott, gave insolent answers and said they would not muster. The crew were then informed of the serious consequences that would follow from the revolt and insubordination.

The eighteen not on duty were ordered to stand aside, while Black and Scott were placed aft and kept there till four a.m. At nine o'clock they were put in irons and ordered to be kept on bread and water for one week. The following morning both men sent word to the Captain that they were sorry for what they had done. They were brought before the Captain and mate, and after apologizing and promising to do duty they were released.

The Scurvy

Symptoms of scurvy began to show in March, and the only cause that can at present be assigned for so many of the crew being taken down with it, is the fault of the sailors. Most of them shipped in Liverpool a few days after their arrival there from New York; when taken sick they would refuse to take the vinegar and other medicines given by the Captain, until they were helpless. They also became demoralized and frightened, as they saw their numbers decreasing one by one. The Carpenter's Mate went to bed quite well at night and the next morning was dead. Another feature was, that as soon as the ship came out of cold weather into warm, the black men went down, the Captain says, 'like sunflowers'.

On the 25th of April the ship was off Cape Horn, and on the 28th of April the Captain gave directions for fresh messes to be served out twice a week instead of twice a month. On May 7th the forecastle was disinfected; still the disease continued and reached an epidemic form, and three-fourths of the crew were helpless.

On May 21st all the sick men were removed from the forecastle into an improvised hospital on the main deck. The food consisted of sago, rice, arrowroot, oatmeal, and fresh meat twice a week. Alum gargle was given for the mouth and port wine and quinine as medicine. The Captain was unremitting in his attentions, but all that he did seemed to be of little avail. The crew were allowed to eat as much vegetables as they liked. The steward says they often refused to eat the vegetables, and on several occasions he told the Captain it was useless to cook any vegetables, as the men would not eat them.

The Crew Were Paralyzed

Horror was depicted on their countenances. On June 3rd the Captain ordered that three times the quantity of lime juice be given to the crew that was required by the Act [the Merchant Shipping Amendment Act of 1867, mainly legislating for the provision of lime juice against scurvy, medicines, care of sick seamen, etc. on British merchant ships], as he had an abundance on board; but the men

Craigerne – Rounding Cape Horn (postcard).

refused to take advice, and on the 20th of June fourteen of the crew positively refused to take any lime juice. On his official log-book the Captain has an entry that some penalty should be attached to seamen who refuse to take lime juice and eat good pressed vegetables.

There was but little complaint on the part of the crew as to the food. There was plenty of good fresh Australian mutton, which was served three times a week, with salt meat and vegetables. Only the latter part of the voyage bread was reduced one-quarter.

Thirteen of the crew died during the voyage; twelve black and one white, the carpenter, who died ten days ago. The last death was the day before the ship entered the port. It has been a terrible time on board, death stalking among the crew, the Captain, his mates and apprentices being compelled to work the ship as best they could, and of these the Captain, two of his mates and the apprentices may be said to have done well; and they rejoiced when they entered the harbor yesterday after their tedious voyage of one hundred and ninety-one days ...

Sickness Count

The first case of sickness was on the 12th of February, and one after the other was taken down, and by the time the Equator in the Pacific was reached, there were only eight well enough to assist in working the ship. There are now twenty-two men laid up. They have been of very little use since passing Cape Horn – about able to be around, but unable to do any laborious work. Thus being shorthanded, and having met with considerable adverse weather, the passage was greatly prolonged, and great praise is due to Captain Leslie for bringing his ship safely to port with so small a crew. The ship in every respect is in first-class order. (*Daily Alta California*, 18 August 1875)

Amongst the list of the thirteen men who died on the voyage, 'all [were] colored, with one exception [the Dane, Paulsen]'. Seven of the dead men 'died of affection of the throat' by which 'there appeared to be more or less scurvy'. At least three and possibly four men 'died of consumption' – tuberculosis (the possible fourth, 'of a disease of the lungs'). One man succumbed to venereal disease.

The *Guiding Star* – A Fever-Poisoned Ship

Guiding Star was a barquentine (square-rigged on the fore-mast, fore-and-aft-rigged on the main and mizzen masts), of 249 tons and 117ft long. On 7 May 1890 she left Mauritius with 300 tons of sugar to deliver to Hobart, Tasmania, under the command of Capt. Joshua Ikin, a native of Hobart. Soon after leaving Port Louis, 'Mauritius fever' (dengue, or possibly yellow fever) began spreading through the crew. The steward/cook was the first to die, followed by Capt. Ikin, and then by mate Isaac Lear. After another seaman died, just six ordinary seamen were left to work the ship as best they could without really knowing how to get to a safe port apart from putting the vessel on a compass course.

Three of those six then came down with the illness, so that the *Guiding Star* was left with just two ordinary seamen and the boatswain to sail her when a British barque, the *Lancefield*, on passage from New York to Hong Kong, fell in with the death-ridden vessel to the south-west of Cape Leeuwin, Western Australia. The *Lancefield*'s master put on board the mate and two seamen to navigate *Guiding Star* to the open roadstead of Anjer in the Sunda Straits between Java and Sumatra, where she arrived around 10 July. Four men made it home – eventually – though not all entirely intact; the ill-starred *Guiding Star* never did:

A Fever-Poisoned Ship

The Hobart *Mercury* of Oct. 29th contains a statement by Alexander Murray, A.B., one of the crew of the barquentine *Guiding Star*, on a miserable and fatal voyage from Mauritius for Hobart, Murray having arrived at Hobart the previous day from Batavia [Jakarta] by steamer. The *Guiding Star*, captain Ikin (both ship and master known in Timaru), went to Port Louis, Mauritius, with a load of flour from Adelaide, to return to Hobart with sugar. Murray commenced his narration by mentioning an incident of Mauritius weather:

'By-the-way, I might tell you that while we were at Port Louis an enormous waterspout collided with one of the mountains near that place. Bursting, the water came down the creeks in floods, carrying everything movable before it. Our vessel came in for such a share of casks of molasses and other merchandise and water rolling down the wharf on to us, that Captain Ikin moored the ship some distance off. After the rush had ceased, we were berthed a short distance from the wharf, while divers were engaged fishing up the sunken goods. The cargo of sugar was then shipped by means of boats.'

'He then proceeded to describe the sufferings of the crew from Mauritius fever, which, in the island itself, is lightly regarded. A local paper says: 'A minute after the most violent attack we do not even think about it. We content ourselves by taking quinine, and continue to go about our business. The whole community is so familiarised with the fever that no one will admit that he is attacked by the disease.

'I was the first to be attacked by the fever, a few days before we sailed from Port Louis. Captain Ikin told me to go and see a doctor, which I did. The captain pressed me to return on the vessel, saying "Come home with me, you will not be comfortable in Mauritius." Of course I went with him. As soon as we set sail I returned to my bunk, very bad indeed, and after we had made a start I got worse and worse until my reason began to leave me. I knew very little of what was going on. The captain was very good to me, and doctored me with quinine.

'The next I can remember is one of the men telling me that the steward had been found dead in his bunk. Then one morning I was told Louis Williams the second mate [*sic* – he was cook/steward] was dead. He had only been ill a few days. It cast an awful gloom over us when our mate's burial took place. The captain said as the body went over the side, "God bless his soul, he has been a good man."

'Captain Ikin next fell ill, and the word was passed around "The old man's queer." He died after being ill about a week. All the crew had done what they could for him. He died on a Sunday. We had no prayer-book and when he was buried the only words used by the men were "God rest his soul. Amen."

'Though the skipper was dead we had no misgivings about the safety of the vessel, for the mate attended to the navigation. But after Captain Ikin's death Mr. Lear [i.e. the mate] began to show signs of the fever, and as it got a proper hold of him he had to give up work. He died some twelve days after the captain. I had been very ill all this time, just able to crawl, but from now began to mend slowly. There was no one left to navigate, and we steered E.N.E. to reach Western Australia.

'Soon after Mr. Lear's death, Kirchoff, a foreigner, ordinary seaman, took sick and died in a few days. There were then only six of us to work the vessel, but we did fairly well by keeping few sails on, and heaving-to every night to get rest. After Kirchoff died, Jones, Goldring, and Richards took it, and did not recover before the *Lancefield* picked us up. Then there were only three men able to do anything. If the mate had lived we would have brought the ship home, but as it was we did not know where we were making for.'

The Lancefield
'One morning a ship appeared in sight to the windward, bearing in our direction. We kept the *Guiding Star* to

until the stranger came on us about dark. We hove-to as usual all night, and the other vessel kept by us. Next morning a boat was put off, and the mate of the *Lancefield*, that being the name of the barque, boarded our vessel. We told him the state of affairs, and he said, "I can't leave you in this distress. I must go on board again and tell the captain." Presently he returned with coat and provisions, and asked if we were agreeable to go to Anjer [Sunda Straits, between Java and Sumatra] with him, and we answered "Yes."

'We were taken off the ship at Anjer and sent to Batavia [Jakarta], and the *Guiding Star* was taken to the same place by a Malay crew. Four of us went to the Hospital. I was in the institution 14 days. I went on board the vessel one day, but had to lay up again in the Hospital for 16 days. The barquentine made a fresh start with Richards on board and a Javanese crew, Jones, Brown, and myself being in the Hospital. The fever broke out again on board and the ship had to put back to Batavia. Another start was made with a fresh crew, but she had to return to Batavia, owing to another appearance of the fever. Richards caught it bad again, and was taken to the hospital. I came away in the [steamer] *Woodonga* with two others, leaving the other three ill at Batavia.' (*Timaru Herald* [New Zealand], 24 November 1890)

Four men were left in the deadly wake of the *Guiding Star* during her passage from Mauritius: Capt. Ikin, mate Lear, cook/steward Williams, and seaman Kirchoff. Joseph Richards, AB ('a Frenchman'), was kept at the hospital in Batavia in 'a very bad way'. The boatswain Henry Brown and the two surviving ordinary seamen, Robert Jones and

Alexander Murray, eventually made it back to Hobart via Sydney.

An obituary for Robert Jones, who died 10 August 1927, noted, with regard to the *Guiding Star*'s disastrous voyage thirty-seven years earlier, 'Two of the [surviving] crew became insane, and the others, except Mr. Jones, never regained normal health.' The *Guiding Star* herself tried to make it back to Hobart, but, some 100 miles out of Anjer, 'She encountered a gale ... and became a total wreck. No lives were lost.'

The *Johanna*'s Dismal Voyage

Equally as calamitous as the *Guiding Star*'s voyage, and for the same malaise, was that of the German schooner *Johanna*, bound from Mauritius for Melbourne around the same time. The vessel had an inauspicious start even before she sailed from Port Louis on 3 April 1890:

> Fourteen days before the *Johanna* sailed she had lain in the Albion dock, Port Louis. Into this dock a large sewer discharges nearly all the filth of the town. Early each morning the stench noticeable on board the *Johanna* was almost overpowering, and a dense steam arose from the mouth of the sewer, which for several hours every morning enveloped the vessel. The germs of the disease are believed to have been thus conveyed to the *Johanna*.
> (*The Press* [Canterbury, New Zealand], 7 August 1890)

Johanna's crew were almost all from Papenburg, in what was then the kingdom of Hanover, now in Lower Saxony state, Germany. Her master was Capt. Meinders. His 27-year-old wife Margherita, and 5-year-old child Susanna, accompanied him. The mate, Herman Hejen (or Heijen), was 'a splendid specimen of a sailor'. His and Mrs Meinders' conduct in safeguarding the voyage of the *Johanna*, in the face of so many deaths amongst her crew and through the wintry storm-battered wastes of the Southern Ocean, was 'heroic'.

Mate Hejen and Mrs Meinders offered their personal stories of the tragic voyage of the *Johanna*:

Narratives of the Survivors
The Mate's Story
Mr. Hejen, who is a splendid specimen of a sailor, his appearance being quite in keeping with the noble spirit he has proved himself to profess, said:

'I have been in the schooner seven years, and we left Mauritius for Melbourne on the 3rd April. The weather at the island was bad and unhealthy, and the crew were not in very good health when the topsails were loosened and a start made. The fresh sea breezes were, however, expected to bring them back to health; but as the days passed the usually smart fellows who composed the crew showed themselves to be very slow, and although a gallant attempt was made to throw off the disease, the second day at sea saw the majority of the men in their bunks.

'On the 5th of April one of the boys, named Herman Reuter, 17 years of age, a native of Papenburg, where his widowed mother resides, got very ill, and I feared he would die. I, therefore, got the forecastle well scrubbed out and endeavoured to drive the disease away from the ship by burning tar, but it was useless. I had just completed the work when I was seized with 'cold fever', and had to go to bed for a few days. The weather becoming bad, I had to come on deck, as the other fellows were far too ill to be about.

'On the 23rd April, when off St. Paul's [St. Paul Island, southern Indian Ocean], H. Borne, an able seaman, died. I buried him, and once more thought the disease had ran itself out; but three days later L. Olat, a seaman who had been in the schooner three years, died. All the while men were bad the weather was quite wintry, howling gales from the north-west to south-west, accompanied by snow and sleet, being with us incessantly. The wind, after blowing for several hours with hurricane force, would then almost die away, and as there was no light canvas set, there was nothing to steady her, the consequence being that she pitched and rolled fearfully. The only men on deck at this time were the captain and a boy, who were both so weak that they could not go aloft. I had therefore to set to work and lower the topgallant-yards myself, a task I accomplished on Sunday, 18th May.

'The lowering of the yards proved of but little avail, for the next gale saw her in the same position as she was before, with green seas breaking clean over her. The captain helped me to lift the covers off the after-hatch, and the three of us, with the assistance of a boy, who, although weak, managed to sling for us in the hold, threw some 300 bags of sugar overboard.'

A Near Miss For Mrs Meinders

'It was late in the afternoon when we finished, and it was then we nearly lost the 'mistress' [Mrs Meinders]. She was standing near the hatchway when a great sea came tumbling over the quarter and swept her clean off her feet and almost over the rail. Fortunately I saw her go, and seizing hold of a stay I caught her arm as she was going over the side.

'On May 1 the cook (J. Hiafer) died, and I almost envied him, for the work and the sickness so increased that I despaired of getting the ship to port. On the night of May 9 there was another death, the victim being a boy named Oarl Helgrindorf, whose home was a little Baltic village. We were in about 39° S. by this time and the weather was terribly cold, and the captain took to his bunk, leaving only Mrs. Meinders, the little girl, and myself to work the ship. As our misfortunes increased Mrs. Meinders improved in spirits, and what with working at the pumps (for the ship began to take water), attending to her sick husband and the little girl, and cooking for the crew, she had enough to do.

'The furling of the foresail, a new piece of canvas and very stiff, was the most difficult job I had, but after eight hours it was accomplished, and we bore away for Fremantle. Had it not been for Mrs. Meinders, however, and the bravery with which she stood by me, the schooner would never have got to port. The death of her husband after we left Fremantle was the saddest part of the whole voyage, for he was always a kind man and a good sailor.'

Post Script

Here the mate ended his little history of the voyage, but the terrible tasks he had to perform so frequently of burying the dead had so impressed him that he could not resist giving vent to his feelings.

'The forecastle,' he said, 'as you know, is small and closed up, as it was in the rough weather, and the air was so fearfully bad that when a man died I had to get the body away at once. When I went into the forecastle the men called out for water, and in their agony threw themselves on the floor. The poor men who died were all young, smart fellows, and we had been together so long that it was a terrible task for me to have to throw them overboard like dogs, but it could not be helped. Then I had to destroy the bedding, and altogether it was a terrible time, the like of which I hope never to experience again.'

Mrs Meinder's Narrative

The sorrows and sufferings of the voyage were told by the captain's wife, who, as she sat in the shadow of the mast, said:

'My name is Margherita Meinders, and I was born in 1863 at Papenburg, in the kingdom of Hanover. In 1882, when I was only 19 years of age, I was married, and I went to sea with my husband at once. I had never been to sea before, and I was afraid at first, but as I grew used to it I ceased to fear. My husband was with me, and I was happy. In 1883 my eldest boy, who is home in Germany, was born, and two years later little Susanna, who has been with me through all the troubles, was born. She was born when the ship was last in Melbourne, but I was at home then. I joined the *Johanna* shortly afterwards and have never been away since.'

The 'Awful' Voyage

'The voyage was the same as usual until after we left Mauritius, and then that awful time commenced. The men were all sick, and my husband was sick, and I thought we would all go to the bottom at once, and sometimes I did not care if we did, but I felt I must do something for the poor sailors who were suffering so, and cooked them meat and rice, and tea and coffee. The mate took it to them at first, but then when they all got bad I had to, and it used to make my heart sore to see them suffering so, and the quinine I gave them would not make them better. They were lying on the wet floor in the forecastle, and when the pain was very bad they would cry out and it made me cry.

'I was very frightened when poor Herman Boras died. I was really afraid then that we would all die off with the fever, but giving way would not help anyone, so I would not think about it. Four poor fellows were then thrown overboard, after dying in great agony. They were always calling for their friends and speaking of people they loved. It made me think whether I would get the fever, and what would become of my Susanna.

'The rough weather then made me forget everything, and one terrible night when I was taking my turn at the pumps a great sea washed me away to the side, and thought I was gone then. My first thought was of my little girl, but before I had time to think again I felt the mate dragging me back again. I don't know how I stood at the pumps after that or what I did at all, but my husband was getting worse and the mate was sickening again. We tied up the wheel then and fixed the sails and let the ship drift as it would.

'All hope appeared gone then, and it seemed wonderful to wake up in the morning and find that we were not wrecked. I cried a great deal then, and when the fourth sailor died I prayed that God would take us all quickly. I did not think my husband would recover then; but he did get better, and he helped the mate and me to throw overboard a lot of cargo. The mate and my husband got it out of the hold, and I threw it overboard. It seemed very heavy at first, but afterwards I did not feel it. The little girl did not know what trouble there was and was always calling to get on deck. It was so trying when we were working for our lives to hear the child crying to be allowed up.'

The Heroic Mate

'I could not do much for the ship – it was the mate. He was never tired and worked himself nearly to death. Sometimes he had to lie down on the wet deck, in the wind and the rain, and sleep. Then the ship would be tossed about every way, and the sea would sweep over her, but he was too tired to care, and when he woke up went back to the wheel and would get the ship back on her course again. There never was another man that suffered and worked as Hejen. He saved all our lives.

'When we got to Fremantle I could not speak for thanksgiving, and my husband got well, and I thought all our troubles were gone. The ship had not much trouble after, for it was all good weather, but my husband seemed to get worse as soon as we got to sea again and had bad cramps. He lost all his voice and could not speak at all, not even to say good-bye. I can't tell you about that time. It is so hard. All my heart was gone then, and I only cried. It did not seem real trouble as long as my husband lived; but it all seemed worse when he died. The ship was all right then and the wind was fair, but there seemed more danger. If it had not been for my little Susanna I would never have lived.

'I felt so thankful when we arrived here [Melbourne] that I could not help crying again. Nearly all belonging to the ship came from Papenburg, and it will be sad news for them – there are so many dead. I don't know what I will do, except go back to Papenburg with the *Johanna* when she sails.' (*South Australian Chronicle* [Adelaide], 2 August 1890)

Capt. Meinders had been 'quite well' when the *Johanna* left Fremantle on 29 June, for Melbourne:

> On the 2nd inst. [July], however, soon after dinner, he was seized with a fit, in which he remained twenty-four hours, and then died. A coffin was made for him, and next evening he was buried at sea, Mr. Hejen, the chief officer, reading the burial service of the Roman Catholic Church, of which the deceased was a member, in the presence of the rest of the crew. The widow was so overcome with grief that she could not attend the ceremony, and remained in the cabin with the child in her arms. (*The Press* [Canterbury, New Zealand], 7 August 1890)

4

HUNGER

Intelligence of a case of suffering and privation at sea, resulting fatally to one of those concerned, reached Noumea [New Caledonia] by the ketch *Rosette*, which arrived there from Ouvea [an island in the New Caledonia group] just prior to the departure of the last French mail boat for Sydney. Two natives, named Tan and Goin, about 20 years of age, embarked on a raft for the purpose of fishing. By means of a pole they pushed the raft along the coast, and managed to secure a good load of fish. So engrossed were they in fishing that they did not notice that the tide was carrying them away from the land, and when they realised this fact they found it impossible to make their way back to land.

The raft was carried away to sea, and for several days the unfortunate men were without food or water. At last, overcome by hunger, Tan decided to eat some of the raw fish, which had become almost entirely putrid. His companion, however, refused to do this, and eventually died from starvation and exposure. For three days and

nights Tan kept the corpse of Goin on the raft, but was then compelled to cast it overboard. At last, after being 20 days at sea, the raft was carried by the current to land at Ouvea, where Tan was rescued in an apparently dying condition. So terribly famished was he that during the last few days he had eaten pieces of wood from the raft.
(*Evening Post* [Wellington, New Zealand], 5 January 1897)

Although British sailing ship crews were not ordinarily forced to eat parts of their vessel from hunger, their staple diet of gristly salt pork and beef was an ordeal in itself. Nineteenth-century seamen survived on an officially pre-scribed diet consisting of: pork and beef (or, as *they* claimed, horsemeat) of the poorest quality that was salted down, brined and stored in wooden casks for years; 'hard tack' that was called 'bread' but was actually iron-hard ships biscuit, or 'pantiles' (including, more often than not, the added protein of weevils); pea soup, which was actually very popular (when it was properly peasy rather than 'being nearly all water'); and an over-stewed vaguely coffee-flavoured hot drink optimistically called *coffee*. A decent ship's cook could make such provisions edible, but he wasn't an alchemist: palatability was not in his job description nor, consequently, part of a sailor's diet.

The Seaman's 'Whack'

A seaman's diet on British ships – their 'whack' – was regu-lated by the Merchant Shipping Act in force at the time. Towards the end of the 1800s that daily ration per man, was: 1lb bread or the equivalent in ship's biscuit; 1½lb salt beef or 1¼lb salt pork, on alternate days; ½lb flour and ¼ pint of peas every other day; ⅛oz tea; ½oz coffee; 2 oz sugar; and 3 quarts fresh water (for cooking, washing and drinking). The 1906 Merchant Shipping Act prescribed a better standard and wider variety of diet and quality of provisions.

The one thing notably absent from a sailor's 'whack' in the nineteenth century was fresh vegetables. Lime juice, issued daily on British merchant vessels from 1844, was supposed to give them a daily dose of vitamin C in lieu of the varied vitamin content of fresh vegetables which could only survive for a few weeks on a voyage that might last four months and often longer. The daily dose of lime juice on British ships (thus 'limejuicers', and 'limeys') was issued to keep scurvy at bay.

Burgoo ('a watery porridge with a flavouring of weevils', from *The Way of A Ship*, by Alan Villiers) was a staple breakfast. 'Dandy funk' was made by pounding ship's biscuits into a coarse powder, mixed with water, jam and fat, and baked in the galley by the cook. 'Cracker' hash was similar: bits of ship's biscuit mixed with leftover anything (pea soup, scraps of meat or fat) and baked. Some livestock of hogs or chickens might be kept in pens on deck to be slaughtered on special occasions to provide the rare rapture of fresh meat.

'Plum duff' was served on British ships on Sundays, holidays and feast days, and was a particular favourite of limejuicers' crews:

*Origin of Plum Duff – How A Famous Dish
of English Sailors Got its Name*

There are many traditions respecting the origin of the name 'plum duff,' the great holiday dish of sailors. No feast on shipboard is considered perfect without it. According to the story given in the history of the British

Rough rations on a trading schooner: a complaint to the mate.
(*The Graphic*, 27 August 1898)

navy, an English brig in the South Pacific was caught in a series of awful hurricanes. All on board were anxious to reach a port in time for Christmas, but the holiday found them still off the Navigator islands [Samoa]. Worst of all, they had shipped a sea that carried away the hencoop containing a few chickens.

When the cook saw the Christmas dinner floating in the lee scuppers and in danger of going overboard he made a gallant charge down the slippery, sloping deck to recover it, but at that moment a great wave rose high over the bulwarks, broke with resistless fury on the very spot where he stood, and when it subsided cook and chickens had both disappeared.

The unfortunate accident left the crew not only without a Christmas dinner, but without anyone to prepare an ordinary meal. The sailors were heartily sick of 'hard tack' and remembered with longing the famous plum pudding of Merry England. They determined that somehow they must have a Christmas pudding and drew lots as to who should be the cook.

The choice fell on the boatswain's mate, a brawny son of the Emerald Isle. In the galley he found an old cookbook. This he solemnly pored over in search of something promising, but for lack of skills or materials found nothing he dared venture upon. At last he settled upon a recipe which began, 'Make a stiff dough.' When he reached the word dough he said to himself, 'If r-o-u-g-h spells ruff, d-o-u-g-h spells duff.'

So he made the pudding, putting in some fine Malaga raisins, and served it out with a generous quantity of rich sauce. The sailors hailed it with delight and appreciation. 'What d'ye call it?' they asked. 'Plum duff,' said the proud cook. And plum duff it has remained from that day to this. (*Amador Ledger* [Jackson, California], 13 May 1904)

The standard supply of casked meats and tinned provisions was only meant to last the average duration of a passage, or a bit more. But no one could predict how long a sailing ship's passage would be. And no matter how much food was provided for, rations sometimes went low – or even ran out altogether. In those cases it wasn't just the pangs of privation that sailors endured; it was the suffering of *real* hunger, and the *real* fear of actual death by starvation.

Famine in the *Peggy*

One of the most infamous incidents of a famished ship's crew concerned the brigantine *Peggy* during a voyage from the Azores to New York in 1765. The *Peggy* loaded a cargo of wine and spirits at Fayal, Azores, and sailed on her return voyage for New York on 24 October 1765. Almost immediately she was assailed by storms, dismasted, and started to leak. Battered and drifting around the North Atlantic, her provisions ran out by mid-December. A passing vessel that promised to send on board some relief provisions decided instead to abandon her, to the dismay, and disdain, of the *Peggy*'s starving crew.

Their ravenous hunger pitted them to catch 'the only animals that remained on board ... a couple of pigeons and a cat, which were devoured in an instant'. Worse was to come. After gnawing through 'oil, candles, and leather', all consumed by the end of December, their attention was drawn to a more nutritious temptation, the ultimate relief and resurrection of starving seamen: the body and flesh of their own shipmates:

Extraordinary Famine in the American Ship Peggy – *On her Return from the Azores to New York in 1765*

Famine frequently leads men to the commission of the most horrible excesses: insensible on such occasions to the appeals of nature and reason, man assumes the character of a beast of prey; he is deaf to every representation, and coolly meditates the death of his fellow-creatures.

One of these scenes so afflicting to humanity was, in the year 1765, exhibited in the brigantine the *Peggy*, David Harrison commander, freighted by certain merchants of

New-York, and bound to the Azores. She arrived without accident at Fayal, one of those islands, and having disposed of her cargo, took on board a lading of wine and spirits. On the 24th of October, of the same year, she set sail on her return to New-York.

On the 29th, the wind, which had till then been favorable, suddenly shifted. Violent storms, which succeeded each other almost without interruption, during the month of November, did much damage to the vessel. In spite of all the exertions of the crew and the experience of the captain, the masts went by the board, and all the sails, excepting one, were torn to rags; and to add to their distress, several leaks were discovered in the hold.

At the beginning of December the wind abated a little, but the vessel was driven out of her course; and, destitute of masts, sails, and rigging, she was perfectly unmanageable, and drifted to and fro at the mercy of the waves. This, however, was the smallest evil; another of a much more alarming nature soon manifested itself. Upon examining the state of the provisions, they were found to be almost totally exhausted. In this deplorable situation the crew had no hope of relief but from chance.

A few days after this unpleasant discovery, two vessels were descried early one morning, and a transient ray of hope cheered the unfortunate crew of the *Peggy*. The sea ran so high as to prevent Captain Harrison from approaching the ships, which were soon out of sight. The disappointed seamen, who were in want of every thing, then fell upon the wine and brandy with which the ship was laden. They allotted to the captain two small jars of water, each containing about a gallon, being the remainder of their stock. Some days elapsed, during which the men in some measure appeased the painful cravings of hunger by incessant intoxication.

On the fourth day a ship was observed bearing toward them in full sail; no time was lost in making signals of distress, and the crew had the inexpressible satisfaction to perceive that they were answered. The sea was sufficiently calm to permit the two vessels to approach each other. The strangers seemed much affected by the account of their sufferings and misfortunes, and promised them a certain quantity of biscuit; but it was not immediately sent on board, the captain alleging, as an excuse for the delay, that he had just begun a nautical observation which he was desirous to finish.

Despair

However unreasonable such a pretext appeared under the present circumstances, the famished crew of the *Peggy* were obliged to submit. The time mentioned by the captain had nearly expired, when, to their extreme mortification, the latter, regardless of his promise, crowded all his sails and bore away. No language is adequate to describe the despair and consternation which then overwhelmed the crew. Enraged and destitute of hope, they fell upon whatever they had spared till then. The only animals that remained on board were a couple of pigeons and a cat, which were devoured in an instant. The only favor they showed the captain was to reserve for him the head of the cat. He afterward declared, that however disgusting it would have been on any other occasion, he thought it at that moment a treat exquisitely delicious.

The unfortunate men then supported their existence by living on oil, candles, and leather, and these were entirely consumed by the 28th of December.

An Execrable Proposition

From that day until the 13th of January [1766] it is impossible to tell in what manner they subsisted. Captain Harrison had been for some time unable to leave his cabin, being confined to his bed by a severe fit of the gout. On the last mentioned day the sailors went to him in a body, with the mate at their head; the latter acted as spokesman, and after an affecting representation of the deplorable state to which they were reduced, declared that it was necessary to sacrifice one in order to save the rest; adding, that their resolution was irrevocably fixed, and that they intended to cast lots for the victim.

The captain, a tender and humane man, could not hear such a barbarous proposition without shuddering; he represented to them that they were men, and ought to regard each other as brethren; that, by such an assassination, they would for ever consign themselves to universal execration; and commanded them, with all his authority, to relinquish the idea of committing such an atrocious crime.

The captain was silent; but he had spoken to deaf men. They all with one voice replied, that it was indifferent to them whether he approved of their resolution or not; that they had only acquainted him with it out of respect, and because he would run the same risk as themselves; adding that, in the general misfortune, all command and distinction were at an end. With these words they left him, and went upon deck, where the lots were drawn.

The Victim

A negro who was on board and belonged to Captain Harrison [this was a hundred years before the abolition of slavery in the United States] was the victim. It is more than probable that the lot had been consulted only for the sake of form, and that the wretched black was proscribed the moment the sailors first formed their resolution. They instantly sacrificed him. One of the crew tore out his liver and devoured it, without having the patience to dress it, by broiling, or in any other manner. He was soon afterward taken ill, and died the following day in convulsions, and with all the symptoms of madness.

Some of his comrades proposed to keep his body to live upon, after the negro was consumed; but this advice was rejected by the majority, doubtless on account of the malady which had carried him off. He was, therefore, thrown overboard, and consigned to the deep.

The captain, in the intervals when he was the least tormented by the gout, was not more exempt from the attacks of hunger than the rest of the crew; but he resisted all the persuasions of his men to partake of their horrid repast. He contented himself with the water which had been assigned to him, mixing with it a small quantity of spirits; and this was the only sustenance he took during the whole period of his distress.

Second Victim

The body of the negro, equally divided, and eaten with the greatest economy, lasted till the 26th of January. On the 29th the famished crew deliberated upon selecting a second victim. They again came to inform the captain of their intention, and he appeared to give his consent, fearing lest the enraged sailors might have recourse to the lot without him. They left it with him to fix upon any method that he should think proper. The captain, summoning all his strength, wrote upon small pieces of paper, the name of each man who was then on board the brigantine, folded them up, and put them into a hat, and shook them well together.

The crew meanwhile preserved an awful silence; each eye was fixed, and each mouth was open, while terror was strongly impressed upon every countenance. With a trembling hand one of them drew from the hat the fatal billet, which he delivered to the captain, who opened it and read aloud the name of *David Flatt*. The unfortunate man on whom the lot had fallen appeared perfectly resigned to his fate. 'My friends,' (said he to his companions,) 'the only favor I request of you is, not to keep me long in pain; dispatch me as speedily as you did the negro.' Then turning to the man who had performed the first execution, he added, 'It is you I choose to give me the mortal blow.'

He requested an hour to prepare himself for death, to which his comrades could only reply with tears. Meanwhile compassion, and the remonstrances of the captain, prevailed over the hunger of the most hardhearted. They unanimously resolved to defer the sacrifice till eleven o'clock the following morning. Such a short reprieve afforded very little consolation to Flatt.

The certainty of dying the next day made such a deep impression upon his mind, that his body, which, for above a month, had withstood the almost total privation of nourishment, sunk beneath it. He was seized with a violent fever, and his state was so much aggravated by a delirium with which it was accompanied, that some of the sailors proposed to kill him immediately, in order to terminate his sufferings. The majority, however, adhered to the resolution which had been taken of waiting till the following morning.

Reprieve and Salvation

At ten o'clock in the morning of the 30th of January a large fire was already made to dress the limbs of the unfortunate victim, when a sail was descried at a distance. A favorable wind drove her toward the *Peggy*, and she proved to be the *Susan*, returning from Virginia and bound to London.

The captain could not refrain from tears at the affecting account of the sufferings endured by the famished crew. He lost no time in affording them relief, supplying them immediately with provisions and rigging, and offered to convoy the *Peggy* to London. The distance from New-York, their proximity to the English coast, together with the miserable state of the brigantine, induced the two captains to proceed to England.

The voyage was prosperous; only two men died, all the others gradually recovered their strength. Flatt himself was restored to perfect health, after having been so near the gates of death. (*The Mariner's Chronicle*, 1834)

The *Hornet* Survivors:
A Wrecked Crew's Hunger

The American clipper ship *Hornet*, 1,426 tons, launched in 1851, was a competitor with other famously speedy American clipper ships of her day, particularly the *Flying Cloud*, along the well-furrowed track round the Horn between New York and other East Coast ports, and San Francisco and other West Coast ports. On what turned out to be her last such passage, *Hornet*, commanded by Capt. Josiah Mitchell, left New York on 15 January 1866 with a highly combustible cargo of kerosene and candles, as well as rope, iron rails and miscellaneous merchandise.

Having rounded the Horn, she took fire on 3 May in the Pacific just north of the equator, 'about 1,000 miles due south from Cape St Lucas, Lower California [Cabo San Lucas, Baja California], 2,500 miles east of Hawaii'. The following day, 'the noble clipper made a plunge forward and went down bow first, leaving no trace of her but a few charred spars and pieces of wood floating about'. Three boats with the crew and Capt. Mitchell took to the lonely wastes of 'the vacant sky and the desolate sea' between Mexico and Hawaii. Only one boat survived, that of Capt. Mitchell, with two passengers, the third mate, and eleven seamen – fifteen souls in all – which arrived at Hawaii on 15 June 1866.

The subsequent narrative of the *Hornet* castaways' odyssey focused more than usual in such narratives on the provisions that kept them alive for over a month, and the privations of hunger and despair they suffered before reaching the safety of their Hawaiian landfall:

A Tale of the Sea

The following is a correspondent's account of the privations the crew of the ship *Hornet* endured after she was burnt in north latitude 2.20, west longitude 112.8, about 1,000 miles due south from Cape St. Lucas, Lower California, and 2,500 miles east of Hawaii. After describing the loss of the vessel, he says:

'I have said that in the few minutes' time allowed him Captain Mitchell was only able to seize upon the few articles of food and other necessaries that happened to lie about the cabin. Here is the list:-

'Four hams, seven pieces of salt pork (each piece weighed about four pounds), one box of raisins, 100lb of bread (about one barrel), twelve 2lb cans of oysters, clams and assorted meats; six buckets of raw potatoes (which rotted so fast they got but little benefit from them), a keg with 4lb of butter in it, twelve gallons of water, in a forty-gallon tierce, or 'scuttle-butt,' four one-gallon demijohns full of water, three bottles of brandy, the property of passengers; some pipes, matches, and 100lb of tobacco; but no medicines.'

'Short Allowance'

'That was all these poor fellows had to live on for forty-three days – the whole thirty-one of them. Each boat had a compass, a quadrant, a copy of 'Bowditch's Navigator,' and a nautical almanac; and the captain's and chief mate's boats had chronometers. Of course, all hands were put on short allowance at once. The day they set sail from the ship each man was allowed a small morsel of salt pork, or a little piece of potato, if he preferred it, and half a sea biscuit three times a day. To understand how very light this ration of bread was it is only necessary to know that it takes seven of these sea biscuits to weigh a pound [so, about 2½ oz per man per day].

'The first two days they only allowed one gill of water [4 fluid oz] a day to each man; but for nearly a fortnight after that, the weather was lowering and stormy, and frequent rain squalls occurred. The rain was caught in canvas, and whenever there was a shower, the forty gallon cask and every other vessel that would hold water was filled – even all the boots that were water-tight were pressed into this service, except such as the matches and tobacco were deposited in to keep dry. So for fourteen days. There were luxurious occasions when there was plenty of water to drink. But after that, how they suffered the agonies of thirst for four long weeks.

'For seven days the boats sailed on, and the starving men ate their fragment of biscuit and morsel of raw pork in the morning, and hungrily counted the tedious hours until noon and night should bring their repetitions of it. And in the long intervals they looked mutely in each other's faces, or turned their wistful eyes across the wild sea, in search of the succoring sail that was never to come.

'"Didn't you talk?" I asked one of the men. "No; we were too down-hearted – that is, the first week or more. We didn't talk; we only looked at each other and over the ocean." And thought, I suppose – thought of home, of shelter from storms, of food, and drink, and rest. The hope of being picked up hung to them constantly, was ever present to them and in their thoughts, like hunger. And in the captain's mind was the hope of making the Clarion Islands [Revillagigedo Islands, 700km off the Mexican coast], and he clung to it many a day.

'The nights were very dark. They had no lantern, and could not see the compass, and there were no stars to steer by. Thomas said of the boat, "She handled easy, and we steered by the feel of the wind in our faces and the heave of the sea." Dark and dismal and lonesome work was that. Sometimes they got a fleeting glimpse of the sailor's friend, the north star, and then they lighted a match and hastened anxiously to see if their compass was faithful to them, for it had to be placed close to an iron ringbolt in the stern, and they were afraid during these first nights, that this might cause it to vary. It proved true to them, however.'

Dolphin for Dinner

'On the fifth day a notable incident occurred. They caught a dolphin [the fish, not the mammal], and while their enthusiasm was still at its highest over this strike of good fortune, they captured another. They made a trifling fire in a tin plate and warmed the prizes – to cook them was not possible – and divided them equally among all hands, and ate them. On the sixth day two more dolphins were caught. Two more were caught on the seventh day, and also a small bonito, and they began to believe they were always going to live in this extravagant way; but it was not to be – these were their last dolphins, and they never could get another bonito, though they saw them and longed for them often afterwards.

'On the eighth day the rations were reduced about one half. Thus breakfast, one-fourth of a biscuit, an ounce of ham, and a gill of water to each man; dinner, same quantity of bread and water, and four oysters or clams; supper, water and bread the same, and twelve large raisins or fourteen small ones to a man. Also, during the first twelve or fifteen days, each man had a spoonful of brandy a day; then it gave out.

'This day, as one of the men was gazing across the dull waste of waters as usual, he saw a small dark object rising and falling upon the waves. He called attention to it, and in a moment every eye was bent upon it in intense interest. When the boat had approached a little nearer it was discovered to be a small green turtle fast asleep. Every noise was hushed as they crept upon the unconscious slumberer. Directions were given and hopes and fears expressed in guarded whispers.

'At the fateful moment – a moment of tremendous consequence to these famishing men – the expert selected for the high and responsible office stretched forth his hand, while his excited comrades bated their breath and trembled for the success of the enterprise, and seized the turtle by the hind leg and hauled him aboard. His delicate flesh was carefully divided among the party, and eagerly devoured, after being 'warmed,' like the dolphin, which went before him.'

Separation

'The eighteenth day was a memorable one to the wanderers on the lonely sea. On that day the boats parted company. The captain said that separate from each other there were three chances for the saving of some of the party, where there could be but one chance if they kept together. The captain told the mates he was still going to try to make the Clarion Isles, and that they could imitate his example if they thought best, but he wished them to freely follow the dictates of their own judgement in the matter. At 11 o'clock in the forenoon the boats were all cast loose from each other, and then, as friends part from friends whom they expect to see no more in life, all hands hailed with a fervent "God bless you, boys; good-bye!" and the two cherished sails drifted away and disappeared from the longing gaze that followed them so sorrowfully.

[The continuation of the narrative concerned the captain's boat only.]

'On the afternoon of this eventful day two 'boobies' were caught – a bird about as large as a duck, but all bones and feathers – not as much meat as there is on a pigeon; not nearly so much, the men say. They ate them raw – bones, entrails, and everything; no single morsel was wasted; they were carefully apportioned among the fifteen men. No fire could be built for cooking purposes;

the wind was so strong and the sea ran so high that it was all a man could do to light his pipe.'

'Sail!'

'On the morning of the twenty-first day, while some of the crew were dozing on the thwarts, and others were buried in reflection, one of the men suddenly sprang to his feet and cried, "A sail! a sail!" Of course, sluggish blood bounded then, and eager eyes were turned to see the welcome vision. But disappointment was their portion as usual. It was only the chief mate's boat drifting across their path after three days' absence. In a short time the two parties were abreast of each other and in hailing distance. They talked twenty minutes; the mate reported 'all well,' and then sailed away, and they never saw him afterwards.

'On the twenty-fourth day Captain Mitchell took an observation, and found that he was in lat. 16 deg. N, and long. 117 deg. W. – about one thousand miles from where his vessel was burned. The hope he had cherished so long that he would be able to make the Clarion Isles deserted him at last; he could only go before the wind, and he was now obliged to attempt the best thing the S.E. trades could do for him – blow him to the "American Group," or to the Sandwich Islands [Hawaii] – and therefore he reluctantly, and with many misgivings, turned his prow towards those distant archipelagoes.

'What these men suffered during the next three weeks no mortal man may hope to describe. Their stomachs and intestines felt to the grasp like a couple of small tough balls, and the gnawing hunger pains and the dreadful thirst that was consuming them in those burning latitudes became almost insupportable.

'And yet, as the men say, the captain said funny things and talked cheerful talk until he got them to converse freely, and then they used to spend hours together describing delicious dinners they had eaten at home, and earnestly planning interminable and preposterous bills of fare for dinners they were going to eat on shore, if they ever lived through their troubles to do it, poor fellows. The captain said plain bread and butter would be good enough for him all the days of his life, if he could only get it.

'But the saddest things were the dreams they had. An unusually intelligent young sailor, named Cox, said: "In those long days and nights we dreamed all the time – not that we ever slept, I don't mean – no, we only sort of dozed, three-fourths of the faculties awake and the other fourth benumbed into the counterfeit of a slumber; oh, no – some of us never slept for twenty-three days, and no man ever saw the captain asleep for upwards of thirty. But we barely dozed that way and dreamed – and always of such feasts! Bread, and fowls, and meat, everything a man could think of, piled along long tables, and smoking hot! And we sat down and seized upon the first dish in our reach, like ravenous wolves, and carried it to our lips – and then we awoke and found the same starving comrades about us, and the vacant sky and the desolate sea."

'These things are terrible even to think of.'

Rations and Flying-fish

'On the twenty-eighth day the rations were: One teaspoonful of bread crumbs, and about an ounce of ham, for the morning meal; a spoonful of bread crumbs alone for the evening meal, and one gill of water three times a day. A kitten would perish eventually under such sustenance. Four little flying-fish, the size of the sardines of these latter days, flew into the boat on the night of the twenty-eighth day. They were divided among the hands and eaten raw. On the twenty-ninth day, they caught another, and divided it into fifteen pieces – less than a teaspoonful apiece.

'On the thirtieth day they caught a third flying-fish, and gave it to the revered old captain – a fish of the same poor little proportions as the others, four inches long – a present a king might be proud of under such circumstances, a present whose value, in the eyes of the men who offered it, was not to be found in the Bank of England – yea, whose vaults were not able to contain it. The old captain refused to take it; the men insisted; the captain said no – he would take his fifteenth – they must take the remainder. They said in substance, though not in words, that they would see him in Jericho first! So the captain had to eat the fish.

'On Monday, the thirtieth day after the disaster, "we had nothing left," said the third mate, "but a pound and a half of ham – the bone was a good deal the heaviest part of it – and one soup and bouilli tin." These things were divided among the fifteen men, and they ate it all – two ounces of food to each man. I do not count the ham bone, as that was saved for next day. For some time now the poor wretches had been cutting their old boots into small pieces and eating them. They would also pound wet rags to a sort of pulp and eat them.

'On the thirty-ninth day, the ham bone was divided up into rations and scraped with knives and eaten. I said, "You say the two sick men remained sick all through, and after a while two or three had to be relieved from standing watch; how did you get along without medicine?"

The reply was, "Oh! we couldn't have kept them if we'd had them; if we'd had boxes of pills, or anything like that, we'd have eaten them. It was just as well; we couldn't have kept them, and we couldn't have given them to the sick men alone; we'd have shared them around all alike, I guess."

'It was said rather in jest, but it was a pretty true jest, no doubt. After apportioning the ham bone, the captain cut the canvas cover that had been around the ham into fifteen square pieces, and each man took his portion. This was the last division of food the captain made. The men broke up the small oken [oak] butter tub and divided the staves among themselves and gnawed them up. The shell of the little green turtle heretofore mentioned, was scraped with knives and eaten to the last shaving. The third mate chewed pieces of boots and spat them out, but ate nothing except the straps of the two pairs of boots – ate one on the 39th day, and saved one for the 40th.

'The men seemed to have thought in their own minds of the shipwrecked mariner's last dreadful resort – cannibalism; but they do not appear to have conversed about it. They only thought of casting lots and killing one of their number as a possibility; but even while they were eating rags, and bone, and boots, and shell, and hard oak wood, they seem to have still had a notion that it was remote. They felt that some one of the company must die soon – which one they well knew; and during the last three or four days of their terrible voyage they were patiently but hungrily waiting for him.

'I wonder if the subject of these anticipations knew what they were thinking of? He must have known it – he must have felt it. They had even calculated how long he

Burning of the California clipper *Hornet*, One Thousand Miles From Land. Our engraving illustrates an unfortunate disaster which occurred to the *Hornet*, one of the finest of the California line of clippers. What story can be more thrilling than that of a ship's crew in open boats, one thousand miles from land, compelled to witness the burning of their ship, and then to drift for days upon the Pacific, almost without hope, and subject to the exposure of sea and sky, and to the peril of starvation? (*Harper's Weekly*, 29 September 1866)

would last; they said to themselves, but not to each other, I think they said, "He will die Saturday – and then?" '

Reprieve and Salvation

'At eleven o'clock on the 15th of June, after suffering all that men may suffer and live for forty-three days in an open boat, on a scorching tropical sea, one of the men feebly shouted the glad tidings, "Land ho!" The "watch below" were lying in the bottom of the boat. What do you suppose they did! They said they had been cruelly disappointed over and over again, and they dreaded to risk another experience of the kind – they could not bear it – they lay still where they were. They said they would not trust to an appearance that might not be land after all. They would wait.

'Shortly it was proved beyond question that they were almost to land. Then there was joy in the party. One man is said to have swooned away. Another said the sight of the green hills is better to him than a day's rations – a strange figure for a man to use who had been fasting for forty days and forty nights.' (*Otago Daily Times* [New Zealand], 14 December 1866)

The *Frances Mary*: Shipwreck and Sufferings of Ann Saunders

In March 1826 the British naval vessel HMS *Blonde* was returning to England after a voyage to the Hawaiian Islands to return the bodies of the Hawaiian monarchs King Kamehameha II and Queen Kamamalu who had died on a visit to England, probably from measles, in 1824. The *Blonde*'s commander was Lord (later Admiral) George Anson Byron, the 7th Baron and cousin of the Romantic poet Lord George Gordon Byron. Around 700 miles northeast of the Azores she came across a virtually derelict ship in distress. It was to be a particularly 'affecting incident' that surpassed 'in horrible interest, all that invention has ever produced to move the sympathies of man':

Wreck of the Frances Mary, *4th February, 1826*

The following affecting account is given of the wreck of the *Frances Mary*, in a narrative of a voyage of H.M.S. *Blonde*:

'On the 28th of January [1826] we left St. Helena, and on the 27th of February we crossed the line [equator], where we experienced nearly three days of calm; after which we continued our course, favoured by the north-east trade wind, until the 7th of March, when one of those affecting incidents occurred which surpass, in horrible interest, all that invention has ever produced to move the sympathies of man.

'The morning was squally, but about noon it cleared up, and the ship's place [position] was ascertained to be in latitude 44° 18' N. and longitude 23° W. About four o'clock, P.M., a strange sail was reported, and though, from the haziness of the weather, she was but indistinctly seen, it was perceived that she was in distress. Our course was immediately altered, and we steered directly for her, being distant about nine miles.

'As we neared her, she proved to be in distress indeed; she was a complete wreck, and waterlogged, but, being laden with timber, had not sunk. Her dismantled rigging indicated how severe had been her struggle with the elements. Her foremast was carried away, but part of her bowsprit and the stump of her main-topmast were still standing, and a topsail-yard was crossed, to which a few shreds of canvas were still hanging. An English jack [union jack flag] reversed [a signal of distress] was attached to the main rigging, and the mizenmast was partly gone. The sea had cleared the decks of every thing. We all now felt the greatest anxiety to reach her.

'The evening was closing in, with every sign of an approaching gale. Thick squalls had already once or twice concealed from us the object of our pursuit; but at length we came near enough to discern two human figures on the wreck, and, presently, four others came out from behind the remnants of a tattered sail, which hung from the main rigging, and which had, as it appeared, been their only shelter from the weather.

'It was late ere our boat reached the wreck, where she remained long; and, as the weather was growing worse, and the night dark, we fired a gun to hasten her return. No words can describe the wretched state of the poor creatures she brought when she did come. Two women and four men were sent up in the arms of the sailors, evidently suffering in the last stage of famine. They were immediately carried below, and supplied with small quantities of tea and bread, then stripped of their wretched clothing, washed, and put to bed.

'Meantime the officer reported the condition in which he had found the wreck. It appeared to have been thirty-two days in the state in which he saw it, during which time most of the crew had died, and the rest had only preserved life by feeding on their late companions. When the officer went on board, the two women rushed towards him, kissed his hands, and hailed him as a deliverer. The men, stupefied, as it appeared, with suffering, scarcely spoke, but hastily gathering their tattered clothes round them, hurried towards the boat.

'The master of the vessel, his wife, a female passenger, two middle-aged men, and one young man, were all that survived of seventeen. One of the women, when brought on the *Blonde*'s deck, fell on her knees and exclaimed – "Great God, where am I! Is it a dream?" But it was not until the next day that we heard the particulars of their sad story.' (*Chronicles Of The Sea*, Vol. I, 1838)

The woman who fell to her knees on the *Blonde*'s deck was a twenty-three year old Englishwoman, Ann Saunders. Her later narration of the horrendous events on board the small (398 tons) ship *Frances* (or *Francis*) *Mary* during her passage from St John's, New Brunswick, to Liverpool, in the winter of 1826, was a harrowing account not only of hardship at sea but of the grisly realities of survival when the spectre of extreme hunger skulked around a starving ship's decks.

After her departure from St John's on 18 January 1826, the timber-laden vessel was constantly assailed by winter North Atlantic storms. The crew were hammered by the exhaustion of struggling against the weather, the cold, and, eventually, the shortage of food. Early in February a 'poor seaman was discovered', early in the morning, 'hanging lifeless by some part of the rigging', overcome by cold and fatigue. About a week later, on 12 February, a second seaman, James Clarke, succumbed from 'no other complaint … than the weakness caused by famine'.

Another nine seamen perished up till 7 March when HMS *Blonde* rescued the remaining six survivors, including Ann Saunders, about 700 miles north-east of the Azores. The awful tragedy that eleven of the original crew of fifteen on the *Francis Mary* died from fatigue and famine was accompanied by the grimmer revelation to Lord Byron's horror that the survivors had subsisted upon the corpses of their brethren, which 'caused tears to bedew those faces' of their rescuers.

Worst of all, though, was that the last man to die was none other than Ann Saunders' fiancé himself, James Frier, cook on the *Francis Mary* – and that she herself 'plead [her] claim to the greater portion of his precious blood, as it oozed half congealed from the wound inflicted upon his lifeless body!!!'

Ann Saunders' Narrative (Extracts)

Narrative of the Shipwreck and Sufferings of Miss Ann Saunders: Who was a Passenger on Board the Ship Francis Mary, *which Foundered at Sea on the 5th Feb. 1826, on Her Passage from New Brunswick to Liverpool ...* (9 February 1827)

'For the information of such of my readers as may be unacquainted with the fact, it may not be unimportant that I commence the narrative of my recent unparalleled sufferings, with stating, that I am a native of Liverpool, [Eng.] where I was born in June, 1802, of reputable parents; who, although as regarded "worldly riches," were ranked with the "poorer class," yet, succeeded in bestowing on me what I now and ever shall conceive a legacy of more inestemable worth, to wit, an education sufficient to enable me to peruse the sacred Scriptures, whereby I was early taught the importance of attending to the concerns of my soul.

'At an early age I had the misfortune to lose my father – but, young as I was, the irreperable [*sic*] loss made a deep and lasting impression upon my mind – by this melancholy and unexpected event, my poor mother was left a widow with five helpless children, and without the means of contributing but scanty pittance to their support – the three oldest were in consequence put out into respectable families in the neighbourhood, where I have reason to believe we were treated with as much tenderness, as young children generally are, who are bound out under similar circumstances.

'When I arrived to the age of eighteen, I was persuaded to take up my abode with a widowed aunt, with whom I remained until sometime in October, 1825. It was while with my aunt, that I became first acquainted with that peculiarly unfortunate youth, James Frier, whose wretched and untimely fate, I shall hereafter have a sad occasion to speak.'

Voyage to Canada

'While with my aunt, I also became intimately acquainted with a Mrs. Kendall, the wife of Capt. John Kendall, a lady of pious and amiable disposition, and who, I believe, was very deservedly respected by all who had the pleasure of her acquaintance. It was by the very strong solicitations of this lady (and those of the unfortunate youth above mentioned) that I consented to accompany her with her husband, on their passage from Liverpool to St. Johns, (New Brunswick,) in the fall of 1825.

'It was early in the morning of the 10th November, that I took an affectionate leave of my mother and sisters, and embarked with Mrs. Kendall, (whose companion I was to be,) and bid adieu for the first time to the shores of my native land. The wind was favorable, but it being the first time in my life that I had ever adventured more than half a mile on the ocean, with seasickness and a depression of spirits, I was confined to my berth, the first three days, after we left port – but, becoming more accustomed to the motion of the vessel, I soon regained my health and spirits, and from this moment enjoyed a pleasant passage, without any very remarkable occurrence attending us, until we reached St. Johns, the port of our destination.'

St. John's to Liverpool

'On the 18th January, 1826, (Capt. Kendall having obtained a cargo of timber, and made every necessary preparation for our departure,) we set sail for Liverpool, with a favorable wind, and with the prospect and joyful expectations of an expeditious passage – on board of the ship were 21 souls, including Mrs. Kendall, and myself – many of the seamen were married men, and had left in Europe numerous families, dependent on them for support – Alas! poor mortals, little did they probably think, when they bid their loving companions and their tender little ones the last adieu, that it was to be a final one, and that they were to behold their faces no more, forever, in this frail world! but, we must not charge an infinitely wise and good God foolishly, who cannot err, but orders every event for the best.

'We enjoyed favorable weather until about the 1st February, when a severe gale was experienced, which blew away some of the yards and spars of our vessel, and washed away one of the boats off the deck, and severely wounded some of the seamen – early in the morning ensuing, the gale having somewhat abated, Mrs. Kendall and myself employed ourselves in dressing the wounds of the poor fellows that were most injured while those who had escaped injury, were employed in clearing the deck of the broken spars, splicing and disentangling the rigging, &c., so that in a few hours they were enabled again to make sail, and with the pleasing hope that they should encounter no more boisterous and contrary winds to impede their passage.

'But, in this they were soon sadly disappointed, for on the 5th, they were visited with a still more severe gale, from E.S.E., which indeed caused the sea to run "mountains high!" The captain gave orders to his men to do everything in their power to do, for the safety of our lives – all sails were clewed up, and the ship hove to, but the gale still increasing, about noon our vessel was struck by a tremendous sea, which swept from her decks almost every moveable article, and washed one of the seamen overboard, (who was providentially saved) and in a few moments after by another tremendous sea the whole of the ship's stern was stove in! this was only the beginning of a scene of horrid calamities! doubly horrible to me, (as the reader must suppose) who had never before witnessed any thing so awful.'

Appeal to the Almighty

'While the captain and officers of the ship were holding a consultation on deck, what was best to be done for the preservation of our lives, Mrs. Kendall and myself were on our knees, on the quarter deck, as earnestly engaged in prayer to the Almighty God that he would in his tender mercy spare our lives, and consistent with his will that he would finally restore us in safety to our friends. And, O my Supreme and Glorious Deliverer who art a prayer hearing and prayer answering God, how shall I acknowledge for the mercy shown me, and in what manner shall I adore thee?

'The ensuing morning presented to our view an aspect the most dreary – not the least appearance of the gale abating, on the contrary it seemed to increase with redoubled vigor; as the sea had rose to an alarming height and frequently dashed against the vessel with great violence– little else was now thought of but the preservation of our lives. Exertions were made by the crew to save as much of the ship's provisions as was possible, and by breaking out the bow port, they succeeded in saving 50 or 60 pounds of bread, and a few pounds of cheese which were stowed in the main top; to which place Mrs. Kendall and myself were conveyed, it being impossible for us to remain below, the cabin being nearly filled with water, and almost every sea breaking over us!

'The night approached with all its dismal horrors – the horizon was obscured by black and angry looking clouds, and about midnight the rain commenced falling in torrents, attended with frightful peals of thunder, and unremitting streams of lightning! But, during the whole of this long and dismal night with all its attending horrors, Mrs. K. and myself were constantly upon our knees, supplicating the mercy of that God,

"Who rides upon the stormy winds, And manages the seas."

Burial at Sea
'Daylight returned, but only to present to our view an additional scene of horror – one of the poor seamen, overcome by fatigue, was discovered hanging lifeless by some part of the rigging – his mortal remains were committed to the deep – as this was the first instance of entombing a human body in the ocean, that I had ever witnessed, the melancholy scene made a deep impression on my mind, as I expected such eventually would be my own fate!

'At 6 A.M. our depressed spirits were a little revived by the appearance of a sail standing toward us; which proved to be an American, who remained in company with us until the next morning; when, in consequence of the roughness of the sea, being unable to afford us any assistance, they left us!

'It would be impossible for me to attempt to describe the feelings of all on board at this moment, on seeing so unexpectedly vanish, the pleasing hope of being rescued by this vessel, from our perilous situation. As the only human means to prolong our miserable existence, a tent of spare canvass was erected by the ship's crew on the forecastle, and all on board put on the short allowance of a quarter of a biscuit a day.

'On the 8th February (the gale still continuing) a brig was seen to leeward but at a great distance, and in the afternoon the same brig (as was supposed) was seen to the windward. Capt. Kendall ordered a signal of distress to be made, and we soon had the satisfaction to see the brig approach us within hail, and inquire very distinctly of Capt. K. how long he had been in that situation, and what he intended to do – if he intended leaving the ship? to which he replied, "yes, with God's assistance," – but, alas the Almighty, for his own wise and good purposes, saw fit once more, to disappoint us in our expectations of relief! – night approaching, and the gale still prevailing to that degree that no boat could have floated in the water, we saw no more of the brig!

'All on board were now reduced to the most deplorable state imaginable! Our miserable bodies were gradually perishing, and the disconsolate spirits of the poor sailors (who were probably like too many of their seafaring brethren, strangers to prayer) overpowered by the horrible prospects of starving without any appearance of relief! – as for myself, altho' I was not insensible that in our deplorable situation I had as much to apprehend as any other one on board, yet my spirits were probably more buoyed up by the reflection that the greatest afflictions which we meet with, are often productive of the greatest blessings, and that they are the means which a merciful Creator often makes use of to bring souls to the knowledge of Jesus ...'

Crisis of Hunger: An 'Awful Extremity'

'We had now arrived at an awful crisis – our provisions were all consumed, and hunger and thirst began to select their victims! – on the 12th, James Clarke, a seaman, died of no other complaint (as was judged) than the weakness caused by famine; whose body, after reading prayers, was committed to the deep – and on the 22nd, John Wilson, another seaman, fell a victim to starvation! – as the calls of hunger had now become too importunate to be resisted, it is a fact, although shocking to relate, that we were reduced to the awful extremity to attempt to support our feeble bodies a while longer by subsisting on the dead body of the deceased – it was cut into slices, then washed in salt water, and after being exposed to and dried a little in the sun, was apportioned to each of the miserable survivors, who partook of it as a sweet morsel – from this revolting food I abstained for 24 hours, when I too was compelled by hunger, to follow their example!

'Alas, how often in my childhood have I read accounts of seafaring people, and others, having been driven to the alternative of either starving, or to satisfy the cravings of nature, subsisting on human flesh or the dead carcases of the meanest animals that were to be obtained! Accounts which are pretty generally discredited by those who have not been placed in a similar situation – but, to such an awful extremity, I can assure my Christian readers, was I and my wretched companions now reduced!

'This is indeed the height of misery, yet such was our deplorable state; we eyed each other with mournful and melancholy looks, as may be supposed of people perishing with hunger and thirst; by all of whom it was now perceived that we had nothing to hope from human aid, but only from the mercy of the Almighty, whose ways are unsearchable – nor did I fail almost constantly to implore his mercy ...'

Deaths by 'Fatigue and Hunger'

'On the 23rd, J. Moore, another seaman died, whose body was committed to the deep after taking therefrom the liver and heart, which was reserved for our subsistence – and in the course of twelve days after (during which our miseries continued without any alleviation) the following persons fell victims to fatigue and hunger, to wit, Henry Davis and John Jones, cabin boys, James Frier, cook, Alexander Kelly, Daniel Jones, John Hutchinson and John James, seamen – the heart-piercing lamentations of these poor creatures (dying for the want of sustenance) was distressing beyond conception; some of them expired raving mad, crying out lamentably for water!

'Hutchinson, who, it appeared, had left a numerous family in Europe, talked of his wife and children as if they were present – repeating the names of the latter, and begged of them to be kind to their poor mother, who, he represented, was about to be separated from him forever!

'Jones became delirious two or three days before his death, and in his ravings, reproached his wife and children as well as his dying companions present, with being the authors of his extreme sufferings, by depriving him of food, and in refusing him even a single drop of water, with which to moisten his parched lips! and, indeed, such now was the thirst of those who were but in a little better condition, that they were driven to the melancholy, distressful horrid act (to procure their blood) of cutting the throats of their deceased companions a moment after the breath of life had left their bodies!'

James Frier: 'An Indissoluble Attachment'

'In the untimely exit of no one of the unhappy sufferers
was I so sensibly affected, as in that of the unfortunate
youth, James Frier – for in the welfare of none on board
did I feel myself so immediately interested, as the reader
may judge, from the circumstances that I shall mention.
I have already stated, that with this ill-fated young man,
I became immediately acquainted in Liverpool – to me
had early made protestations of love, and more than once
intimated an inclination to select me as the partner of his
bosom; and never had I any reason to doubt his sincerity
– it was partly by his solicitations that I had been induced
to comply with the wishes of Mrs. Kendall, to accompany
her in this unfortunate voyage; in the course of which, by
frequent interviews, my attachment for this unfortunate
youth was rather increased than diminished; and before
this dreadful calamity befell us, he had obtained my consent, and we had mutually agreed and avowed to each
other our determination to unite in marriage, as soon as
we should reach our destined port!

'Judge then, my Christian female readers (for it is you
that best judge) what must have been my feelings, to see
a youth for whom I had formed an indissoluble attachment – him with whom I expected so soon to be joined
in wedlock, and to spend the remainder of my days,
expiring before my eyes, for the want of that sustenance
which nature requires for the support of life, and which
it was not in my power to afford him! And myself at the
same moment so far reduced by hunger and thirst, as to
be driven to the horrid alternative to preserve my own
life (O! God of Heaven! the lamentable fact is known
to thee, and why should I attempt to conceal it from
the world?) to plead my claim to the greater portion of

his precious blood, as it oozed half congealed from the wound inflicted upon his lifeless body!!

'Oh, this was a bitter cup indeed! But it was God's will that it should not pass me – and God's will must be done ...'

Another Brig – 'Hopes Vanished'

'About the 26th February, an English brig hove in sight, on which the usual signals of distress were made, and, although the winds had become less boisterous, and the sea more smooth, to our inexpressible grief, she did not approach to afford us any assistance! Our longing eyes followed her until she was out of sight; leaving us in a situation doubly calamitous from our disappointment in not receiving the relief which appeared so near, and the wretched uncertainty of the approach of any other vessel, in time to save our existence; our hopes vanished with the brig, and from the highest summit of expectation, they now (with most of the survivors) sunk into a state of the most dismal despair!

'Nature indeed seemed now to have abandoned her functions! Never could human beings be reduced to a more wretched situation; my readers must have been a witness of it to form any adequate idea of our distress, and that which I am attempting now to describe, falls infinitely short of the reality!

'More than two-thirds of the crew had already perished, and the surviving few, weak, distracted, and destitute of almost every thing, envied the fate of those whose lifeless corpses no longer wanted sustenance. The sense of hunger was almost lost, but a parching thirst consumed our vitals! Our mouths had become so dry for want of moisture for three or four days, that we were

'The Last Toss': Burial at sea. (*The Graphic*, 28 July 1894)

obliged to wash them every few hours with salt water, to prevent our lips glueing together ...'

HMS Blonde: *'The Hour of Our Deliverance' by 'Unerring Providence'*

'Early in the morning of the 7th March, a sail was discovered to windward – the ship's crew (with my assistance) made all the signals of distress that the little remaining strength of their bodies would enable them to do; they were indeed the last efforts of expiring nature – but, praised be God, yea, ever ought we to praise Him, for his mercy endureth forever – the hour of our deliverance had now arrived!! The ship was soon within hail (which proved to be his Majesty's ship *Blonde*, Lord Byron) when her boat was manned and sent to our relief ...

The Rescue. (*Harper's Weekly*, supplement, 27 November 1875)

'When relieved but a small part of the body of the last person deceased remained, and this I had cut as usual into slices and spread on the quarter deck, which being noticed by the Lieutenant of the *Blonde* (who with others had been dispatched from the ship to our relief) and before we had time to state to him to what extremities we had been driven, he observed "you have yet, I perceive, fresh meat!" But his horror can be better conceived than described when he was informed that what he saw, was the remains of the dead body of one of our unfortunate companions, and that on this, our only remaining food, it was our intention to have put ourselves on an allowance the ensuing evening, had not unerring Providence directed him to our relief.

'When we reached the *Blonde*, the narrative of our sufferings, as well as a view of our weak and emaciated bodies, caused tears to bedew those faces which probably are not used to turn pale at the approach of death.

'By Lord Byron, and his officers and crew, we were treated with all possible kindness and humanity; insomuch that we soon gained our strength to that degree, as to be able in ten days after to go on board of a vessel spoken [met], bound to Europe; and it was on the 20th March following that I was landed in safety at Portsmouth, where for twelve days I was treated with that hospitality, by both sexes, as ought not, and I trust will not, pass without its merited reward; and on the 5th April following, I was conveyed by my Christian friends and restored to the arms of my dear mother, after an absence of nearly five months; in which time I think I can truly say, I had witnessed and endured more of the heavy judgements and afflictions of this world, than any other of its female inhabitants.' (*Narrative of the Shipwreck and Sufferings of Miss Ann Saunders*, written by herself, 1827)

5

'HELL SHIPS': CRUEL CAPTAINS, MALEVOLENT MATES

American sailing ships, in their prime, were renowned – or rather ill-famed – the world over for the brutal treatment their crews received on board them. There were exceptions, no doubt; but the majority of these Yankee packets richly deserved the title of 'hell ships,' 'blood boats,' and the like. Their hard-case skippers and bucko mates, possessed by some diabolical and inhuman bloodlust, were experts in the art of 'working-up' and 'man-handling' refractory [mutinous] crews; and many cases are on record of their beating a man to death with their belaying-pins or knuckledusters, or of subjecting him to such methods of refined cruelty that he went mad, or jumped overboard to escape from them. In rare instances these human gorillas were brought to justice and executed, or sent to penal servitude for long terms.

But so difficult was it for the prosecuting attorneys to collect evidence against them ... that in the majority of cases they went free, to perpetrate fresh outrages elsewhere upon long-suffering and down-trodden sailormen. (*Square-Rigger Days: Autobiographies of Sail*, by C.W. Domville-Fife, 1938)

The *Harvester* was another Pacific ship with a bad record. Her captain had one man put in a barrel, the head of which was then fastened up, and nails were driven into the sides of the barrel. When the captain thought it had enough spikes, he rolled the barrel up and down the deck. The unfortunate victim was nearly dead when released. (*In The Days of the Tall Ships*, by R.A. Fletcher, 1928)

'The Red Record'

In December 1895 The National Seamen's Union of America published a pamphlet titled 'The Red Record' (*'Ecce! Tyrannus* ['Here be Tyranny!'] – *The Symbol of Discipline on the American Hell-Ship – A brief resume of some of the cruelties perpetrated upon American Seamen at the present time.'*) The 'Record' cited sixty-four cases of abuses and excessive cruelty on American vessels in the previous seven years as evidence to support a proposed Congressional bill to eradicate such treatment by American ships' officers of their crews. It noted:

The state of affairs prevailing aboard American ships is incompatible with the conceptions of justice which prevail among men ashore. We believe that the dissemination of the facts in the case must necessarily result in the abolition of buckoism ['appertaining to a brutal ship's officer': a *bucko* mate] by Congressional action and by the power of public opinion brought to bear upon shipowners.

And:

It is claimed that seamen in American ships suffer more from brutality and poor food than the seamen of any other nationality; and [Treasury Commission Special Agent] Mr. Baldwin says that he found it to be only too true that American seamen are underpaid, underfed, overworked and generally driven about like slaves. The proposed new laws will be modelled after those established by the British Board of Trade.

The litany of tyrannical cruelty, even torture cited by 'The Red Record' included a gamut of violent abuse, from severe 'knocking about', savage assaults with belaying pins, capstan bars, 'knuckledusters', calloused fists and heavy-booted stamping and kicking, to such miscellaneous other 'punishments' that usually left a ship's deck spattered with blood and sometimes caused the death of seamen.

Some of 'The Red Record's' citations of shipboard barbarism included:

HELCA, Captain Snow, arrived in Tacoma [Washington state], November 1, 1888. Sixteen seamen being all hands forward, entered complaint of cruelty in the District Court. Near Cape Horn captain attacked the carpenter; struck him with a heavy instrument, breaking his jaw and knocking out several teeth. Captain nearly killed another man, and with the aid of the first-mate, beat several of the crew. Crew were put in the hold for forty-eight hours and secured in such a manner that they could neither stand erect, sit nor lie down. One man was tied to a stanchion four days and kept without food. The latter [i.e. food] was placed within sight but out of reach. In Acapulco the crew was imprisoned ashore until the ship was ready to sail. Application was made to the Consul for assistance, but the latter refused, saying the only thing to be done was to 'rough it.' Captain Snow boasted that he had never been beaten in any difficulty with seamen ashore, and refused to pay his crew the wages due them ($600 in all) for the passage from Cardiff.

COMMODORE T.H. ALLEN, Captain Merriam, arrived in San Francisco, April, 1889. A seaman, McDonald, reported that while expostulating against the vile language of the third mate he was struck several times by that officer and thrown against the rail with such violence that his shoulder was dislocated. Captain remarked, when appealed to: 'Serves you damned right,' and ordered the mate to confine McDonald in the carpenter's shop. As treatment for his wounds he was given a dose of salts. Another seaman fell sick and was confined with McDonald in the carpenter's shop – a combination of hospital and prison. There being only one bunk in the place, the weakest man had to sleep on the deck. Diet for the sick man, common ship's fare; medicine, salts. For four days he ate nothing. Finally he died. Interviewed about the matter, the third-mate acknowledged McDonald was a good seaman, but that he (the third-mate) was 'down' on him'.

FINANCE, steamer, Captain Zollinger. First-mate Evelyn examined by United States Commissioner in Brooklyn, August, 1889, on the charge preferred by a passenger, of brutally assaulting four negro stowaways. Captain and mate took hold of one negro boy and threw him violently to the deck. Evelyn then kicked him twice in the face; boy ran forward; Evelyn followed and beat him over the head with a belaying-pin. Boy took refuge among the passengers, but he was dragged away and made to stand on his head blindfolded and say his prayers till he fell from exhaustion. Captain fired at the boy with a pistol, and the mate kicked him in the chest to make believe he had been shot. Captain beat the four negro stowaways over their heads with a plank until they bled and pleaded for mercy. Three of these boys were landed on a desert island twelve miles from St. Thomas Island. Captain instructed the boat's crew to pitch the negroes overboard and let them swim. Second-mate Martin disobeyed this order until within thirty yards of the island. Then it was discovered that one of the boys could not swim, and if he had not been pulled into the boat again would assuredly have drowned. Captain Zollinger disappeared upon arrival in New York.

TAM O'SHANTER, Captain Peabody, arrived in San Francisco, July, 1893. Charges of the grossest brutality made against second-mate R. Crocker (late of the Commodore T.H. Allen). Crocker stands 6 feet 3 in height and weighs 260 pounds. Crocker assaulted several seamen. One in particular Harry Hill, bore nine wounds, five of them still unhealed. A piece was bitten out of his left palm, a mouthful of flesh was bitten out of his left arm, and his left nostril torn away as far as the bridge of his nose. Crocker is reported to have kicked the seamen from 'pure devilment.' He attempted to kick one man from aloft; seaman slid down to the deck, Crocker followed him and administered a beating, the marks of which he showed in court. Crocker held on $500 bail. Case tried, usual verdict, acquittal.

ROANOKE, Captain Hamilton, arrived at New York, March 13, 1895, from Manila. Crew charged that while the vessel was lying in Shanghai Edwin Davis, able seaman, fell from aloft, through fright at the threats of Second-Mate Taylor, and was killed. The second-mate is reported to have laughed at this, and said that 'it served the fellow right, as he was too slow to be of any use.' The day following this fatality Arthur Baker, able seaman, was working under the hatches. A bale of cotton was in danger of falling on him, and when the attention of First-Mate 'Black' Taylor was called to this he swore at the crew and ordered them to 'go ahead,' at the same time saying that Baker must look out for himself. The bale fell on Baker, injuring him seriously. The first-mate, with another oath, ordered the man hoisted on deck. When Baker tried to stand he fell overboard, through weakness, and narrowly escaped drowning. The first-mate accused Frank McQueeney of being asleep on the lookout, and pounded him into insensibility with a belaying-pin. Captain Hamilton struck Carpenter Hansen on the head and face with a bottle, inflicting deep wounds, and afterwards put him in irons and triced him up to the spanker-boom, where he was kept till nearly dead. Crew accused Captain Hamilton of drunkeness and neglect of his officers' conduct.

SUSQUEHANNA, Captain [Joe] Sewall, (late of *Solitaire*), arrived in San Francisco, November 12, 1895, from New York. The crew charged the usual ill-treatment against the captain and officers. James Whelan, able-seaman, swore out a warrant for the arrest of First-Mate Ross on a charge of brutally beating. Captain Sewall threatened that if Ross was convicted he would have the crew arrested on a charge of mutiny. The case of Ross was heard before United States Commissioner Heacock and, as usual, dismissed.

Captain Sewall is one of the most notorious brutes in charge of an American ship. This is his fourth appearance in the 'Red Record' in less than seven years. He has openly boasted that he would beat his seamen whenever he felt inclined. Well-sustained charges of murder have been made against him, but he has gone scot-free every time. Once, in Philadelphia in 1889 when he was in danger of conviction, he 'disappeared' for a time, and afterward 'healed the wounds' of the complainants in cash. His threat in the present case is simply a repetition of an old dodge to embarrass the officials.

Arthur Sewall's Ships: 'Red Record' Regulars

Arthur Sewall was the scion of a well-known shipbuilding family from Bath, Maine. Arthur Sewall & Co. operated a fleet of thirteen big deep-sea sailing ships (one, the four-masted, 3,539 ton *Roanoke*, launched in 1892, was the largest wooden sailing ship of the time). Sewall's vessels were 'beautiful specimens of the shipbuilder's art, as stanch as they are swift'. But there were amongst them, too, 'hell ships', as remarked upon by *The New York Times* in July 1896, which cited pertinent cases published in 'The Red Record' (14 of the 64 cases listed in 'The Red Record' involved Sewall ships).

Cruelty on Sewall Ships – Some Cases That Are Cited in 'The Red Record' – An Explanation of Why Sailormen Prefer to Ship on Vessels That Are Not Such Fine Examples of the Shipbuilder's Art – Case of the Solitaire, *Commanded by a Son of the Free-Silver Vice Presidential Candidate [i.e. Sewall]*

The candidacy of Arthur Sewall, of Bath, Me., for the Vice Presidency* on a platform which makes humanity its pretense, would cause amusement among many shipping people and seamen did it not incite to a feeling of indignation at the hypocrisy of the thing.

The New-York Times, on the day after Mr. Sewall's nomination, in giving his record, credited his firm with building and owning some of the finest sailing craft that fly the American flag ... Commendable as the Sewall fleet is, however, from the standpoint of commerce and art, sailors have a different opinion of it, and vastly prefer to ship on dingier, smaller, slower, and unsafer craft.

For it has been a tradition among sailormen that these noble vessels are floating hells, that on them men are starved and abused to a more outrageous extent than on any other American ships that sail the high seas. There is an organization known as the National Seamen's Union of America, which issues a pamphlet known as The Red Record, and described as 'a brief resumé of some of the cruelties perpetrated upon American seamen at the present time.' The introduction to this book sets forth that considerations, not only of humanity, but of business expediency, as evidenced by the scarcity of seamen, demand public attention to the cause and cure of brutality to seamen.

The opinion is expressed that public ignorance is at once the cause and perpetuation of brutality to seamen, and that the dissemination of the facts must result in the abolition of 'buckoism' – appertaining to a brutal ship's

---

* In 1896 William Jennings Bryan, the Democratic candidate for the presidency of the United States, chose Arthur Sewall to be his running mate for the vice presidency. There never was, of course, a President Bryan, much less a Vice-President Sewall.

officer – by Congressional action, and by the power of public opinion brought to bear on ship owners. The Red Record cites sixty-four cases of cruelty that have been especially investigated. Of these fourteen relate to ships owned by Arthur Sewall & Co. of Bath, Me.

That of the ship Willie Rosenfeld has already been instanced in The New-York Times. Though the cases of outrage were proved, and the master and mate were indicted by the Federal Grand Jury, both avoided the processes of the courts, and Capt. Dunphy sailed away again to the Pacific coast. Sewall & Co. evidenced no concern. [It is reported that Captain Sewall 'healed the wounds of all complainants' with $440 in cash and proceeded on his way.]

The following examples are taken from The Red Record's list covering the last seven years:

The Solitaire

'*Solitaire*, Captain Sewall (son of the Bath shipbuilder and owner of that ilk), arrived in Dunkirk, France, about January, 1889. In the Channel the mate called a seaman from aloft, knocked him down, jumped on his breast, and inflicted wounds from which he died next day. The body was kept in the after hatch for four days. When the corpse was so black that the bruises could not be distinguished, the story was given out to the local authorities that the man died of consumption.

'The Captain beat two men for talking while at work. The first mate also set upon them and broke one man's nose. The second mate beat one of the boatswains with knuckle dusters, because the latter omitted the usual 'Sir' from his address. Another seaman accidentally spat on the deck. He was made to go down on his knees and lick it up.

'Boatswains were beaten for refusing or being unable to beat the seamen. An old seaman was given liquor and then plied to tell tales about the crew. With the cues thus received, the officers made occasions to beat the seamen.'

There is a second case recorded against the *Solitaire*, as follows:

'*Solitaire*, Capt. Sewall, arrived in Philadelphia April 18, 1889. Warrants were sworn out for the arrest of the Captain, First Mate F. Ryan, and Second Mate J.W. Robins, on complaint of brutality on the passage from Dunkirk. One man was hit aloft by the second mate and fell eighty feet. He fell in the buntlines and was thus saved. Another man was also struck off the yard and fell to the deck. He was killed outright.

'When the seamen made complaint to the officials at Philadelphia, they bore upon them the marks of their sufferings. The mates deserted the ship while towing up the Delaware [River]. Capt. Sewall also disappeared for a time.'

The Rappahannock

Here are two reports on the short-lived ship *Rappahannock* [built 1890 at Bath, Maine; burned at Juan Fernandez Island on 11 November 1891], Capt. Dickinson:

'Loaded at Philadelphia, on her maiden voyage, April 1890. Got aground towing down the Delaware. Crew complained of vessel being undermanned. Captain went ashore, got crimps aboard, and beat the seamen; then put them in irons and locked them in the forecastle, where they remained with little food for two weeks. A detective got aboard and saw the men – one with an arm broken and another with his head smashed. A United States Marshal boarded the ship and took Capt. Dickinson back to Wilmington, where he was examined by the Commissioner. Case dismissed on ground of 'justifiable discipline.'

The *Rappahannock* arrived in San Francisco from Japan in January, 1891. The Red Record says:

'Crew report having shipped in Baltimore to sail in a pilot boat; *Rappahannock* was then in Philadelphia: only twenty men to man a 5,000-ton-burden ship. Beating, kicking, belaying pins, and pistols were the order from the day of sailing. One man was washed off the jibboom and drowned; no attempt made to pick him up. Another man fell from the mizzen crosstrees and was killed. Crew refused to go to law about it. "No use to bother the courts," they said.' (*The New York Times*, 14 July 1896)

And so on and so forth: brutality as business as usual.

The *Willie Rosenfeld* – A 'Hard Ship'

At the time of her launch in 1895 the *Willie Rosenfeld* was the largest ship Arthur Sewall & Co. had ever built: 2,455 tons, 266' long by 45' wide (beam) by 19' deep. (A predecessor, the *John Rosenfeld*, 2,374 tons, had also been the largest Sewall vessel when launched, in 1884.) The *Willie Rosenfeld*'s figurehead was of her eponymous namesake, the son of John Rosenfeld, a prominent San Francisco shipping merchant. (The young man died just before the ship was launched. An omen?)

With the exception of one voyage under the command of Capt. Wylie Dickinson, the *Rosenfeld* was commanded by Capt. William H. Dunphy throughout her sailing life until she was lost in a storm off the coast of Brazil in 1896.

Capt. Dunphy had a sound reputation as a shipmaster – at least by some accounts:

Capt. William H. Dunphy ... was one of the best known and most experienced American merchant shipmasters of his time, *genial and intelligent and a brave seaman*. He was born in Gardiner, Maine, and first went to sea in 1856, at the age of thirteen, in the bark *San Jacinto*, on a voyage to Kronstadt, Russia. In the summer of 1867, as master of the brig *Nellie Mitchell*, he sailed from Aspinwall [Panama] for Swan Island. When four days at sea the crew were stricken with Isthmian fever [yellow fever or malaria], all being prostrated but Captain Dunphy and one man. This pair cared for the others for two days and at the same time kept the brig on her course. Within some fifty miles of their destination they, too, were stricken. Captain Dunphy attached a letter to the bulkhead explaining the circumstances, just before he collapsed.

For two days the vessel sailed her own drunken course with no hand at the wheel. The Captain then recovered sufficiently to crawl about upon hands and knees and attempt to aid his less fortunate fellows. A friendly sail then showed up and the vessel was navigated into port. For a year it was feared that the Captain might not recover but he did and then took command of the ship *Henry S. Sanford*, in which he continued some four years, then taking the *Occidental*. From the latter he went to the ship *Willie Rosenfeld* which, except for one passage, he commanded during her whole sea life of nearly twelve years. (*American Merchant Ships 1850–1900*, by Frederick C. Matthews)

Captain Courageous

On another occasion Capt. Dunphy revealed personal courage and dutiful stamina in the face of extreme adversity. The *Willie Rosenfeld* left San Francisco on 5 September 1893 for Queenstown, Ireland. All went well until 8 January 1894:

> On that date the ship was running by the Azores, trimmed down to two lower topsails, with two men at the wheel and Captain Dunphy standing in the wheel house directing the steering. Suddenly the wind, which had been blowing with hurricane force, ceased and a flat calm ensued but almost immediately a small tidal wave struck the stern of the ship, picking up and heaving the wheel house against the end of the after house. The ceiling fell in and Captain Dunphy was washed across the deck a couple of times, semi-conscious and half drowned.
>
> Starting to clear himself from the wreckage, the Captain discovered that his right leg had been knocked out of its socket. With the help of the cabin boy he got on top of the after house and made himself fast to the mizzenmast. The mate and the watch below were called and extricated the two steersmen out of the wrecked wheel house to find that one had a leg and an arm broken and the other a leg and both arms broken. The wheel itself was found to be broken in twelve pieces.
>
> Captain Dunphy got the boy and the steward to assist in pulling his leg back into position but the steward flunked. The boy then stretched a line along the spanker boom and after hard work the leg was reset. The Captain finally got below where he set the broken limbs of his men.
>
> It was found that a seaman had been caught between the after and forward houses when the wave came aboard,

and killed outright [one newspaper report said: 'Two seamen were killed instantly, their brains being dashed out.'; another said: 'Two of her crew were swept overboard.'], while eight others had been severely injured. Many sails had been blown away and two days later others were lost in a heavy squall. A crutch was fashioned for Captain Dunphy who navigated the ship while the mate attended to the sailing and two weeks later the ship reached Queenstown. (*American Merchant Ships 1850–1900*, by Frederick C. Matthews)

Capt. Dunphy's reputation as a seaman was doubtless rock solid amongst his peers. As a disciplinarian he was, in truth, probably not much different from most hard-bitten American shipmasters of the time, brought up through the hawsepipe by rough-and-tumble seafaring traditions. Still, just before the *Rosenfeld*'s fateful last voyage, her crew brought charges of cruelty against him and his officers during a voyage from Newport News, Virginia, round the Horn to Port Townsend, Washington state, in 1895–96.

Battered Seamen These – Complaints of Cruelty on the Ship Willie Rosenfeld – Knocked Down With Belaying Pins – So Men Testify Before Deputy Shipping Commissioner Keenan – One Jumped Overboard to Escape

In The Red Record, a crimson stained pamphlet issued by The Coast Seamen's Journal, appears, in a list of disgraceful happenings at sea, this memorandum of the American Ship *Willie Rosenfeld* and her master, Dunphy:

'*Willie Rosenfeld*, Capt. Dunphy, arrived at Port Townsend, Washington, January 24, 1895, from Newport News, via Acapulco. Crew charge that First Mate

Gillespie struck William McNally, able seaman, on the head with a belaying pin, knocking him down and cutting his head in several places. [The same officer compelled another seaman, John Barton, to besmear his own face with the contents of the water closet.] Further abuse drove this man [John Barton] crazy, so that he stole food from the pigpen. For this offence he was triced up. First Mate Gillespie also assaulted Ivor Iversen, able seaman, once with a belaying pin and again with a handspike, knocking him senseless. Second Mate Sullivan assaulted Mike Patterson, able seaman, knocking him down and kicking him repeatedly while he was on deck. Boatswain [John] Kelly assaulted Charles Green, knocking him down, causing blood to spurt from mouth and nose.

Such were the amenities of sailor life on the Rosenfeld's outward voyage. The ship returned to port [New York] last Sunday, and yesterday her crew of fourteen men filed into the office of Shipping Commissioner Power and told of some of the episodes of the homeward trip.

They are sombre-visaged mariners, and look as if hard usage had been theirs. One had a ghastly wound in his head, opened four months ago, he said, by a blow given with an iron block in the hands of the mate, and which has never healed. Harsh treatment seemed to be written on the features of all the others, and the tales they told appeared merely as a confirming supplement to visual evidence. Those moralists who advise for the sea bully the same treatment which is meted out to the wife-beater should have been there to listen.

In addition to instigating and authorizing brutal treatment of the men, Capt. Dunphy is accused by them of sailing the ship out of port shorthanded, and of supplying insufficient food. When questioned by Deputy

Commissioner Keenan about the shorthanded charge, Capt. Dunphy replied surlily:

'Well, I've been going to sea long enough to know my business. I know how many it takes to man a ship.'

'But the men say that both watches had to be called to take in royals; that one watch was too weakhanded for the work, and that all hands ...'

'I know my business,' was the curt interruption.

Witnesses' Statements

Howard Gould, able seaman, was among the first witnesses called. He is a quiet-spoken, youngish-looking man, and unconcerned listeners felt he spoke the truth. Gould testified that while lying in the harbor of Caleta Buena, Chile, Mate Gillespie ordered him to take off his coat:

'I started in for to tell Mr. Gillespie that I had a cold and sore throat, when he up and hit me with a belaying pin, and then tore the coat off'n me,' he said. 'Then he ordered me to go below an' work at the cargo. He followed me, and, picking up a scantling [piece of timber board], commenced beating me again. I run for the deck, for I had seen the Captain up there, but he stood by and saw the mate knock me down and kick me, and being 'fraid he was going to murder me, I scrambled to the railing and jumped overboard.

'Then I struck out and swam for the Allerton, a British ship anchored about 600 yards away. I don't know how I ever got to her, for I was nearly dead when I got in the water, but the water freshened me up a bit and I reached her at last, but plumb played out. They took me on board, and I tell you they treated me well. Then the next day [second] Mate Sullivan and a shore policeman came after me and took me back to the ship. I had hardly got my foot on deck before Mr. Sullivan turned, and, without saying a word, hit me below the ear, knocking me flat on deck.

'Did you appeal to the Captain?' Deputy Commissioner Keenan asked.

'I did not for I knew I would only get more if I did.'

'Want to ask the witness any questions?' Capt. Dunphy was asked.

The burly seaman shook his head, and Thomas Gavin was called.

Assaults on Thomas Gavin

Gavin is an able seaman. His sworn affidavit is to the effect that on the morning of Oct. 7, 1895, he received orders from Mate Sullivan to do a job of work on the main yard, and when that was finished to go to the topsail yard and send down certain blocks. He had completed his task on the yard and was ascending the topmast rigging when hailed by Mate Gillespie with 'Where you going?' Gavin told him where, and the mate ordered him on deck, Gavin says. He came down the rigging, and as he was swinging to the deck from the sheerpole, Gavin says he received a blow to the face from Gillespie. Then, as he got to his feet, he got another blow and a kick, and was told to go forward and remove a tarpaulin from a hatch.

Gavin says he staggered forward, and while groping for the hatch, with eyes blinded with blood and pain, Gillespie, following him, and cursing him for his slowness, picked up a hammer, and then dropping that implement, seized a heavy block and struck him on the head. Capt. Dunphy, he says, was looking on. He besought him for protection.

'You want braining,' he says was the master's reply.

'Want to ask the witness any questions?' asked the Commissioner.

'Na-w!' grunted the skipper.

Fitzimmons' Beatings, 'Brute' Captain

James Fitzsimmons, a seaman, well along in years, and of anything but robust build, says that he was at the wheel one day when the Captain came along and asked the course.

'I told him,' said Fitzsimmons, 'and then he walked on aft, and then hailed me and asked the time. I told him just as respectful as I knew how, an', mor'n that, I was 'fraid of him. I tell you I was afraid of that man. I don't know what made him mad, but he comes back storming to me, and says he to me, 'I can't clout you myself, but I can get someone who will.' And he did – he give me my dose, and when he was through with me (Mr. Gillespie it was) I was carried forward by some of my mates.

'The Captain, you see, he goes below swearing at me, and another minute, up comes Mr. Gillespie, and he catches me one in the mouth, and then after knocking me down he kicked and beat me until I didn't know nothing. And then some of the men takes me forward, after he had knocked every bit of life out of me, and couldn't move a peg myself.'

'You say it was by the Captain's order that you were beaten?' Fitzimmons was asked.

'I didn't hear him give the order, but I know it was him that done it. He is the most inhuman brute I ever sailed with. And I have been going to sea for mor'n thirty years now.'

Capt. Dunphy had no questions to ask the witness.

Richard Gyles said he had been assaulted by the mate 170 times during the voyage, as nearly as he could calculate.

'How many times?' asked the Deputy Commissioner, in amazement.

'About 170, Sir,' the man replied. 'I calculate it this way: I was set upon two or three times every time my watch was on deck. The mate would come along and order me to do this or that, and then give me clout, and sometimes he would give me clout first, and then the order. I told the Captain I was being abused by mate, and he turned on his heel and walked away.'

Gyles testified as others had, that he had been defrauded when shipped. He was beaten by boarding-house runners, who took him on board in Port Townsend, and compelled him to sign papers. Capt. Dunphy had no question to ask.

Capt. Dunphy's Version

Dunphy was then told he could make a statement. 'The men charge you with brutal treatment,' said the Deputy Commissioner, to start him going.

'I say they haven't been brutally treated,' was the dictum of the Captain.

'Did the man who had his head split open have any medical treatment?' the Captain was asked.

'Yes: I had a doctor for him,' replied the Captain, unguardedly. 'When the ship anchored off Caleta Buena, I engaged a doctor from shore for the ship.'

'Do you know,' continued his questioner, 'that the wound has been open for four months?'

'No, I know nothing about it. The doctor came aboard, and he could have had the wound treated if he wanted to.'

The men had claimed that the Mate, Gillespie, had been got rid of by the Captain in Caleta Buena, along with two other seamen, whose testimony, the men say would have been more damaging than any given yesterday. The Deputy Commissioner asked the Captain what had become of the Mate.

'I had some words with him,' the Captain said, 'and discharged him. He gave me insolence, and said he was going to burn the ship, and I put him ashore.'

'Did you,' the Deputy Commissioner asked, 'make any efforts to have the man punished for his treatment of the men?'

'No.'

'Did you ask the [American] Consul to have him prosecuted?'

'No.'

'How long did you remain in port?'

'About a month – no, let me see, about eighteen, no, seventeen, days.'

The Food Supply: The Cook's Evidence

Continuing, Capt. Dunphy said it was false that he had ordered the mate to attack the man Fitzsimmons. 'And it's a lie about there not being enough food on board,' he said. 'There was plenty of it. One man came to me just before we got in and wanted some sugar. That's all the complaint about food I heard. I gave them fresh meat twice a week.'

Exclamations of 'Phaw!' long and low, whistles, and looks of amazement from the crew.

'What kind of fresh meat?'–from the Deputy Commissioner.

'Canned goods,' said the Captain. 'The cook, he ought to be here. He can tell you there was plenty to eat on board.'

The cook was called, and a little cross-eyed negro, very deaf and very stupid, made answer. He manifested some fear of the Captain. His deafness had prevented him from hearing what the Captain had said about a redundancy of provisions.

'Did you have plenty of food?' he was asked.

'No, sah! Didn't have enough 'taters.'

'Short of anything else?'

'Yes, sah – short of beans, short of flour, short of salt horse, short of sugar.'

'How did you feed the men – by the scale or by your judgement?'

'Fed 'em the best way I could, sah.'

'Any complaints?'

'Yes, sah! Dey didn't like cracker hash.'

'What's that?' demanded the Deputy. 'Is that a luxury?'

'Yes, sah, dat's him.'

For the benefit of the uninformed it should be explained that cracker hash is a mixture of hard tack [hard ship's biscuit, bread] and water, baked in an oven with a bit of 'slush' [rendered fat] spread thinly over it to give a taste to the mess. The cook testified that there were plenty of provisions on board now. (*The New York Times*, 31 January 1896)

Guilty

At the end of January 1896 the United States Shipping Commissioner concluded that 'the charges brought by the crew of the American ship *Willie Rosenfeld* against the vessel's master and his brutal mates' were proved. Indeed, 'every charge they had brought was true'. The Commissioners reported that mates Gillespie and Sullivan did assault members of the crew at various times; 'that the master, William

H. Dunphy, knew of the assaults and refused to interfere; that the vessel was short of provisions, and that the men did not receive the amounts [of pay] they were scheduled'.

The Commissioners ordered that $5 be paid to each crew member for the shortage of provisions. There was no particular penalty or punishment imposed on Capt. Dunphy or his 'brutal mates' Gillman and Sullivan (though a warrant was issued for Mate Sullivan). The real act of justice – divine retribution, perhaps – came shortly afterwards ...

Foundered in the Southern Seas – Fate of the Clipper Willie Rosenfeld – Many Days in Open Boats

Freighted with a general cargo and rigged with curses dark, the *Willie Rosenfeld*, a Bath-built clipper of the Sewall fleet, sailed from New York on April 23, bound for San Francisco. The ship and her master, W.H. Dunphy, and his mate had come into much notoriety, because of charges of incredible brutality which had been made before the Shipping Commissioner by the old crew, which had brought the ship from San Francisco to New York.

The mate evaded arrest, the captain gave bonds for appearance when wanted, shipping masters got together another crew, and the vessel sailed away, bearing the maledictions of her older men, some of whom had been left in hospital. And on October 7 one boat-load of castaways from the *Rosenfeld* returned to New York on board the steamship *Carib Prince*, and told how the ship had foundered on the Antarctic's verge. Two other boats put off from the wreck. One of these is supposed [believed] to have been saved. The other has yet to be heard from. [In fact both boats were lost. The only survivors were the twelve in Capt. Dunphy's boat.]

Those who arrived on the *Carib Prince* are: Mate
Gillespie and his wife, Steward Burnham and his wife
(who was the stewardess), the carpenter, boatswain, and
five men. Captain Dunphy was in command with these
castaways, but when the boat made a landing on the
Brazilian coast he left the others and remained behind.

Final Voyage
It was a narrative of blood, of misadventure, of blue lights
[distress signals], and shipwreck that the returned castaways had to tell.

The voyage was ill-fated from the very start. Two days
out from port Charles Simpson, an able seaman, cut his
throat. A week later Jacob German, who had been sent
aloft to furl the foreroyal [the royal, highest sail, on the
foremast], lost his footing, and plunged headlong into
the sea.

The days filed by with the latitudes, and when three
months out from port, the ship was shouldering her
way through the long Antarctic heavings [south of Cape
Horn]. There a gale was met, and a dangerous leak was
sprung. The pumps could not keep the craft afloat, and
she was headed for the Falkland Islands. There was
another gale, which left the ship with 14 feet of water
in her hold, and then there was an abandoning of the
sodden wreck, the crew dividing itself among the three
boats. Second Mate Baldwin and six men manned one
and Third Mate Smith, with six men, took the other.
The composition of the first boat has been given [above].

The wreck sunk soon after it had been abandoned. A
south-west gale swept the boats well to the northward,
and it was decided to head up for Rio Janeiro. While the
gale was on, the lights of a steamship were seen, and blue

The Passage Round Cape Horn. (*Gleason's Pictorial*, Boston, Saturday, 30 July 1853)

lights were burned from the boats but the signals were unheeded or unseen.

In the captain's boat canvas was stretched over the after part, making a shelter for the women. The gale grew wilder, and a sea anchor was improvised from a bread bag and tossed over the bow, attached to a line. Riding to that drag the boat outlived the storm, though for thirty hours she swung to it, every moment in imminent danger of being swamped.

The three boats became separated in the tumult. The captain's boat landed at a point ninety miles south of Imbutula [Imbituba, Santa Catarina State], Brazil, and from there the party made its way to Rio Janeiro, where they embarked on the *Carib Prince*. (*Grey River Argus* [Greymouth, New Zealand], 30 November 1896)

The *Willie Rosenfeld* 'was known as a "hard ship", and sailors as a rule are not sorry that she is gone so long as they are satisfied no lives were lost'. So, at her final farewell, the *Rosenfeld* gave scant satisfaction to the brethren of seafarers who were bound to those lost by the perils of the sea and rough trade of rogue masters and mates of similar 'Red Record' vessels, but who, indeed, would not rue her passing.

Brutality on the *George Stetson*

Built at Bath, Maine and launched in 1880, the *George Stetson* was another of Sewal's big American clippers (1,845 tons). She was renowned for her speed and employed primarily in the busy trade between East Coast and Pacific West Coast ports. On a voyage from Baltimore, Maryland, to Astoria, Oregon, in 1897–98, one of the crew, a seaman named Amos Stone, was the subject of such brutality by the *Stetson*'s mate as to render Stone 'a raving maniac' by the time the vessel reached her destination after a prolonged voyage of 174 days:

Made a Maniac by the Brutality of a Ship's Mate –
Seamen of the George Stetson *Tell a Story of Awful Cruelty to One of Their Number*

Portland [Oregon], Jan. 31. – If the story of John Burke, who came around the Horn on the American ship *George Stetson* in the capacity of sailor, can be believed, the officers of this ship are guilty of the most barbarous cruelties that have been reported at this port in many a day. The *Stetson* arrived at Astoria with a cargo of coal on Thursday, being 174 days out from Baltimore, where she took on cargo. Captain Murphy is in command and George Harvey is first officer [first mate].

Amos Stone

The victim of the alleged brutality of the officers, and especially that of First Mate Harvey, is a seaman named Amos Stone, son of a wealthy jewellery merchant of Boston. Stone is said to have been taken off the Stetson at Astoria a raving maniac, having arrived at this condition as a result of the treatment he received on the voyage.

'Stone was singled out as the especial object of Harvey's brutality soon after we left Baltimore,' said Burke, in narrating his story. 'Harvey, for some reason, knocked him insensible with an iron topmaul [heavy iron hammer], and as the rest of us feared we would be treated likewise, we were at the point of turning back four hours after we left port. As soon as we saw what had happened we scampered up the masts to turn to. The mate, however, informed the captain [Capt. Ebed Murphy], who bullied us into remaining with the ship.

'Stone, as the result of the injury he received, was laid up for some days, during which time he was given little to eat. As soon as he recovered sufficiently to venture out and report for duty Harvey kicked him off the forecastle. From that time on Stone was unable to leave his cabin. He was starved and beaten almost daily, and by the time we reached Astoria he was skin and bones and a raving maniac.

'As we were rounding the Horn, where the seas were very bad, Harvey would open the door of Stone's cabin so as to let the water in to soak his clothes and bedding. I have also seen Harvey open the door of Stone's cabin and with a heavy leather strap beat him until big welts stood out on his legs and back. Stone, who was already losing his reason, would not wince under this scourging and stood like a statue, without saying a word in remonstrance.

'An effort was made to obliterate the marks on Stone's body before the ship reached Astoria, but without success, and he will carry the marks with him to the grave. During much of the time Stone was cooped up in his cabin he had nothing but refuse to eat, and the place was the most foul-smelling I was ever in. He was abused like a dog, even during the time he was in irons. It made me sick to look at him, accustomed as I was to seeing displays of brutality on the high seas.' (*San Francisco Call*, 1 February 1898)

Mate George Harvey was arrested on evidence given by the *Stetson*'s crew of his brutality against Amos Stone. Capt. Murphy was indicted on similar charges. Both were tried at Portland, Oregon, in January 1899. On 5 January of that year, however, Capt. Ebed Murphy died suddenly from 'brain fever' (probably pneumonia), aged just 45, thereby evading secular if not divine justice for his thuggish treatment of Amos Stone. As for the officers' 'victim of the outrage': 'Amos Stone had to be removed to the insane asylum at Salem, where he has been ever since, but now, it is said, he has recovered his mental, if not altogether his physical health.' (*The Dalles Weekly Chronicle* [Oregon], 7 January 1899)

Murder on the *P.J. Williams*

Two brothers, Capt. George Layton and mate Arthur Layton, from Nova Scotia, together with the second mate,

Alexander Cummings, were charged with murder on the
high seas during a voyage by the British ship *P.J. Williams*
from Wilmington, North Carolina, to the Tyne on the
north-east coast of England, in 1885. Other 'various cruelties' were inflicted upon the victim, a young Swedish sailor
named Hugo Limborg, before he eventually succumbed to
the cumulative effects of the officers' combined assaults:

Extraordinary Cruelty on the High Seas

At the Northumberland [northeast England] Assizes,
before Mr. Justice Mathew, a case of gross cruelty the
details of which were of a revolting character, Geo.
[George] Noble Layton (captain), Arthur Layton (chief
mate), Alexander Cummings (licensed [second] mate), of
the British ship *P.J. Williams*, were charged with having
on the high seas, between the 9th and 26th of March
[1885], whilst on a voyage from Wilmington, North
Carolina, to the River Tyne, murdered one of the crew,
a young Swede, named Hugo Limborg. The evidence of
the rest of the crew showed that Limborg was kicked and
beaten by the officers of the ship, he not being, in their
opinion, an efficient seaman.

Various cruelties were practised upon the man during
the voyage. According to the evidence for the prosecu-
tion it was a bad voyage, and the men had to work at
the pumps, the vessel having sprung a leak. Once when
Limborg was sick the chief mate and Cummings pulled
him out of his bunk, kicked him, and threw him out of
the forecastle. Limborg never retaliated; he would put
his arms high up very like a child. The deceased, who
was between 12 and 14 stones weight [76–89kg] when he
joined the ship at Wilmington, failed in strength and
weight, and on the day he died was in a weak condition.

On the morning of that day the first mate was seen to seize Limborg and kick him into the lee scuppers, the man being too weak to resist. He cried like a child, and was unable to raise himself. He was given some soup at dinner time, but was unable to swallow it owing to the swelling in his mouth from ill-treatment, and fell from his seat to the deck. He tried to get up but failed.

The captain said, 'You Dutch son of a ---, you have eaten your dinner and must work.' The captain and mate then slung a rope round the deceased's body and dragged him on deck. The deceased fell between some casks, and the mate kicked him. The mate then got a bucket of water, and dashed it into Limborg's face. Immediately afterwards he gave a long breath and expired.

The Cruelty Defense

Mr. Waddy, Q.C., in defending the captain and mate, contended that in ships of this class cruelty to some extent was always seen, and the prisoners were not guilty of intentionally causing the death of this man. He called the North Sea pilot who boarded the vessel in the Downs on her arrival and other witnesses to show that the crew did not complain of any murder having been committed, although they reported that the man Limborg had died on the voyage. The captain, in recording the death of Limborg, who was buried in the Atlantic, attributed his death to heart disease.

Ultimately, the jury found the captain and chief mate guilty of manslaughter, and acquitted the second mate, Cummings. Mr. Justice Mathew, in passing sentence on the two Laytons, who were brothers, and belonging to [i.e. from] Nova Scotia, said he concurred in the verdict given. It had been advanced on behalf of the prisoners that those who were in charge of ships of this description (usually called starvation ships) could only maintain order by rough usage and brutal treatment of the crew. He did not believe it; but if it were so, the sooner such ships ceased to be sent to sea, the better. It was said there must be a reign of terror. His Worship did not believe it.

He then sentenced the two Laytons to undergo seven years of penal servitude. Cummings was discharged. (*Evening Post* [Wellington, New Zealand], 26 September 1885)

The 'Hellship' Voyage of the *T.F. Oakes*

The clipper ship *T.F. Oakes* was the first ship built by the American Shipbuilding Company, at Philadelphia. She was launched in September 1883 'in the presence of 3,000 spectators', including Miss Grace Oakes. She was the daughter of Thomas Fletcher Oakes, at the time vice-president of the Northern Pacific Railway and for whom the *T.F. Oakes* was named, and christened the new ship with a bottle of champagne. The *Oakes* was intended to be employed 'in the Pacific freight trade, plying between New York and Portland, Oregon'.

Capt. Reed
Capt. Edward W. Reed ('a paralytic') was the *Oakes'* master in the 1890s. During that time he was cited by some of his crews for cruelty resulting sometimes in the death of some seamen. The prolonged passage of the *Oakes* from Hong Kong to New York in 1896–97 – almost nine months for a voyage that would normally have taken four to five months – was shrouded by illness and death amongst the *Oakes'*

crew. The surviving crew members blamed Capt. Reed for the ship's troubles, including the death of six men from illness and hunger, and most of the rest laid up with scurvy:

Clipper T.F. Oakes *Reaches Port Nine Months Overdue – Storm, Hunger and Scurvy Disable the Ship and Kill Most of the Crew – The Captain's Plucky Wife Saves the Ship by Taking Her Trick at the Wheel Till Rescue Comes*

New York, March 21. – The long overdue American Clipper ship *T.F. Oakes*, which left Hongkong on July 4, 259 days ago [i.e. 4 July 1896], with a general cargo for this port, and which had been given up as lost, was towed into port this morning by the British tank steamer *Kasbeck*, Capt. Muir, who picked her up last Thursday in latitude 38.10 [N], longitude 68.44 [W – about 350 miles southeast of New York City]. The crew were sick with scurvy and six had died. The *Kasbeck* was bound from Philadelphia for Fiume, Austria, with a cargo of oil, and left the former port on Saturday, March 13.

On the following evening at 11 o'clock blue lights were seen, and Capt. Muir ordered the steamer's course altered, and the steamer bore up to the distress signal. At 1 o'clock she was close alongside the ship and stood by until daybreak, when signals were observed flying from the ship, asking that a boat be sent alongside, as the ship's crew were so helpless as to be unable to man their own boats. Chief Officer C.P. Helshem and three seamen at once put off in the *Kasbeck*'s yawl, and when within speaking distance heard a tale of suffering and sickness from those aboard the ship such as made them shudder.

Capt. Reed of the *Oakes* reported that his crew were all laid up with scurvy and that the provisions were well nigh exhausted. He was unable to navigate the ship with the few hands he had at his command, and begged that he be at once supplied with fresh food and taken in tow for the nearest port. Mate Helshem returned to the *Kasbeck* with the message, and Capt. Muir at once decided to take the vessel in tow.

The weather, which had been threatening, now became boisterous and a northerly gale sprang up. Nevertheless, preparations were made to pass a hawser to the *Oakes* when the boat with a load of provisions was sent. A manila hawser was paid out over the *Kasbeck's* stern to the yawl, but a tremendous wave washed it into the propeller, which was turning slowly at the time, and before the engines could be stopped, the screw was so entangled that the engines with the full power of steam could not move it again. An effort was at once made to free the screw, but as it was so deeply submerged and the sea running so high, it was found impossible.

For eight hours the engineer's staff labored to clear the propeller and finally disconnected the shaft, and found that by placing a small block of wood between the couplings, the screws could be made to turn. By that time the *Oakes* had drifted out of sight, and Capt. Muir, despairing of being able to tow her with his disabled screw, determined at least to find her and supply her with provisions. All night he searched the horizon for a trace of her, and at 6 a.m. Tuesday she was again sighted. The sea was rough at the time, but Chief Officer Helshem again volunteered to attempt to board her, and, as the engineers reported the propeller to be working well, it was decided to send a hawser aboard.

Accordingly a line was dragged by the boat, and after a deal of hard work, two hawsers were made fast.

Mr. Helshem and his boat's crew of three did most of the work on the ship. They found only the second and third mates able to help them. The provisions they brought were a Godsend to the scurvy-stricken survivors of the ship's crew, and they began to gather hope that they might live to see land again. From the time the hawser was passed until New York was reached no incidence of importance occurred.

A Hellship Voyage

Captain Reed of the *Oakes* told a terrible story of suffering and privation. When the *Oakes* sailed from Hong Kong the crew were apparently in the best of health with the exception of Captain Reed, who had been ailing for some time, but who, under the careful nursing of his devoted wife, thought himself on the high road to recovery. When about six days out in the China Sea a terrific typhoon was encountered, lasting several days, during which the fore and main topmasts were sprung. The vessel was obliged to run before the gale which had no sooner blown itself out than it was followed by a second typhoon which blew with great fury for twenty-four days.

The vessel had then got well out in the North Pacific and so far off her course that Captain Reed decided to shape his course via Cape Horn rather than by the Cape of Good Hope, hoping thereby to make better time. The weather remained fine until Cape Horn was rounded, 167 days out.

In the meantime the Chinese cook had been taken down with a severe cold and died on November 11. Afterwards a seaman named Thomas King was taken down with what appeared to be scurvy, and died

December 20 [*sic* – 26th]. In quick succession Seaman Thomas Olsen was taken down and died January 12. Thomas Judge, another seaman, was taken ill with cancer of the stomach, and later Mate Stephen Bunker showed symptoms of scurvy. The latter died February 4 and was quickly followed by George King, an old man [Thomas King's older brother], who died on the 9th. On the 17th Judge succumbed, making in all six deaths.

One by one the other sailors were obliged to quit work until, on March 1, nobody was left except the second and third mates, the captain and his wife. All were well nigh exhausted, and when a strong northerly gale blew up that day the brave woman was obliged to take the wheel and for eight hours without relief and without so much as a drink of water she kept the ship on her course.

The provisions were running short, although a supply had been obtained on January 12 from the American ship *Governor Robie*, from New York for Melbourne, when off the island of Trinidad [off the coast of Brazil], and the crew were left without other than the barest necessities. [The *Governor Robie* left Hong Kong four days before the *Oakes*, arrived at New York via the Cape of Good Hope, discharged her cargo, and was outward bound again when she met the *Oakes* still on passage!]

A sharp lookout was kept for passing vessels, but none were seen until the *Kasbeck* hove in sight. The only vessel previously sighted during the entire voyage, with the exception of the ship *Governor Robie*, was a north-bound Lamport and Holt steamer which passed the *Oakes* off Pernambuco [Recife, Brazil], but was too far off to distinguish signals. (*Los Angeles Herald*, 22 March 1897)

Hannah Reed

Capt. Reed's wife, Hannah, claimed to play an integral part in working the severely under-manned ship to port, particularly in the latter weeks of the voyage when most of the crew were ill and disabled, and 'the provisions were well nigh exhausted'.

The Captain's Brave Wife

Mrs. Reed, wife of the Captain of the *Oakes*, is a woman of masculine proportions. She told last night of her experience during the gale, that commenced on March 1. She had previously lent a hand at the wheel and at the halyards and sheets, and after the death of the cook she worked in the galley and attended besides as best she could to the sick men in the forecastle. Her husband said that she was the best man on board the ship. From the time the trouble began she bore a man's part and shared with the others the privations of the voyage. When the time came she showed also that she was a good sailor.

The *Oakes* was off [Cape] Hatteras when the gale of March 1 was encountered.

'I went on deck,' she said, 'and asked Capt. Reed if I could help him. Mr. Abrams and Mr. Regan, the two mates, and one seaman were aloft trying to furl the main topsails, and the two Chinese servants were doing their best to haul the clew lines. Capt. Reed asked me to take the wheel while he helped those on deck, and I did so. It was bitterly cold, and I was not prepared for the weather, but I stuck it out till my husband ran aft to see how I was getting on, and gave me a chance to run below and get a big ulster [overcoat] of his to wrap myself in.

'From that time until noon I was steadily at it. The work was not very hard for me, as I am pretty strong, and the ship was speeding before the gale, but I was tired before I was relieved. Then we had something to eat, and afterward I went back to the wheel. Altogether I was at it eight hours that day.'

Mrs. Reed lives at Haverhill, Mass., and a telegram awaited her at Quarantine, announcing the death of her daughter, but it was charitably withheld until she should be stronger. (*The New York Times*, 22 March 1897)

Statements and notes written by some of the crew testified to the nature of Capt. Reed's rough treatment of and severe attitude towards his crew, the poor provisioning of the vessel, and reappointing of the officers according to their subservience to or insubordination of Capt. Reed's command:

Told by the Oakes's Mate – Samuel A. Frazer's Statement Concerning the Horrors of the Long Voyage from China

Samuel Alexander Frazer, for a time the third mate of the clipper ship *T.F. Oakes*, the long overdue vessel which arrived in port Sunday, lay in his cot at the Marine Hospital on Staten Island yesterday afternoon. Around him were his eleven companions from the vessel, and all of them, Dr. Stoner said, were doing reasonably well. Frazer is a Long Island man, and his brother, John N. Frazer, is the Postmaster in Islip. Frazer said that he shipped at Hongkong against the advice of Mr. Meyers, Superintendent of the Hongkong Sailors' Home, who said to him: 'Frazer, you don't want to go home in that ship.'

He insisted that there were no vegetables taken on board at Hongkong except a ton of sweet potatoes. There were no onions on board. As for lime juice, the men were given stuff from bottles, he said, which bore a

West Indies label declaring that it was lime juice cordial. When he was asked about wages he thrust his hand under a small table beside the bed, and, drawing out a memorandum book, opened it and drew therefrom a piece of paper, on which was written in a scrawling hand the last will of Thomas King, who died on Dec. 26. The writing was dated Nov. 15 and read:

'I, Thomas King, do will my clothes to the men in the forecastle, and my wages to Samuel Frazer.

(Signed) 'Thomas King'

'Witnesses, Albert Larson, Hans Arro.'

Thomas Judge's 'Communication'

Frazer, after he had shown the document, said that the clothing had all been thrown overboard by order of Capt. Reed. He also had another bit of paper, which contained a declaration from Thomas Judge, written before the one which was published, in which he quoted from the Psalms. This communication was intended for the United States Shipping Commissioner at New York, and was written with a lead pencil. Parts of it were well nigh indecipherable. It was dated Jan. 16, and Judge died on Feb. 17. The writer said:

'My Dear Sir: I am very sorry to relate to you such a story for it is one which we do not hear every day, or even year. We left Hong Kong on the 4th of July [1896] for the port of New York in the ship *T.F. Oakes*, and while we were in the China Seas the crew were very badly treated by the Captain. We were very poorly fed from the time we left port. The whole of us were sick with the exception of two or three, the sickness being swellings all over the body, with sore mouths and swelled gums, with bad feelings all over the body, and when a man died he went without warning. We have had three, the cook, King, and Olsen.

'The Captain said to myself that he would fix the pair of them – meaning King and Olsen – before he reached New York. That is nothing. He said he would fix all of us hungry hounds, and all such bad words. Now I should like to live to know whether a sick man can be treated like this. He gets nothing extra, only a little mush, and he has to give up his [ration of] beef and pork before he can get that. Medicine he gets very little. Of quinine one dose a week, and if we ask for more the Captain gets up on his pins and says he has got no more. We get about one-quarter of a pound of beef, and less pork. This is what I call bad treatment ...'

Plug Tobacco for Weights

Third Mate Harry Regan, who is a native of New York City, says the *Oakes* was the hardest ship that he ever had a billet on. He said last night that the statement of Judge in regard to forfeiting his beef and pork in order to get a small quantity of mush was true. The men went aft and complained of the quantity of food while they were still in the China Sea. They selected Frazer to see that the food was properly weighed.

Frazer and Regan both say that the scales on which the bread was weighed were not in good condition, and that the skipper and his wife used as weights two six-and-a-half ounce plugs of tobacco, when they should have used a sixteen-ounce weight. The men were thus cheated out of three ounces of bread, and Regan said that he would make an effort to get the value of that returned to him when he goes before the Shipping Commissioner to receive his pay.

There was a good deal of shifting of officers on the first half of the voyage, he [Regan] says. Abrams, the second mate, had a quarrel with the Captain, who put him off the bridge, and ordered him to go forward and do duty as a seaman. Regan was then made second mate, and held the billet for forty-one days. Frazer got the job of third mate. Regan had a disagreement with the Captain, and was sent forward [i.e. demoted to ordinary seaman]. Boatswain Robinson took his place, and the old English sailor, Judge, fell into the berth of the boatswain.

Robinson and the skipper could not agree, and after twelve days' service aft was also sent to the forecastle. Abrams then resumed his old place as second mate, Frazer was sent forward, and Regan was brought aft once more. Judge and the mate had a fight over the job of patching a topsail, and on the mate's complaint Judge was sent forward. Robinson got his old place again, and the ship was officered just as she left Hongkong.

Rations

Regan said the men received three quarts of water a day each, and every day of the voyage each man had served to him a small wineglass full of diluted lime juice. There were many gallons of water, some of which had been shipped at this port [New York] nearly two years before, when the ship reached Quarantine.

Regan said that while he was in the forecastle Thomas King and the Norwegian sailor, Olsen, both of whom died, asked the mate for something nourishing, suggesting that beef tea would be good. The mate told the Captain this, and the Captain came into the forecastle, looked at the men, intimated that they were loafing, and remarking to them: 'Beef tea is only good for dead men,' turned and went out on deck. (*The New York Times*, 24 March 1897)

Other stories of brutality on the *Oakes* were recounted by former *Oakes* seaman Arthur Smith during a voyage from Astoria, Oregon, to Le Havre, France, in 1893–94. His accusations concerning 'cruelty and starvation' by Capt. Reed rang with a familiar echo of her later 'hellship' voyage from Hong Kong:

Sailors Cruelly Treated – Arthur C. Smith's Story of a Former Voyage of the Ship T.F. Oakes *– He Makes Serious Charges – The Scanty Food, He Asserts, Forced the Sailors to Steal Wheat from the Cargo to Eat Uncooked – Men Beaten Without Reason – A Denial from Capt. Reed*

Arthur C. Smith, a seaman on the schooner *Goodwin Stoddard*, arriving in this port last Wednesday from Fernandina, Fla., tells a story of cruelty and starvation which he says was inflicted on the crew of the clipper ship *T.F. Oakes* by Capt. Reed on a voyage in 1893 … Smith, who was born in Oregon, stated yesterday to a reporter for *The New York Times*, when seen at the offices of the Coast Seamen's Union, at 51 South Street, that he shipped in the *Oakes* at Astoria, Oregon, Oct. 14, 1893, for a voyage to Havre, France. The voyage lasted four months:

'It was my first experience at sea,' said he, 'and it came very near being my last. I had applied to a boarding-house keeper to get on a deep water ship, and he sent me to the *Oakes* as able seaman, notwithstanding the fact that I had never seen salt water. My advance money, amounting to $40, I never saw. Capt. Reed was master of the *Oakes* then, as now, and Mrs. Reed was with him, and I will say that from the first day out to the end of the voyage I had but one full meal, and that was on Thanksgiving Day, when we had a double allowance of meat and boiled duff.

'When the vessel started out, we were put on what Capt. Reed called a "full and plenty" allowance. This differs from the regular allowance prescribed by law, and, instead of being better, is a great deal worse. The legal scale calls for one pound of bread daily. This means hardtack [ship's hard biscuit], but Capt. Reed had the cook bake a heavy, soggy bread, and gave us a pound of that. For breakfast and supper, we had what is called "lobscouse," consisting of meat and potatoes boiled in water and very thin. For dinner we had our regular one-third of a pound of bread and a piece of salt beef about one-fourth the size of an ordinary beefsteak. Twice a week we had pea soup, but this was such in name only, being nearly all water. At the end of the fourth week we were so weak that we begged the Captain to change our allowance to the regular legal scale. Mrs. Reed told us that too much meat would give us the scurvy, and the Captain said we were getting too fat.

'However, we got the regular provision list for a few weeks. The day's allowances of one pound and a half of salt beef was served out to each man at 12 o'clock; this included the bone, which made up fully one half the weight. At 4 o'clock in the afternoon our day's allowance of bread was served out, and we were usually so hungry that we ate the entire day's allowance on the spot.'

Knocked About

'One night I was sent to swab some water from the floor in the boatswain's room, and when I came out he accused me of stealing his bread, and beat me, breaking my nose.

Later in the day he came into the forecastle and assaulted me again, throwing me against the bulkhead and knocking me senseless. Next morning Capt. Reed only told the boatswain to be more careful.

'"Kick him, or push him," he said, "or hit him with the bight of a rope, but not on a part of his body where the marks can be seen."

'When we reached Cape Horn, where the weather was bitter cold, the Captain again put us on his "full and plenty" allowance, because he had several tons of potatoes which were rotting, and these could be boiled with a small piece of salt meat and served to us. I was so hungry that when sent abaft to grease a mast, I have eaten the grease, though it was half rotten. Once, while doing a job in the forehold, I stole three potatoes and ate them. The boatswain reported me to Capt. Reed, who beat me over the head with a piece of water-soaked rope. I was so weak from starvation and abuse that I staggered when I walked. The Captain comforted me with, "Smith, you are getting loggy; you are too fat. I will have to shut down on your beef."'

They Ate Raw Wheat

'The vessel was loaded with wheat, but we were watched to prevent us from stealing it. Still, we did steal it, and mixing it with our bread, would pound the mess up in a bag and get the cook to bake it. When he found that the wheat was stolen, he refused to bake it, and after that we ate it raw. I have often spent a half hour at night eating raw wheat to allay the pangs of hunger before I could go to sleep.

'John Kaski, a Finn, who could speak very little English, was also singled out for abuse. He was struck in the side by the boatswain, the blow breaking his rib. Subsequently the officers made a practice of striking him in the same place to save labor; a great deal of pain could be inflicted with slight exertion. Capt. Reed never reprimanded an officer for assaulting the men. John Graham, who was boatswain when the *Oakes* left port, refused to strike the men without cause, and was disrated [demoted] and sent to the forecastle. I, being a green hand, was kicked and beaten until I was covered with marks and bruises.

'When we arrived in Havre, Capt. Reed had me charged with $42 in the "slop chest," although I never drew $10 worth of clothing. There was $4 due me according to the statement of the Captain, and this I refused to accept. After leaving the *Oakes* I sailed two years in foreign vessels and received good food and treatment.'

Denied by the Captain
Capt. and Mrs. Reed, when asked about the statement of Smith, could not remember of ever having had him on board, and denied that trouble of any kind was experienced on the voyage mentioned. 'I suppose half the sailors on South Street will have a yarn to tell now,' said Mrs. Reed, 'and the newspapers will believe them.' (*The New York Times*, 27 March 1897)

It wasn't the first or even the only time Reed had been charged with cruelty to his crew. In May 1893 he and the *Oakes*' first mate at the time, a Mr McKay, were acquitted in San Francisco on the charge of cruelty to which six seamen had testified. In February 1895, again at San Francisco, Capt. Reed, this time with the second mate, faced claims of cruelty to his crew after a voyage from New York:

It was alleged that Frederick Owens, seaman, was assaulted, dragged out of the forecastle and compelled to work during extremely cold weather off Cape Horn, despite his illness, on Dec. 3, 1894. The captain, according to testimony, ordered Owens to 'walk the deck even though he couldn't work.' The man died Dec. 5. J. Johnson testified that he was knocked down and kicked in the eye by Reed for failure to address the second mate as 'sir.' The captain was acquitted in the Owens case because no 'official' charge had been made. (*Rockland County Journal* [Nyack, New York], 3 April 1897)

Arrest

At the end of March 1897, Capt. Reed was arrested on the basis of an affidavit by Samuel Frazer on behalf of the *Oakes'* crew that he, Capt. Edward W. Reed, 'did unlawfully, willfully and knowingly, from malice and without justifiable cause, withhold suitable food and nourishment from one Hans Arro and from divers others' of the crew of the *Oakes* on her voyage from Hong Kong to New York'.

After the official investigation into and hearing of the charges, Reed was 'censured, [but] he was not punished in any way'. ('The Red Record' reported that 'illtreatment [on the *Oakes*] was justified on the grounds that ... "a shipmaster has the right to beat a seaman who is unruly".')

Revenge for that, and, one suspects, other injustices, came shortly after when Capt. Reed's house at Haverhill, Massachusetts, burned (or was burned) down under mysterious circumstances. Although Reed 'escaped in his nightshirt', he 'caught pneumonia and died shortly afterwards'. His wife, the 'heroic' Hannah, who had been awarded by Lloyd's with their silver Meritorious Service medal for her bravery during the *Oakes'* notoriously hellish voyage, survived the conflagration, but 'what happened to her after that is unknown'. The *Oakes* herself survived for just another four years: she was 'stranded on the Californian coast near San Francisco in 1901'.

'The Bloody *Gatherer*': Barbarity at Sea

The American full-rigged ship *Gatherer* became notorious for her 'hard-case' captain and equally iron-fisted 'bucko' mates during a voyage from Antwerp, Belgium, round the Horn to Wilmington, California, in 1881–82. The *Gatherer*'s first mate William Watts (also known as Charlie and 'Black' Watts) and second mate Cornelius (George) Curtis were worse than bullies; in their assaults upon the ship's crew, they verged on being psychopathic brutes.

'Black' Charlie Watts was most adept at using as weapons his fists and belaying-pins, the hard wooden or metal pins around which ropes were secured (belayed), to beat seamen senseless. Second mate Curtis was only a whimper less brutal, wielding 'a rope knotted and soaked in tar' to assault a young Danish sailor named Gustave Adlung. The third mate, a kindly man named Driscoll, stated that 'Watts was the most brutal of the two mates, but Curtis was the most beastly in his treatment of the crew'.

Capt. Charles Newell Sparks, master of the *Gatherer*, was more like the gangmaster of that evil duo than shipmaster of a late-nineteenth-century deep-sea sailing vessel. Sparks complied with the atrocities more by his willing abetment than by direct participation, though his personal assault on the young Danish seaman Adlung confirmed his readiness to wield a belaying-pin for purposes other than those prescribed in seamanship manuals.

Barbarity at Sea – Brutality of the Officers of the Ship
Gatherer *– A Harrowing Story of the Cruelties Suffered by Her*
Crew on the Passage from Antwerp to Wilmington [California]
– Arrest of the Miscreants

The story of cruelty at sea on the *Gatherer* is one of the most horrible of the many horrible stories of diabolical abuse of seamen. The *Gatherer* sailed from Antwerp in September last [1881], officered by C. N. Sparks, Wm. Watts, Cornelius Curtis and John Driscoll, respectively Captain, first, second and third mates. The vessel, according to the sailors' stories, was scarcely off the coast of Holland when the first and second mates began their acts of barbarity, which consisted in treating the sailors in a most inhuman and brutal manner.

A sailor named Clarke was the first victim and received a hard beating at the hands of Watts for the misconstruction of an order. A few days afterward a sailor named Turner so displeased the mate and second mate that the two model officers attacked the unfortunate man in a shameful manner, maltreating him to such an extent that it was months before his wounds healed.

Then in rapid succession, so the complaint states, the remainder of the crew incurred the anger of the first and second mates, and were summarily dealt with in the presence of Captain Sparks, who did not raise his voice in behalf of the unfortunate crew.

Beaten With Brass Knuckles

A Belgian sailor who can only speak a few words of English nearly lost an eye by a beating at the hands of Watts, who a few days subsequently called a sailor named Burns to account for some trivial offense, and did so in such a harsh manner that Burns revolted, and was, by order of Watts, lashed to the rail of the ship. Having his victim thus at his mercy, the officer adorned his hands with a pair of brass knuckles, and with them beat and lacerated Burns about the face, and otherwise disfigured him.

The ship's boy, a Dane, who witnessed the brutal treatment of his shipmate, was indiscreet enough to express his horror thereat, and was in turn beaten with the knuckles about the head, one of the blows injuring the tympanum of the ear, and it is said that his hearing is destroyed forever.

A sailor-boy named Adlung was knocked down upon the deck, beaten and trampled upon by the first mate, whom he accuses of kicking out his eyes, at all events the young man is blind. The sailors state that the third mate, Driscoll, did all in his power to prevent the outrages, but that being a minor officer he was powerless. The ship's boy, named George, and another man, it is said, jumped overboard rather than endure the cruelty which was daily inflicted upon them.

Tommy Ung Stang, a Chinaman who was steward on the vessel, was sick one day and told the captain he could not work. The captain then took him by the hair and dragged him out of his bunk and beat him with knotted ropes, after which he stamped on him and left him lying senseless. He was taken to another place to lie, the captain refusing to allow him to be placed back in his old bunk. The Chinaman kept his bed for the rest of the voyage, and was often heard to cry.

While lying off Wilmington the Chinaman was found lying in the hold of the iron rails [i.e. the cargo of iron rails], his head being crushed and bleeding and the iron wet with blood. It was not known how he came to be in the hold. When he recovered consciousness he was crazy, and was brought to our jail and kept in confinement till he was taken to the Napa Insane Asylum last Friday by Deputy Sheriff Huber.

Arrest of the Captain

The *Gatherer* arrived in the harbor of San Francisco on Tuesday [14 March 1882], and as soon as she cast anchor Deputy U.S. Marshal Favor proceeded on board armed with a warrant for the arrest of Captain Sparks. The Captain took the information that he was wanted very coolly, and at first refused to recognize the officer or his authority. But other parties coming on board, he submitted to their advice and proceeded ashore with the Deputy, who locked him up.

On his way to the prison the Captain declined to make any explanation of the conduct of his subordinates, being content to heap maledictions upon their heads, and accusing them generally of being devils incarnate. He finally admitted having the worst mates that he had ever seen or heard of. Arrived at the prison the Captain was escorted to a cell in murderers' row. (*Los Angeles Herald*, 17 March 1882)

Another report described in more graphic detail the 'punishments' inflicted on the crew by Watts and Curtis:

Human Fiends

A revolting tale of cruelty and outrage by the officers of a ship is told in the San Francisco papers. The vessel was called the *Gatherer*, and was commanded by a scoundrel named Sparks, with two ruffians considerably worse than himself as first and second mates.

On the day of sailing, while the *Gatherer* had not even left the harbor of Antwerp, the brutality of Watts, the first mate, and Curtis, the second mate, began to manifest itself. Peter Anderson, one of the sailors, being slightly under the influence of liquor, as most sailors are when a ship leaves the harbor, was given a severe beating by the first mate. Turner, a Scotchman, another sailor, being also somewhat under the influence of liquor, was pitched by Curtis, the second mate, head foremost from the forecastle head, down into the forecastle.

On September 15, John Hansen, a Belgian sailor, who was unable to understand all the orders given him in the mate's English, was beaten by the second mate Curtis in a brutal manner; one of his eyes was nearly gouged out.

Five days later a German sailor named William Olsner, who had shipped under the name of John Burns, and who understood very little English, became the victim of Watts's wrath and was lashed to the rail, while his tormentor disfigured his face with brass knuckles, fracturing his nose. Charley, a Danish boy, standing by and seeing the brutal treatment, expressed his compassion, when the mate struck him on the side of the head. The boy was rendered entirely deaf in one ear, and the injury resulted in impairing the other.

'Revolting' and 'Monstrous' Cruelty

On October 1 Watts lashed a heavy capstan bar to the back of Olsner, and made him walk up and down the deck, kicking him as he passed in review. Not content with that, Watts called up a sailor named McCue, another named Peter Anderson, and a boy named George, and together with Olsner subjected them to treatment of the most revolting nature. The day following, Watts caused McCue and the boy George to be partially stripped, and, after fastening straps around their waists, caused one to drag the other along the deck, the mate meanwhile sitting on the one being dragged.

The boy George, who was only eighteen years of age, became thoroughly discouraged, and shortly after fell into the sea from the mizzen-topsail and was drowned. Whether he sought death voluntarily or whether it was accidental is not known. It is also stated that the seaman John Hansen, who was beaten when only about fourteen days out at sea, continued to be treated with monstrous brutality by both mates, until, no longer able to endure the torture, being one mass of sores from head to foot, he jumped into the sea and was drowned.

Jack de Briand, a French sailor nicknamed 'Frenchy' by the crew, was struck with a belaying-pin by the mate, the blow breaking his nose and injuring his ear. The steward of the ship was also struck over the head and put in confinement, and left without food for five days. He is now in the county gaol of Los Angeles, a raving lunatic.

On November 15 McCue was partially stripped and fastened by a strap to his waist and raised to the mizzen stay, where he hung with his face downward until he was black in the face from the rush of the blood to his head. Old Henry, nicknamed 'Baby-face,' and William Olsner were also treated with brutality during the entire voyage, the former receiving a blow on his head with a belaying-pin, which has rendered him partially demented.

Gustave Adlung, a German boy about eighteen years of age, was also brutally treated and kicked in the eye by the first mate, Watts, which has rendered him almost blind.

An 'Alta' [*Alta California* newspaper] reporter found Adlung in the United States Marshal's office. Although only eighteen years of age, the boy's frame was naturally strong and powerful, but he was as helpless as a child. When asked in regard to the nature of the treatment of the crew, he told the following pitiful story.

Gustave Adlung's Account

The ill-treatment of the crew began while the ship was still in the harbor, and Peter Anderson and a sailor named Turner were beaten by both mates. On the second day out Curtis, the second mate, told Adlung to put canvas around the hawsers, after which he went aft. He came back afterwards, and as the work did not suit the mate, he struck the boy in the eye, knocking him down and giving him a black eye. John Hansen, a Belgian, was repeatedly subjected to most brutal treatment, his flesh being lacerated on his back and legs. The boy had heard Hansen say that if he could not get relief from his cruel punishment he would commit suicide.

The captain witnessed many of the acts, but took no part to prevent the outrages; on the contrary, he assisted in the atrocities.

On October 27, Adlung accidentally spilled some tar water on the railing, which was painted white, but he did not notice at the time that he had done so. The next morning, about eight o'clock, Watts asked him why he had spilled the tar on the rail. He replied: 'I don't know; I didn't see.' The mate then hit him, knocking him down against the bulwarks. While in that position, and unable to help himself, Watts kicked him in the eyes and on the face, and also beat him with his fist. The captain saw the act, but instead of interfering, turned around and laughed. The mate finally ordered Adlung below to his bunk. He [Adlung] asked the captain for medicine, when the latter replied: 'Go to --- and go to work.'

The next morning, while lying in his bunk, unable to see the least thing, with his left eye swollen in such a manner as to form a huge ball, the second mate, Curtis, came down and struck him in the back of the neck, saying, 'Get out and go on your watch.'

'I thought he had killed me,' said the boy, 'my eyes seemed to me like burning balls of fire, and the pain of the blow was terrible.'

Adlung was four weeks in bed, during which time the third mate, Driscoll, who was the only friend the sailors had on deck, poulticed the boy's eye, and relieved his sufferings as best he could. After four weeks, when still unable to see anything, he was ordered on deck. At night, when everything was dark, the mates would order him aloft, there being nothing to do, but merely out of pure devilry, and he heard them say, 'I hope the --- will fall down and kill himself.' He had to feel his way up, and always succeeded in making his dangerous trips without the desire of the brutal mates being accomplished.

Chinese Steward Driven Mad

Tommy Ung Stang, a Chinaman, who was steward on the vessel, was sick one day, and told the captain he could not work. The captain then took him by the hair and dragged him out of his bunk and beat him with knotted ropes, after which he stamped on him, and left him lying senseless. He was taken to another place to lie, the captain refusing to allow him to be placed back in his old bunk. The Chinaman kept his bed for the rest of the voyage, and was often heard to cry. While lying off Wilmington the Chinaman was found lying in the hold on the iron rails, his head being crushed and bleeding, and the iron wet with blood. It was not known how he came to be in the hold. When he recovered consciousness he was crazy, and he is now at Los Angeles, insane.

William Olsner complained that he did not get anything to eat, when the first mate tied him against the rail and stuffed his mouth with hard-tack [hard ship's biscuit], after which he rammed it down with a belaying-pin. The captain and the second mate witnessed the cruel act, but seemed to think it a good joke, and laughed at it.

Jack De Briand was struck on the head with a belaying-pin in the hands of the first mate, splitting the weapon. One time Charley, the Danish boy, was at the wheel, when the captain hit him on the side of the head with a belaying-pin; he could not hear well after that, and there was a discharge from his ear.

Adlung … said the first mate always used a belaying-pin in striking, while Curtis used a rope knotted and soaked in tar. When the ship arrived at Wilmington Adlung asked the captain to be allowed to go on shore to see the doctor, when he replied, 'You can't go; go to work.'

Adlung's Blindness
The next day both mates were allowed to land. The men, upon arriving in port, refused to work, and demanded their discharge, which was due there, when the captain refused to give them anything to eat, so they were compelled to work. The boy Adlung stated that his sight was perfect when he boarded the ship. He is now unable to walk unassisted, he being totally blind in one eye. 'The other eye is getting worse all the time,' continued Adlung. 'I can scarcely see anything now.' He also

stated that the men were afraid to defend themselves, because the mates always wore a brace of pistols, and Watts had often bragged of being 'master of the beasts,' referring to the crew. After being two weeks on board a man named Kelley, living in Wilmington, took Adlung ashore, together with three others, after which they were sent to the Marine Hospital. Oculists have examined his eyes, and decided that the injuries are incurable, and that he will become permanently blind.

Third Mate Driscoll

The third mate, John Driscoll, on being interviewed by an 'Alta' reporter, substantiated the statements made by the sailors. He said that the crew, consisting of fourteen men and three boys, were all subjected to cruelty, except a man named Lindsay, who was only protected by virtue of Driscoll declaring to the mates that if they ill-treated Lindsay they had also to ill-treat him, when he put Lindsay in the cabin to do work. He stated that the boy George did not jump overboard, but fell from the mizzen-mast, he (Driscoll) being near him at the time but unable to catch him.

The man Hansen, he said, committed suicide because of the cruelty to which he was subjected. Hansen showed him the condition of his body, and Driscoll was horrified to find the body mutilated in a shocking manner. There were cuts large enough to lay a finger in, and at some places the flesh was in shreds. With tears in his eyes Hansen had begged Driscoll to protect him from the mates, but Driscoll was unable to help him, and one evening Hansen deliberately jumped overboard.

In regard to the German boy Adlung, Driscoll stated that the boy's face was terrible to look upon. The white of the eye had turned black, and but slowly regained its usual color. Driscoll stated that Watts was the most brutal of the two mates, but Curtis was the most beastly in his treatment of the crew. Driscoll stated that he had tried to prevent the men from being punished as much was in his power, but he could do very little.

Arrest of the Perpetrators

Curtis, after some difficulty, was hunted down and arrested in San Francisco, and the captain was seized as soon as the *Gatherer* visited the port again. Watts, the worst of all, got away on a vessel bound for Queenstown [Ireland], and extradition papers were sent after him. The grand jury found the following indictments against the prisoners:– Twenty-seven for offences committed on the high seas, fourteen under the revenue laws, four for forgery, three for offences under the postal laws, three for selling liquor to Indians, two for cutting timber on Government lands, and one each for counterfeiting coin, for attempting to bribe a Custom-house official, for smuggling and for perjury.

All the officers, it was ascertained, bore a reputation for cruelty to sailors, and Watts had been in gaol for offences of the kind. (*Evening Star* [Dunedin, New Zealand], 16 May 1882)

Capt. Sparks

Capt. Sparks was 'a thick, heavy-set man, about 5 feet 10 inches in height ... about 200 pounds' who had form for his wicked ways:

He is about 45 years of age, very dark complexion, and apparently possesses an iron will and a wicked temper. He is reported to have served a term in San Quentin [prison] some ten years ago. A few years later he left this port [San Francisco] as mate of the bark *Penang*, and had to leave the ship at Sydney to avoid arrest at Australia, whither he was bound. Soon after his return to San Francisco he sailed as mate of the schooner *Lovett Peacock*, and was obliged to leave her before his agreement was up, owing to threatened arrest for abuse to seamen. Last year he sailed as Captain of the ship *Hagerstown*, and a similar fate attended that voyage. (*Sacramento Daily Union*, 16 March 1882)

A United States Grand Jury indicted Capt. Sparks and second mate Curtis for numerous individual and joint assaults on members of the *Gatherer*'s crew 'between the 1st of September 1881, and January 5th, 1882'. At the subsequent trial, 18-year-old Gustave Adlung testified to the brutality inflicted upon him, describing how he came to be blinded in one eye and was 'struck by both the First and Second Mates often during the voyage':

I made a loud outcry when I was injured. My blood flowed on the deck. I wiped it up, by orders of the Mate. The Mate attacked me for spilling some tar water on deck. While below, the Captain visited me and asked me about my eyes. When I went on deck the Mate made me go to work. I cannot see to read. My eyes are getting worse. Cannot distinguish one juror from another. (*Los Angeles Herald*, 8 April 1882)

Another young seaman, Carl Rasmussen, aged 17, testified to the extent of the cruelty inflicted upon him and the other crew by the captain and mates of the *Gatherer*, corroborating young Adlung's and others' accounts.

Capt. Sparks was acquitted and escaped punishment for his devilry on the *Gatherer*, largely on his claim that there was no evidence of his direct assaults on the crew. He accused his malicious mates of being 'devils incarnate', and that he was not guilty of any of their acts of brutality 'unless he ordered it'.

He was relieved of his command of the *Gatherer* but eventually, in 1884, got command of another ship, the *Red Cross*, for a voyage from Portland, Oregon, for Liverpool. Though the *Red Cross* arrived in Liverpool towards the end of November 1884, Capt. Sparks never did:

Suicide of Captain Sparks

Advices by telegraph report the arrival in Liverpool on November 28th of the American ship *Red Cross* from Portland, Or. During the voyage, Captain Sparks, the master, committed suicide by jumping into the sea. Captain Sparks will be remembered as being the master of the ship *Gatherer*, and who figured in our Courts while being on trial for cruelty to his crew. Captain Sparks was acquitted, but two of his mates are now serving their sentences out at San Quentin Prison.

Shortly after his arrival at Portland, Captain Sparks wrote a letter to a merchant in this city [San Francisco] stating that he had been tendered the command of the ship *Ontario*, but preferred to take command of the *Red Cross*, then at Portland loading for Liverpool. He also stated that he had expected to meet his wife at Liverpool, whence she has gone from their home in Bath, Me [Maine]. The letter showed no evidence of mental disorder, and no reason could be given for his rash act. (*Daily Alta California*, 2 December 1884)

Mates Curtis and Watts

Second mate Curtis was sentenced to six years' imprisonment at San Quentin State Prison, just north of San Francisco.

'Black' Charlie Watts was paid off from the *Gatherer* in San Francisco and, 'fearing trouble for his acts', escaped immediate arrest by signing on the ship *Imperial*, bound for Queenstown, Ireland. He was arrested there and subsequently extradited to the United States for trial. A technicality got him off, but he was kept in prison and tried a second time in 1884.

Watts was found guilty for his criminality on the *Gatherer*, but only for the assaults on two of the crew (and those the youngest) amongst the multitude of others he actually perpetrated. Though he did not satisfy the public's putative desire to see his neck stretched by a length of 'five-eighths manilla rope' (hemp) he did spend time inside San Quentin, his terms overlapping Curtis's six-year stretch:

Six Years – Watts Sentenced to San Quentin for that Term – The Judge Wonders that the World Proved Large Enough to Hold Him and His Late Crew – The Convict Reviled by the Crowd

The jury ... convicted Watts of but two of the charges,... but those two were the most serious of any, one being the blinding of the boy Gustave Adlung [18 years old], the other the beating of the sailor [Carl] Rasmussen [17 years old] with brass knuckles. He [prosecuting Assistant District Attorney] did not think that the case was one for clemency.

He [the Judge] then sentenced Watts to four years in San Quentin for putting out the eye of Gustave Adlung, and two years for beating Rasmussen with the brass knuckles ... When sentence was pronounced, a murmur of satisfaction ran through the assembled audience. Watts himself appeared unmoved. As he passed through the wall in charge of the Marshal, even though accompanied by his wife and baby, the crowd jeered and taunted him.

So ends the notorious *Gatherer* case. (*The San Francisco Daily Repository*, 5 March 1884)

Watts virtually embodied the Biblical utterance that he who lived by the sword, died by the sword. *The New York Times* of 25 August 1906 reported that the *Gatherer* ('known for years as "the bloodiest ship afloat"') arrived in New York after a voyage of 140 days from Tacoma, Washington, 'her first peaceful voyage since she was built'. It included the observation on the notorious reputation of the 'bloody' *Gatherer* from her 1881–82 blood-soaked voyage that, 'After being imprisoned for brutality towards the sailors on the *Gatherer*, Watts fled to the lumber camps and met a violent death in one of the northern logging settlements'.

The *Cyrus Wakefield* – Cruelty on the High Seas

The American ship *Cyrus Wakefield*, of just over 2,000 tons, was built and owned by Samuel Watts (no relation to 'Black' Charlie) of Thomaston, Maine, and launched on 30 September 1882. The *Wakefield* was renowned for some very fast runs. Most notable was a round-trip-voyage of just over eight months under the command of Capt. Isaac N. Hibberd – the *Wakefield* left San Francisco in May 1887 and arrived in Liverpool 116 days later, returning to San Francisco on 30 January 1888. It was under her next master, however, Capt. Fred T. Henry, and with a brace of brutal mates, by which she earned her 'hell ship' moniker, on a passage from Baltimore to San Francisco in 1898.

The incidents of the voyage bore similarities to the *Gatherer* case, including the liberal infliction of the belaying pin upon the body of the crew, and the absconding of one of the mates soon after the *Wakefield* reached port:

Cruelty on the High Seas – The Cyrus Wakefield *a 'Hell Ship' – Officers to be Prosecuted – Second Mate Leonard Has Left the Vessel – Sailors Say They Were Beaten, Wounded and Ill-Treated from the Time the Ship Left Baltimore*

Another 'hell ship' reached port yesterday [30 August 1898]. According to the crew of the *Cyrus Wakefield* a tougher set of officers never commanded a vessel, and if there is any law in the land the sailors intend to make Captain Henry, First Mate Williamson and Second Mate Leonard answer for their brutality. The record of the voyage from Baltimore to San Francisco is to be laid before the United States District Attorney to-day and warrants sworn out for their arrest. United States Marshal Shine will have some trouble in locating Second Mate Leonard, as he disappeared yesterday as soon as the ship dropped anchor.

The *Cyrus Wakefield* left Baltimore four months ago [on 1 May 1898], and during the entire passage, according to the sailors, there was hardly a day passed but one of them was beaten and ill used. J.A. Jansen came ashore yesterday afternoon with his nose swollen and his face marked with blood from a blow he received from the mate while the ship was entering port. His offense was letting a drop of varnish fall on the deck, and for that he was knocked down and kicked.

Assaults

'I have travelled in some pretty hard ships, but the *Cyrus Wakefield* takes the cake,' said the boatswain yesterday. 'The first day out Paul Peterson was knocked down with a knuckle duster and brutally beaten by the captain, mate and second mate. I really believe they would have killed him if the unfortunate fellow had not escaped aloft. Charlie Mattson was on the main crosstrees doing some work and was not getting along fast enough to suit the second mate. Leonard went aloft and struck him a blow with a scraper, almost knocking him overboard. Had it not been for P. Webb, who caught him when he stumbled, Mattson would surely have gone to Davy Jones' locker.

'A few days later Second Mate Leonard had a row with Webb and struck the latter on the face with an iron punch, almost putting his eye out. While he was down First Mate Williamson called out, "Kick the life out of the lazy sailor," and the second mate answered, "I'd kill him if we were only going to Hongkong."

'When they got tired of beating us they started in and threw our clothes overboard, and when the men said they would have the law on them Second Mate Leonard laughed and said, "We're going to Frisco; there's no law in that hole."

'Part of the evidence we have against them is the belaying pin which did most of the damage. There is hardly one of us but has felt its weight, and nearly all of us have marks on some portion of our body left by it. Herman Lensky secured it before he left the ship. The second mate hit him over the arm with it on one occasion and laid him up for a week. Leonard has been known on other ships and was formerly known as O'Connor. He went ashore first thing with the captain yesterday morning, but we will catch him if we have to hunt him from one end of California to the other.

'We tried to have the harbor police arrest the three officers, but they would not do it, saying we would have to get the United States Marshal to do that. Well, we are going to do that, and we will soon find out whether there is any law in California or not.

'Captain Henry says that the men were the worst lot of kickers that ever sailed on a ship. Many of them had never been to sea before, and only two or three of them were 'A.B.'s'. He denies the stories of brutality in toto, and says that while one or two of them may have got an occasional cuff they did not get half what they deserved. The chances are that the whole matter will be aired before United States Commissioner Heacock tomorrow.' (*San Francisco Call*, 31 August 1898)

There was no evidence that any of the *Wakefield*'s officers were actually prosecuted, much less held to account, for their ill-treatment of the crew on that miserable voyage. Capt. Henry was certainly still in command and mate Williamson, still first officer when the *Wakefield*, sailed from San Francisco on 27 September 1898, with a cargo of wine, for New York, where she arrived on 5 January 1899 after a fast passage of just 100 days.

The next voyage of the *Cyrus Wakefield*, from New York (sailed 4 April 1899) round the Horn for San Francisco, was to prove rather more eventful – particularly for Capt. Henry and, subsequently, mate Williamson:

Henry Was Slain by the Mate – New Version of the Death of the Captain of the Ship Cyrus Wakefield – Was Hit on the Head

Port Townsend, Wash., Sept. 4. – The fate of Captain Henry of the American ship *Cyrus Wakefield*, while rounding Cape Horn, seems to be shrouded in mystery, according to mail advices received here to-day from Port Stanley, Falkland Island. On August 14 reports reached this city to the effect that Captain Henry of the *Cyrus Wakefield*, while rounding Cape Horn, was killed by being dashed against the cabin of his vessel by an immense sea, which swept the deck of the ship.

Possible Alternative Cause of Death

According to letters received here to-day by E.T. Biggs from his brother, Alfred Biggs, who is an undertaker at Port Stanley, it appears that Captain Henry met death at the hands of his mate, who, during the heat of passion, hit Captain Henry on the head with a carpenter's hammer, and after the deed was committed looted the cabin of all valuables.

According to the letter, Captain Henry had been dead three days when the vessel put into Port Stanley, and the sailors say that the mate wanted to run to Montevideo [Uruguay], but the sailors absolutely refused to do duty unless the first port was made, as they claimed that by running to Montevideo the body would have decomposed and necessitated a burial at sea.

Dastardly Mate

Upon arrival at Port Stanley the body was taken ashore and turned over to the Coroner. The mate refused to allow the sailors to go ashore, and he was the only one who gave testimony at the inquest. Just before the *Wakefield* arrived at Port Stanley, the man at the wheel when Captain Henry was supposed [believed] to have been killed by the shipping of a heavy sea, was hit on the head by the mate and knocked senseless, and when he came to himself the mate threatened to kill him unless he kept quiet.

According to the letter, after the body of Captain Henry was taken ashore at Port Stanley and the inquest was held, the only witness being the mate, a verdict was rendered that the captain met death by being thrown against the cabin by the vessel shipping a sea.

The mate forsook his post of duty and took the first steamer leaving port, when he was the proper person to take the vessel to the port of destination.

Suspicions

Biggs, the writer of the letter, says the action of the mate caused a suspicion of foul play. The mate was smoking high-priced cigars and was spending money elaborately until after the inquest was held over the remains of the captain, when he suddenly disappeared, leaving the ship without a master. Captain Chapman of the wrecked ship *John R. Kelly*, with the crew of that vessel, took command [of the *Wakefield*] and sailed for San Francisco. The crew of the *Wakefield* left here say that the mate was responsible for the death of Captain Henry.

'I took charge of the body,' says Biggs, 'and placed it in a lead coffin. While handling the body I noticed a hole in the head, which had the appearance of having been made with a blunt instrument, but there were no other bruises on the body. Upon the arrival of the body of Captain Henry at San Francisco the casket should be opened, and an examination of the remains made, and I am certain that the fact would be revealed that Captain Henry met death through foul play. The captain had a big hole in the back of his head and since the inquest, the ship carpenter says his hammer has disappeared.' (*San Francisco Call*, 5 September 1899)

A hole in the skull caused most likely by 'a blunt instrument'; no bruises on the body of a man supposed to have been *killed* – not just *bruised*, but *killed*! – by a Cape Horn greybeard knocking him senseless; and the ostentatiously suspicious character of mate Williamson – more than enough, indeed, to suspect 'foul play' in the death of Capt. Henry.

The *Wakefield* arrived at Port Stanley, Falkland Islands, on 18 June 1899. Capt. Chapman, master from the ship *John R. Kelly* which wrecked at Port Stanley in May 1899, assumed command of the *Wakefield*. He brought her, with some of his own crew, and with Capt. Henry's body, to San Francisco where they arrived 11 November 1899. The only *Wakefield* seaman still aboard the ship from when Capt. Henry was killed was the steward, Thomas Visiga – the only witness to Capt. Henry's demise:

Captain Henry Killed by the Chief Officer – Murderer Takes Advantage of a Storm off the Horn – Ship Cyrus Wakefield *Arrives with but One Member of the Crew that Was Aboard when the Tragedy Occurred*

Was Captain F.T. Henry of the American ship *Cyrus Wakefield* murdered off Cape Horn, or was he killed by being washed by a sea off the poop to the deck below?

The *Wakefield* arrived in port [San Francisco] yesterday [11 November 1899], and the log shows that 'on June 15, about 7:30 p.m., shipped a heavy sea on the port quarter, which struck Captain Henry and knocked him off the after-house down on the deck. He struck against some iron and received some terrible injuries to his chest, back and hips, and his head was cut to pieces. We carried him into the cabin and did everything in our power to restore consciousness, but failed, and Captain Henry died at 8:20 p.m.' This entry was made on the log by First Mate Williamson.

Thomas Visiga, the steward of the *Cyrus Wakefield*, is the only man left aboard who knows anything about the tragedy, and he says Captain Henry was murdered. Furthermore, he says the killing was done by Mate Williamson with a hammer, and that the man at the wheel and other witnesses of the tragedy were all paid off at Port Stanley and are now scattered to the four quarters of the globe.

The Wakefield's Voyage

The *Cyrus Wakefield* left New York for San Francisco on April 4 last with a general cargo. Captain F.T. Henry was in command, and his first and second officers were H. Williamson and A. Johnson. The vessel had fair weather to the Horn, and then in a succession of gales the vessel began to leak and the pumps broke down. Captain Henry and Mate Williamson had been quarrelling almost from the time the ship left New York, and on June 15, when the captain was killed, the mate decided to put into Port Stanley, in the Falkland Islands.

There he paid off the five men who had been on deck when Captain Henry was killed, and left the ship himself.

The American ship *John R. Kelly* had been wrecked in Port William, near Port Stanley, just before the arrival of the *Cyrus Wakefield*, so Captain Chapman took command of her, and finding her to be very much strained came to San Francisco via the Cape of Good Hope [the reason why the ship took so long to get to San Francisco; in October 1899 it was feared that 'some disaster has befallen the ship *Cyrus Wakefield*', it then being 89 days after she left the Falklands].

Thomas Visiga's Narrative

The tale of the killing of Captain Henry is thus told by Steward Thomas Visiga:

'The captain and mate were always quarrelling,' said he yesterday. 'Mate Williamson did not like the old man, and told him so on numerous occasions. On the night of the killing the mate got a hammer from the carpenter at a quarter to 7 and when he came down from the poop he still had the hammer in his hand and there was blood on it. I had supper on the table, and I said, "Will you have something to eat, Mr. Williamson?" and he said, "By and by," and went into his room. Ten minutes later I asked him again, and he said, "By and by I will send two men to help you."

'Between the time I asked him first and the time he told me he would send two men to help me a big sea had broke aboard and flooded the cabin. Second Mate Johnson ran into the cabin and said: "Mr. Williamson, Mr. Williamson, the captain is hurt." "All right," said Mr. Williamson, "bring him down here." Now, there was no need to bring him down, as he had been washed from the after-house down on the deck.'

Death of Capt. Henry

'A few minutes passed and then Mr. Johnson rushed in again and said, "Mr. Williamson, the captain is dying." "All right," answered the mate again; "bring him down here and lay him on his bed." Captain Henry was carried in from the deck and laid out on the cabin floor. The mate went to the medicine chest and, making up a mixture, tried to get the captain to take it. The dying man rolled his head and I heard him say, "No, no! don't let him, Mr. Johnson." His mouth was forced open, however, and Mr. Williamson made him swallow it, saying, "Drink it down; it will do you good." About 8:30 p.m. the captain died.

'When we got into Port Stanley the mate took possession of the ship's money and paid off the man who was at the wheel when the captain and mate were quarrelling near the wheelhouse. He also paid off the four men who took refuge in the rigging just before the sea broke aboard and who had seen everything that took place. Then he left the ship himself and Captain Chapman of the *John R. Kelly* took command. Captain Henry's head was terribly battered and I am certain he never got the wounds by being washed from the after-house to the deck. I think the mate tried to kill him with the hammer and finished him with a dose of laudanum.

'The remains of Captain Henry are now aboard the *Cyrus Wakefield* and an autopsy may show whether the wounds on the head were accidental or inflicted with a hammer.'

The Wakefield's Onward Voyage to San Francisco

Captain Chapman, the present commander of the *Cyrus Wakefield*, is accompanied by his wife and daughter and

Miss Lydia F. Keene, who is acting as governess and companion for Miss Chapman. They all left New York for San Francisco in the *John R. Kelly* and had a delightful voyage until Cape Horn was reached. There very heavy weather was encountered and the vessel sprang a leak. Captain Chapman decided to run into Port Stanley for repairs and reached Port William in safety on May 24.

The next day, accompanied by Mrs. and Miss Chapman and Miss Keene, he went ashore at Stanley to enter his ship. The party had not been an hour ashore before a sudden storm came up and the *Kelly* parting her anchors was driven ashore on a reef. Almost before the watchers on the shore could express their consternation the ship's back was broken and the waves were washing over her fore and aft. The men took to the rigging and were finally rescued, but the ship became a total wreck.

Everything that the captain and his family owned in the world went down in the wreck and just as they were prepared to take passage for Valparaiso, the *Cyrus Wakefield* put into port with Captain Henry dead. Captain Chapman then took command and brought the *Wakefield* to San Francisco. He reported to the owners that the ship was strained and that he would come here via the Cape of Good Hope. The voyage from Stanley was uneventful except that a young man named David Dean fell overboard a week ago and was drowned. He was a great favorite with everybody on the ship, and officers and crew have not yet recovered from the shock caused by his death. (*San Francisco Call*, 12 November 1899)

Postscript

The inquest into the death of Capt. Henry, at Stanley, accepted that mate Williamson's entry in the log, that the master died from injuries caused by the devastating effects of a sea shipped by the *Wakefield*, constituted 'authoritative evidence' of cause of death. Case closed; Williamson was reprieved of suspected murder.

After the inquest at Stanley, mate Williamson apparently took the first steamer out, for New York. Whatever his ultimate fate after that, few, if any, would have mourned his passing if they knew about his brutality in the *Cyrus Wakefield*.

The *Arran* Stowaways: 'Shocking Cruelty at Sea'

On 7 April 1868 the wooden ship *Arran*, of 1,063 tons, sailed from Greenock at the mouth of the River Clyde, south-west Scotland, with a cargo of coal and oakum (old rope and similar stuff used to caulk ships' seams), under the command of Capt. Robert Watt, bound for Quebec. Before the tug towing the *Arran* had slipped her tow-rope, two stowaways were discovered, handcuffed and put ashore. Later the same day two more stowaways were found below deck and the next day five more were turned out. It being too late to turn back to land them, the seven lads, ranging in age from 11 to 22 years, were given menial tasks such as washing the decks and the light work meted out to ships' boys, as the *Arran* started her voyage across the North Atlantic.

The seven stowaways, all from Greenock, were: Hugh McEwan and John Paul ('wee Pauley'), both aged 11; Peter Currie and Hugh McGinnes, 12; James Bryson and David Jolly Brand, 16; and Bernard (Barney) Reilly, 22. The boys were 'thinly clad, and were not able to stand the severe cold. The men could hardly stand it, let alone them.' (From 'The "Arran" Stowaways', in *The Stowaways and Other Sea Sketches*, by John Donald, 1928). The youngest,

Hugh McGinnes and 'wee Pauley', were barefoot the whole voyage, and beyond.

Capt. Watt and Mate Kerr

Capt. Watt, from Saltcoats, Ayrshire, was 'quite a pleasant-looking man, twenty-eight years of age, about five feet eight inches in height, with dark brown hair, his slight beard and moustache being a shade lighter in colour. His conversation was agreeable, and he had the reputation of dealing kindly with those under his command.'

The mate Kerr, by contrast, was 'a rough-looking man, about five feet seven inches high, thin, of determined mien, with dark hair, full beard and moustache, and of a coarse, unfeeling, and dominating nature, [and] he vented an unwarranted spite against those poor stowaways, with one exception – the lad Currie, whose father was said to be a friend of the mate. When passing the boys he kicked them without the slightest provocation, and when he found them in fault, their punishment was cruelly excessive.'

Capt. Watt authorised 'an ample provision of rations' of beef (5lbs/day), coffee (14oz/week), tea (7oz/week) and sugar (5lbs/week) for the stowaway lads, 'so that it appears the captain's intention at the outset was to treat the boys reasonably well'. That might indeed have been Watt's good intention, despite the added burden of feeding seven mouths on the voyage for which the vessel was not provisioned. 'Unfortunately for those boys ... the master was as putty in the hands of his mate, and weakly allowed the latter to override his orders.'

The brutal and casual barbarity that mate Kerr inflicted upon them was accompanied on occasion by Capt. Watt's own harsh treatment, though the master did show some latent evidence of an underlying care about the boys towards the end of the voyage in the ice off Newfoundland.

That misery of shivering bitter cold, the cruel snarl of the mate's constant onslaught upon them, and brutally sadistic assaults upon the 16-year-old lad Bryson in particular, were the boys' constant companions all the way to the coast of Newfoundland. The vessel there became stuck in the sea ice for about a week. Six of the stowaways were put off the ship on to the ice, to make the best they could of getting to land. Four boys, against the odds, did reach safety. Two others perished: one, the barefoot McGinnes, most painfully and tearfully ('Mother, mother, oh, mother!'); the other, McEwan (whose 'mother ... had sent him from Glasgow on an errand: and this was the end of it.'), drowned.

When the *Arran* returned to Greenock the atrocious cruelties inflicted upon the young lads were by then well known to the populace and the authorities; an *Arran* crew member had included that information in a letter that he sent home to his family from Quebec. Captain Watt and mate Kerr were held to account for their barbarity, though justice was considerably more sparing of them than was their ill-treatment of the young Greenock innocents who stole aboard the *Arran* as a bit of juvenile mischief that fateful April day:

Shocking Cruelty At Sea

For a number of days past vague rumours were abroad in Greenock that several stowaway boys had been put on a field of ice off the coast of Newfoundland, from the ship *Arran*, of Greenock, and that two of them had perished. Little credence was, however, given to the story, few people being willing to believe that any shipmaster or his officers could be guilty of such inhumanity. We regret to state, however, that since the ship's arrival on July 30, from Quebec, sufficient evidence has been collected by the authorities in Greenock to warrant the apprehension of the master and mate of the ship on a very serious charge.

The *Arran's Stowaways*

The ship *Arran*, of Greenock, upwards of 1,000 tons register, Captain Robert Watt, sailed from the Tail of the Bank [just off Greenock] for Quebec with a cargo of coals on 7th April last. Before the tug left the ship, off the Cumbrae Heads, two stowaways were discovered on board, and they were accordingly sent back with the steamer [tug]. It was believed by the officers and crew that no other stowaways were on board, but towards nightfall of the same day some of the crew heard a knocking beneath the fore hatch, and upon examination, several other lads were discovered.

Next morning, after carefully searching the ship, seven stowaway boys in all were found on board. As is customary, the officers of the ship gave them some work to do, and it would appear that on board the *Arran* for a number of days the lads were pretty well treated. It seems, however, that the boys ultimately became sea-sick, and from that time till they went on the ice they were treated in the most barbarous manner.

Barbarity

From the statements of the crew it would appear that the chief mate, named James Kerr, was more conspicuous in uniform cruelty to the lads than Captain Watt, but the latter was not only often present, but refused to interfere when severe punishment was being inflicted upon them. The lads were supplied with about half a biscuit a day, and when it became known that the crew in their compassion, with their emaciated appearance, were supplying them with a portion of their own food, the officers ordered the steward to place the crew on a fixed allowance for each man, in order to prevent any addition being made to their scanty supply.

The stowaways had no beds given them, and they were compelled to sleep in the hold in all weather, on the top of the coals. By day or night the boys were brought on deck and were compelled to march about carrying a handspike, and every time they crossed the deck were made to cry out, 'All's well,' 'Ice ahead,' &c., and if they failed to give the monotonous cry they were instantly flogged. The cravings of hunger becoming so keen, the boys eventually burst a flour barrel and appeased their appetite by swallowing a portion of the flour. For this they were unmercifully flogged, and they were afterwards placed in irons.

One of the lads, named James Bryson, was ordered to strip while the snow was falling, and lie down on deck, and one of the crew was compelled to draw a bucket of water, while another with a broom was forced to scrub the poor boy's body till the blood trickled from his back. He was then turned on his back and his stomach and breast were scrubbed in a like manner. (*The Glasgow Herald*, 4 August 1868)

Flogged and Scrubbed

Later, at the trial of Capt. Watt and mate Kerr, 16-year-old James Bryson testified in his own words how he had suffered from being flogged with the ship's lead-line (a rope with lead weight attached used to determine the depth of water), and his body scrubbed with deck brushes shortly before the vessel became iced in off the coast of Newfoundland:

'Before the ship was fast to the ice I was scrubbed. I was flogged before that by the lead-line. The mate flogged me for making a mess of my trousers. I was flogged for sitting on one of the hatches aft. I was made to take off my jacket, vest, and shirt. The mate ordered me to take them off. I do not remember if there was any other body present. My trousers were on at that time.

'I think the cord of the lead-line was half an inch thick. The mate struck me heavily. He continued to flog me for about three minutes. I could not say how many blows I got, but they were very painful. There was nothing between the rope and my skin except the semmet [undershirt]. I cried out with the pain.

'The master came forward when I was screaming. When the mate was flogging me I ran forward, and then the master came to me and told me to strip off. I ran forward as far as the house on the deck. The master made me strip off the rest of my clothes. I was then ordered to lie down on deck. I do not know whether it was the captain or mate ordered me to do that, as both were present. It was one of them.

'I lay down. I was quite naked. One of the men [of the crew], Robert Hunter, was ordered to go upon the rail and draw [sea] water. He was called "Big Bob Hunter". He drew the water in a bucket, and threw it about me, when ordered by the mate. Several buckets of water were thrown about me. The weather was very cold. It was freezing. The captain during the time the water was thrown about me scrubbed me with a broom. It was a hard broom. I was lying both on my face and back. The broom was roughly applied. It occasioned pain. I could not tell how long he continued scrubbing me.

'After the master was done scrubbing he laid down the broom and the mate took it up. He then scrubbed me harder than the captain. I attempted to rise while the captain was scrubbing me. The mate had a rope in his hand, and he said if I rose he would draw it over me. The mate scrubbed me some minutes. The mate then gave the broom to Brand [the other 16-year-old stowaway], one of the stowaways, and told him to scrub me, which he did, and it was during all this time that the buckets of water were thrown over me.

'I was then ordered to the forecastle head by the mate. I was naked. I was there stark naked for an hour when I got my semmit. I suffered very much from the cold. My body had not been dried in any way. The ship shortly after this got fast in the ice.' (*The Otago Witness* [Otago, New Zealand], 6 March 1869)

The boy's testimony was all the more poignant for its understatement of the torturous pain inflicted upon him by a hard brush normally used to scrub the decks, the almost freezing-cold salt water thrown upon his sorely wounded body, and his naked exposure to the bitterly cold North Atlantic weather.

While the ship was labouring in a heavy sea, the boys were put in irons and their hands were manacled behind their backs. They were then placed on the forecastle. The decks were slippery with ice and the cold was intense. The sea was washing over the ship, and the sufferings of the lads are described as being horrible. Every time they slipped to the lee side of the vessel they were lashed with a rope till they managed to crawl to windward. For the most trivial offence they were lashed by the mate with the lead line:

In – and On – the Ice

This kind of treatment was continued for a length of time till the ship got bound in the ice off St. George's Bay on the coast of Newfoundland. The lads were badly clad, and two of them had neither shoes nor stockings. The crew could not spare them any portion of their food, as their allowance was comparatively small. The mate kicked them upon every occasion, and exposed them to all kinds of dangers and hardships.

While the ship was embedded in the ice the lads were for several days ordered to take exercise on it. On the 15th of May, after the ship had been about a week in the ice, some of the boys were ordered to make for the land, which was distant, according to various statements, from five to fifteen miles. About 8 o'clock in the morning six of the boys left the vessel, a biscuit each being thrown after them. Two of the little fellows were barefooted, and their cries are stated to have been heartrending.

Land could be seen from the mast-head, but between the ship and the land it was ascertained by the aid of the glass [telescope] that the ice was detached, and that a broad sheet of water intervened. After the boys had left some time, the captain, it would appear, repented of the course he had adopted, and he went to the mast-head in order to see if he could discover their whereabouts. One of the crew, named Magnus Tait, who was subsequently drowned in the St. Lawrence [River], was also placed at the mast-head, in order, if possible, to make them out, but the lads were never again seen.

On the ship's arrival at Quebec the crew were at once informed by the crew of the ship *Myrtle*, of Greenock, which had also been detained in the ice some distance from the *Arran*, that only four of the boys had survived, and they were taken off the ice by a Newfoundland schooner. One of the lads was reported drowned and another had died from exhaustion; another is stated to have been severely frostbitten. The seventh boy was kept on board the ship when his companions were put on the ice, and he has returned with the ship to Greenock.

No official information relative to the fate of the boys has been received by the authorities here, but immediate inquiry will be made at Newfoundland. Meantime the master and mate of the ship have been apprehended, and committed for further examination. (*The Glasgow Herald*, 4 August 1868)

Beaten Again

In the first week of May, a month after leaving Greenock, the *Arran* became stuck fast in the ice just off the coast of Newfoundland. Shortly afterwards, while Capt. Watt and Kerr had gone off the ship on to the ice, James Bryson and David Brand, famished like all the stowaways from meagre rations, went to look for food. The consequence of that desperate endeavour was yet another brutal punishment inflicted by the master and mate upon the wretched Bryson:

'That day Brand and I went into one of the cabins. We went to seek something to eat. Brand got some biscuits in the cabin. I was on the poop [deck] scraping. Brand said he had got a pocket full of biscuits. I also went into the cabin, but could not get biscuits, and took the currants. I took them because I could get nothing else. I was very hungry. I took about a fistful, and putting them into my pocket, went on deck. That was in the afternoon.

'The mate in coming up the vessel's side saw me coming out of the cabin, and then he ordered my hands to be tied and Brand to be searched by the steward, but nothing was found upon him. My pocket was cut down the side and the currants taken out, and the captain gave them to the rest of the boys. I was immediately afterwards stripped quite naked by the order of the mate, who with the master stood by and saw it done.

'The mate then put my head downwards to the deck and my feet up to my throat, and the captain took a line and flogged me with a lead-line about half-an-inch thick, and of the same sort previously used to flog me. The blows were very sore, as the captain hit very hard. He continued to flog me for several minutes, and gave me from 15 to 20 lashes. I felt pain after the flogging had ceased. The weather was very cold at the time, and the ship was surrounded by ice.' (*The Otago Witness*, 6 March 1869)

On the Ice

The denouement of the stowaways' sufferings came when six of them were put off the ship on to the ice field that gripped the *Arran* from about 9 May. The only boy who stayed on board was 12-year-old Peter Currie, who had avoided ill-treatment on the voyage apparently by dint of his father's friendship with mate Kerr. He returned on the *Arran* to Scotland but died just two years later of 'consumption' (tuberculosis).

Bryson continued his trial deposition with his account of the boys' departure from the ship around the middle of May (the 15th, apparently, at around 8 a.m. 'of a day of gloom over the Gulf of St. Lawrence'). Some of the boys, Reilly (the oldest) and Bryson in particular, were keen to get away from the hell of the *Arran* and her officers. The youngest – McGinnes, McEwan and 'poor wee Pauley' – 'were almost hysterical with fright', and 'crying most dreadfully' when they were put off. Brand was reluctant to go but went when ordered to:

'It was on a Tuesday when I left [the ship], and was the Tuesday after the last flogging. I left the ship, because that morning the captain took Barney Reilly forward, and wished him to look through a telescope, as he said he could see the houses and the people on the shore. I said, if I thought there were any houses I would go ashore with Reilly. Reilly went on to the ice, and I looked over the vessel's side. Paul went and hid. The captain came forward and asked for Paul, and at the same time asked Brand if he was going ashore; but Brand said he would not go till he was made to. The captain then said he would make him, and he pulled him forward to the bows of the vessel.'

'Might as well die on the ice ...'
'The captain then asked Currie for Paul, and was told that he was in the forecastle; he went in and brought him out, holding him by the collar of the coat. Paul cryingly asked the mate to keep him on board the vessel, and the mate said he had nothing to do with putting us on the ice. McEwan ["a delicate boy, who had been spitting up blood during the passage out"], who was in the galley, commenced to cry, and the captain told him he might as well die on the ice as die on board the vessel, as he would get no meat till he got to Quebec. Several of the other stowaways heard that statement.'

Capt. Watt later testified that the reason the boys were put off the ship was because there was not enough food aboard to get them all to Quebec. His allegation was countered by one of the ship's owners and by the cook; both said that 'there was ample food for all'. Bryson continued:

'Afterwards all but Currie went on the ice. I saw nobody lifted on to the rails, or anybody struck. Currie remained on board; but I don't know why McGinnes and McEwan were crying when they left the vessel for the ice. I was dressed at the time with a topcoat, trousers, vest, a cravat, and shoes; but Paul had no shoes. McGinnes had no shoes, and his clothes were all ragged and torn. McEwan was better clothed than either of us.

'We had no provisions when we left the ship; but after we got on the ice a biscuit each was thrown to us by order of the mate. It was because we asked for it that we had the biscuits thrown to us. It was between eight and nine o'clock in the morning, and we had coffee given us before that, and three small pieces of biscuit. We were very hungry at the time. We had had no food at all the previous day. We could not appease our hunger even after eating the biscuits thrown to us.

'We saw nothing of land at the time. We did not know at the time how far land was off, but the fishermen [who rescued them] told us it was from 15 to 20 miles. At the time we set out from the ship I did not think the journey was a dangerous one over the ice, but I left the vessel because I thought I might as well die on the ice as remain on board to die, and I thought we might die on board the vessel if we remained, in consequence of getting no food.

'We all set out together. I was on the ice twelve hours that day, and found the journey a dangerous one. We had gone all that distance before we met any danger, but then we found the ice all broken. There were some broken portions of ice before that. While near the shore we went up to the neck in water between the pieces of ice. I fell into the water by jumping from one piece of ice to another. We got out the best way we could.'

McEwan 'did not rise again' – Drowned

'It was about six o'clock at night when we came to the broken part. My clothes were all wet and frozen. At one time or another we all fell in the water. We left the vessel and remained together for some time; but when the ice became broken we were obliged to separate. Paul and McGinnes had difficulty from having no shoes. McEwan fell in once and I pulled him out, and he fell in a second time and he got out, but the third time he fell in he did not rise again, the ice just closing over him, and it appeared to me a perfectly hopeless thing to attempt to save him. I was about three yards from the spot at the time, and I remained a short time to see if he would come up.

'I then went after my companions, and did not look again.'

McGinnes 'left on the ice'

'The others were a long way ahead of me at the time. About two or three hours after, McGinnes became fatigued. It was about the middle of the day when McEwan was drowned. It was before we got to the bad ice; but the ice was not extra good any of the way. McGinnes sat down on the ice, and said he could not go any farther. We did not render him any assistance, because we had enough to do to assist ourselves. We urged him to come on, and told him if he did not he was sure to die. His clothes were frozen on him at the time, and he said he could not come forward.

'He was left on the ice, and we heard his cries after we had proceeded a long way. He was crying loudly. When we left him we were unable to give him any assistance.'
(*The Otago Witness*, 6 March 1869)

John Donald, in 'The "Arran" Stowaways', wrote:

Need I ask my reader to picture the plight of that boy? Eleven years of age, barefooted, in rags, and frozen; thousands of miles away from home and the mother he vainly called for; alone, utterly alone in a desert of ice; merely a tiny speck in a great white desolation; his ineffable weariness only varied by pain. Poor wee fellow. He was seen no more.

Towards Rescue
Before the boys left the *Arran*, Capt. Watt 'directed them to the ship *Myrtle* which, he said, lay embedded in the ice a mile or two away, and where they would be able to get some more food. The boys doubted the captain's statement, as no ship was visible, but they dared not say so ...' The boys persevered, struggling to find the ship. They never did, though she was, in fact, where the captain had said she was. Bryson's testimony continued:

'We guided ourselves by direction of the captain, who told us in which direction the *Myrtle*, a barque, was lying, where he said we would get some more provisions. We went for about 300 yards, and then changed our course, because we thought it would be better to take another course. We did not see the *Myrtle* at all. We were in sight of the *Arran* at the time we changed our course, but I could not say if we could be seen from the *Arran*.

'It was not possible to walk across when we came near the land. We then saw the houses and commenced to cry out, when a woman saw us. It was about seven o'clock at night. Brand set out on a piece of ice to try to reach the shore, and paddled himself with a piece of wood. Reilly set off also on another piece of ice. The distance between the ice and the shore at that point was about a mile.

'The woman who saw us despatched a boat for us, and Brand by that time was got about half-way ashore. The sun was just going down at that time. If the woman had not seen us I saw no way of getting to shore. We had neither of us tasted food from the time we left the vessel till we reached the shore. The people took us to their houses. I noticed Paul's feet bleeding when he came to the end of the ice, and Brand gave him a pair of socks, but he would not wear them. I was ice-blind the following day, and two of my toes were frostbitten.

'The place where we landed, between eight and nine at night, turned out to be the bay of St. George. I got work there and remained for about four months. Reilly went to Halifax, but I don't know where he is now.' (*The Otago Witness*, 6 March 1869)

Salvation and Retribution

The five fishermen in a small boat who rescued the four surviving stowaways – Reilly, Brand, Bryson, and 'poor wee Pauley' – took them to the farmhouse on shore for 'warmth and nourishment'. The farmer, a Mr McInnes who 'hailed from Cape Breton', despatched a party to search for McGinnes and, 'if possible, ... some trace of McEwan ... No trace of either boy was ever found.'

The boys had come ashore at St George's Bay on the south-west coast of Newfoundland island. Sandy Point was across the bay, where three of them worked at fishing and farming for about four months. Barney Reilly had travelled on to Halifax, Nova Scotia, 'where, it is understood, he obtained employment and settled down' (he worked on the railway there).

Return Of The Arran

Meanwhile, the *Arran* reached Quebec. There the crew of the *Myrtle* told the *Arran* men about the fate of the stowaways, including, 'in a general way', that two boys had 'succumbed'. At Quebec a crewman on the *Arran* wrote a letter, dated 10 June 1868, to his family in Scotland, describing the ill-treatment inflicted on the boys during the voyage (a letter which would be instrumental later in the trial of Watt and Kerr).

When the *Arran* returned to Scotland and came up to dock at Greenock at the end of July, Capt. Watt and mate Kerr were assailed by 'a tremendous outburst of yells, hisses, and other unequivocal tokens of execration' by the crowds, who by then knew about their cruelties from the letter written in Quebec.

The local sheriff held a preliminary examination of the allegations against Watt and Kerr. He then 'committed [them] to prison pending further enquiry', on a general charge of 'cruelly and maliciously' forcing the stowaways off the ship and on to the ice, 'to the imminent risk and permanent injury' of the boys; there was, at first, no charge of murder or the like. That changed after the St John's, Newfoundland, chief of police informed the Greenock authorities about the deaths of McEwan and McGinnes, for which the captain and his mate were held to account.

Ultimately, the capital charge of murder against Watt and Kerr was changed to culpable homicide ('the Scots version of manslaughter') for which, and including 'cruel and barbarous usage', they were tried at Edinburgh's High Court of Justiciary from 23 to 25 November 1868.

The Stowaways' Return

James Bryson, David Brand and John Paul were wanted back in Greenock as soon as possible, not just on the compassionate grounds of reuniting them with their families, but so that they could testify in the trial against Watt and Kerr. The local MP, James Johnston Grieve, offered them free passage in his company's own vessel, the brigantine *Hannah and Bennie*. She sailed from St John's on 12 September 1868 and arrived at Greenock with her three stowaway survivors, compassionately cared for on this voyage, on 1 October.

At the subsequent trial, one of the crew of the *Arran*, George Henry, remarked when questioned by a member of the jury why he or any of his twenty-three shipmates 'did not interfere to save the boys from the cruelty of the officers'. It was not their place, he said, 'to interfere with my master and mate'. It was, he continued, 'very uncertain to think anything' about the boys' chances after they were put on the ice. Indeed, a seaman's contradiction of the orders, or interference in the behaviour of his officers – even if it involved extreme cruelty, even death – on board the vessel, was tantamount to insurrection … mutiny.

Justice?

Kerr was allowed to change his plea to guilty solely to the charge of assault upon the stowaways. He was nevertheless cleared of that charge and instead found guilty of culpable homicide, 'with a recommendation to the leniency of the Court on account of his previous good character, the verdict being unanimous'. Capt. Watt was found guilty of the same charge and sentenced to eighteen months' imprisonment. Kerr got just four months.

Public reaction to the rather lenient sentences, as they were widely perceived to be, incited caustic observations upon the justice of 'The Greenock Stowaways' case:

> If ever there was murder done on earth, that lad [McGinnes] was murdered; but the Edinburgh jury found the Captain had a reputation for being 'kind and gentle,' – indeed, that reputation had originally tempted the lads – and they added a recommendation to mercy to their verdict of culpable homicide, and the Lord Justice Clerk, who had charged dead against the Captain, sentenced him to eighteen months imprisonment, the most astounding failure of justice in a British Court it has ever been our lot to record, the more astounding because Watt's only defence, that he urged the boys on to the ice in the full expectation that they would return, was exposed by the learned judge himself. (*The Spectator*, 5 December 1868)

The only explanation, the above writer said, was that the master of a merchant vessel 'must never be held responsible for violence like another man', in order to maintain discipline on his ship:

> Everywhere a feeling is manifested that were verdicts severe, discipline at sea could never be maintained; that a captain, with his limited legal power, must be allowed occasionally to use force; that in fact cruelty and needful control run into one another on board ship, until it is difficult or impossible to punish the crime without occasionally impeding performance of the duty.

'The Stowaways' – engraved from the picture by A. Dixon in the Walker Art Gallery, Liverpool. The subject of this picture is one which is familiar to the inhabitants of large seaport towns, such as Liverpool, where, in the Walker Art Gallery, the original is exhibited ... Not many years ago the captain of a ship set some boy stowaways ashore (if it could be called 'ashore') on a floe of ice off the coast of Nova Scotia or Newfoundland. The account of the circumstances caused great indignation at the time. It is to be hoped that, fierce as the captain looks, there are better things in store for the poor little trembling wretch in Mr. Dixon's picture. (*The Graphic*, 31 January 1885)

The 'captain's will' and obedience of the crew to that power was paramount for the maintenance of the ship and her crew as 'an intelligent machine'. It was 'impossible to invest the crew with any right of resistance, even in a case so extreme as this; the utmost we can do is to leave such resistance to the judgement of a jury'. The 'steady exercise of legal authority' (the law, in other words) was the sole arbiter in the administration of justice for any case brought before it. The leniency of the verdict against Watt and Kerr could only be attributed to imperfections in the law, which mitigated the consequences of extreme violence at sea: 'a law so imperfect that while it produces daily acts of cruelty, it produces also the state of opinion evident in the verdict of the Edinburgh jury, and the otherwise incredible sentence of the judge':

What Became of the Survivors

Reilly, we know, went to Halifax, N.S.; Bryson emigrated with his father and family to America, where [in Philadelphia] James obtained employment as a street car conductor; Peter Currie died of consumption about two years after he came home; John Paul became a foreman riveter and removed to Itchen, Southampton, where he died some years ago; and David Jolly Brand proceeded to Townsville, North Queensland, where he founded the flourishing engineering firm of Brand, Dryborough & Burns, and died suddenly and unexpectedly in the month of November, 1897 ...

Soon after leaving prison, both Watt and Kerr quickly got to sea again as master and mate respectively – in different vessels, of course. The former is said to have died at Pensacola [Florida], a year or two after his release; but Kerr sailed for many years as a shipmaster before retiring to rest ashore. He died over twenty years ago. (From 'The "Arran" Stowaways', in *The Stowaways and Other Sea Sketches*, by John Donald, 1928)

6

OVERBOARD

Seamen in sailing ships could go overboard by being struck and carried away by a particularly vicious sea coming aboard, knocked over by a flailing boom or other rigging, or, perhaps most commonly, by falling from aloft from one of the vessel's yardarms. The chances of survival depended on whether the vessel was in cold or warm water, whether the man could swim (most could not, or not very well), whether they were wearing heavy boots and clothing that dragged them under, or how speedily – or, more likely, if – a boat could be launched to save them. In stormy, frigid seas a man overboard would probably be wearing such heavy clothing and boots that drowning was inevitable, and quick. Big square-riggers, too, could not be turned around easily in any weather, much less in a storm; it would, as often, have endangered the ship to do so.

So most seamen were abandoned to, they hoped, a quick death by drowning when they found themselves flailing in the open sea as they watched their ship sailing on – if they were conscious: a fall from 100 feet or more off a spar into a tumultuous sea could easily knock them senseless. And most sailing-ship men never learned to swim, deliberately, so that they would drown almost immediately, guaranteed to minimise their suffering.

The fate of an apprentice swept overboard by a huge sea that crashed on board the *Garthsnaid* on a voyage from Sydney for Falmouth in 1921 was like that of most seamen in such circumstances:

> His end was no doubt short and merciful in such weather conditions, but the subject reminds one that many old seamen deliberately refrained from learning to swim so that they would be spared the agony of a lingering death if washed overboard. (From *Four Captains*, by Capt. George V. Clark; Brown, Son & Ferguson, 1975)

By a combination of good fortune, benevolent weather, a quick-thinking captain, and the experienced seamanship of their shipmates, some did survive – those lucky few salvaged from amongst a much larger cohort who never surfaced from beneath the merciless (or merciful?) waves. Resurrection and redemption were far less common in sailing-ship days than brutal annihilation by a godless sea.

Eleven Men Swept Overboard from Barque *Charles Ward*

In mid-November 1872 the Cunard steamer *Batavia* was approaching the Canadian east coast on a voyage from Liverpool, bound for Boston, Massachusetts. In tempestuous weather described by the *Batavia* seamen as encountered 'once in five or ten years', they came across the British barque *Charles Ward*, dismasted and in distress. The *Batavia*'s master, Capt. John Mouland, successfully accomplished the rescue of the nine seamen barely alive from the *Charles Ward*; eleven of her crew had previously been washed overboard and drowned.

Amongst the passengers on the *Batavia* was the renowned American author Mark Twain. In a letter to The Royal Humane Society in London he wrote the day after, Twain described the rescue, and petitioned for the Society to grant to Capt. Mouland and the lifeboat crew of the *Batavia* its highest award of commendation for the men's courageous action that day:

Perils of the Sea – Dismantling of a British Bark in a Hurricane – Eleven Men Washed from the Wreck and Drowned – Sufferings of Four Others Found in the Rigging – Mark Twain's Account of the Rescue of the Survivors

---

Boston, Nov. 25.– The Cunard steamship *Batavia*, Capt. Mouland, arrived at this port today, and reports that on the 19th of November, when in latitude 49° 16' north, longitude 41° 27' west [just east of the Newfoundland Grand Banks], she fell in with the British bark *Charles Ward*, of Newcastle, England, water-logged and dismasted in a hurricane, on the morning of the 18th, and took off the survivors of the bark's complement of twenty men, the other eleven having been washed off the deck.

Mark Twain, who was a passenger on the *Batavia*, addresses a communication to the Royal Humane Society, giving a detailed account of the wreck, and bestowing the warmest praise on the officers of the *Batavia*. (*The New York Times*, 26 November 1872)

A Man Overboard In Southern Seas: 'Saved!' – Drawn by Joseph
Nash, R.I. (*The Graphic*, 3 December 1892)

Mark Twain wrote his letter to The Royal Humane Society
in London on 20 November 1872 while he was still on board
the *Batavia*, and with the rescue of the *Charles Ward*'s survivors still fresh, indeed, uppermost in his mind:

To the Royal Humane Society, 20 November 1872

SS *Batavia* en route from Liverpool, England, to
Boston, Mass.

On Board Cunard Steamer *Batavia*, At Sea, November
20, 1872

Gentlemen,– The *Batavia* sailed from Liverpool on
Tuesday, November 12. On Sunday night [17 November]
a strong west wind began to blow, & not long after midnight it increased to a gale. By four o'clock the sea was
running very high; at half-past seven our starboard bulwarks were stove in & the water entered the main saloon;
at a later hour the gangway on the port side came in
with a crash & the sea followed, flooding many of the

staterooms on that side. At the same time a sea crossed the roof of the vessel & carried away one of our boats, splintering it to pieces & taking one of the davits with it. At half-past nine the glass [barometer] was down to 28.35, & the gale was blowing with a severity which the officers say is not experienced oftener than once in five or ten years. The storm continued during the day & all night, & also all day yesterday, but with moderated violence.

At 4 P.M. a dismasted vessel was sighted. A furious squall had just broken upon us & the sea was running mountains high, to use the popular expression. Nevertheless Capt. Mouland immediately bore up for the wreck (which was making signals of distress), ordered out a life-boat & called for volunteers. To a landsman it seemed like deliberate suicide to go out in such a storm. But our third & fourth officers & eight men answered to the call with a promptness that compelled a cheer. Two of the men lost heart at the last moment, but the others stood fast & were started on their generous enterprise with another cheer. They carried a long line with them, several life buoys, & a lighted lantern, for the atmosphere was murky with the storm, & sunset was not far off.

The wreck, a barque, was in a pitiable condition. Her mainmast was naked, her mizen-mast & bowsprit were gone, & her foremast was but a stump, wreathed & cumbered with a ruin of sails & cordage from the fallen fore-top & fore-top gallant masts & yards. We could see nine men clinging to the rigging. The stern of the vessel was gone & the sea made a clean breach over her, pouring in a cataract out of the broken stern & spouting through the parted planks of her bow.

Our boat pulled 300 yards & approached the wreck on the lee side. Then it had a hard fight, for the waves

& the wind beat it constantly back. I do not know when anything has alternately so stirred me through & through & then disheartened me, as it did to see the boat every little while get *almost* close enough & then be hurled three lengths away again by a prodigious wave. And the darkness settling down all the time. But at last they got the line & buoy aboard, & after that we could make out nothing more.

But presently we discovered the boat approaching us, & found she had saved every soul – nine men. They had had to drag those men, one at a time, through the sea to the life-boat with the line & buoy – for of course they did not dare to touch the plunging vessel with the boat. The peril increased now, for every time the boat got close to our lee our ship rolled over on her & hid her from sight. But our people managed to haul the party aboard one at a time without losing a man, though I said they would lose every single one of them – I am therefore but a poor success as a prophet. As the fury of the squall had not diminished, & as the sea was so heavy it was feared we might lose some men if we tried to hoist the life-boat aboard, so she was turned adrift by the captain's order, poor thing, after helping in such a gallant deed. But we have plenty more boats, & very few passengers.

To speak by the log, & be accurate, Captain Mouland gave the order to change our ship's course & bear down toward the wreck at 4.15 P.M.; at 5.15 our ship was under way again with those nine poor devils on board. That is to say, this admirable thing was done in a tremendous sea & in the face of a hurricane, in sixty minutes by the watch, – & if your honourable society should be moved to give to Captain Mouland & his boat's crew that reward which a sailor prizes & covets above all other distinctions, the Royal Humane Society's medal, the parties whose names are signed to this paper [i.e. passengers on the Batavia] will feel as grateful as if they themselves were the recipients of this great honor.

Those who know him say that Captain Mouland has risked his life many times to rescue shipwrecked men – in the days when he occupied a subordinate position – & we hopefully trust that the seed sown then is about to ripen its harvest now.

Twain continued with the facts of the wrecked ship and her crew, including the revelation that eleven men – more than half the vessel's crew – were washed overboard and drowned in a single boarding by a sea that came over her as she was lying on her beam-ends (on her side), half-capsized, and the gallantry of the eight men who rescued the *Charles Ward*'s men:

If I have been of any service toward rescuing these nine ship-wrecked human beings by standing around the deck in a furious storm, without any umbrella [!], keeping an eye on things & seeing that they were done right, & yelling whenever a cheer seemed to be the important thing, I am glad, & I am satisfied. I ask no reward. I would do it again under the same circumstances. But what I *do* plead for, & earnestly & sincerely, is that the Royal Humane Society will remember our captain & our life-boat crew; &, in so remembering them, increase the high honor & esteem in which the society is held all over the civilized world.

In this appeal our passengers *all* join with hearty sincerity, & in testimony thereof will sign their names. Begging that you will pardon me, a stranger, for addressing your honored society with such confidence & such absence of sincerity, & trusting that my motive may redeem my manner,

I am, gentlemen, Your ob't [obedient] servant,

Mark Twain (Samuel L. Clemens), Hartford, Conn.

In a characteristically *Twain-ish* colourful rendition of the brave events he witnessed on the *Batavia* the previous November, the author painted a vivid picture of the rescue, in a letter to the editor of *The New York Tribune* of 27 January 1873:

The storm lasted two days with us; then subsided for a few brief hours; then burst forth again; and while the last effort was in full swing we came upon a dismasted vessel, the barque *Charles Ward*. She was nothing but a bursted and spouting hulk, surmounted with a chaos of broken spars and bits of fluttering rags – a sort of ruined flower-pot hung with last year's spider webs, so to speak. The vast seas swept over her, burying her from sight, and then she would rise again and spew volumes of water through cracks in her sides and bows, and discharge white floods through the gateway that was left where her stern had been.

Her captain and eight men were lashed in the remains of the main rigging. They were pretty well famished and frozen, for they had been there two nights and a part of two days of stormy winter weather.

Captain Mouland brought up broadside to wind and sea, and called for volunteers to man the life-boat. D. Gillies, third officer; H. Kyle, fourth officer, and six seamen answered instantly. It was worth any money to see that life-boat climb those dizzy mountains of water, in a driving mist of spume-flakes, and fight its way inch by inch in the teeth of the gale.

'After The Gale' (dismasted vessel). (*The Graphic*, 8 October 1892)

Just the mere memory of it stirs a body so, that I would swing my hat and disgorge a cheer now, if I could do it without waking the baby [his daughter Olivia Susan ('Susy') Clemens, born 19 March 1872]. But if you get a baby awake once you never can get it asleep again, and then you get into trouble with the whole family. Somehow I don't seem to have a chance to yell, now, the way I used to.

Well, in just one hour's time that life-boat crew had rescued those shipwrecked men; and during thirty minutes of the time, their own lives were not worth purchase at a sixpence, their peril was so great.

Twain then acknowledged that The Royal Humane Society had indeed honoured the *Batavia*'s Capt. Mouland with its gold medal ('and a vote of thanks'), her two officers, Gillies and Kyle, with the silver medal ('and a money reward suited to their official grade, and thanked them'), and '£7 gold' to each of the six volunteer seamen ('say somewhere about two months' wages') for their heroic rescue of the *Charles Ward*'s men.

The *Claverdon*: Five Men Washed from her Deck into the Sea

Losing a few men overboard during a sailing-ship voyage, by treacherous seas or a fall from aloft, was not an uncommon thing. Losing a whole crowd of men overboard at one time, however, was rare. But it did happen on the British full-rigged ship *Claverdon* during her voyage in 1902 from Hamburg round the Horn (or so it should have been) to San Francisco, when she lost five men in a single swipe of the sea.

Claverdon was launched in 1884 as the *Alexandra*, a big ship, at just over 2,500 tons. She was renamed *Claverdon* when her original owners, J. Coupland, of London, sold her in 1890 to F&A Nodin, of Liverpool. On her 1902 voyage she spent nineteen days battered by westerly gales off Cape Horn. Her master Capt. Robert Thomas determined they would be better off running eastwards to their destination by way of the Cape of Good Hope and across the Indian and Pacific Oceans. Her 218-day, 32,000-mile voyage from Hamburg to San Francisco that year was, for that reason, exceptionally long; the direct Cape Horn route of about 17,000 miles (half the distance) should have taken anything from 100 to 150 days. The *San Francisco Call* newspaper reported on the *Claverdon*'s voyage as follows:

Ship Claverdon *Arrives in Port – Five Men Are Washed
From Her Deck into the Sea – Nearly Complete Circuit of Globe
During Her Voyage*

The ship *Claverdon* arrived in port yesterday at noon,
after an eventful voyage from Hamburg, which took
218 days to complete. The *Claverdon* left Hamburg on
February 22 with a crew of 30 men and carrying a cargo
of 3,600 tons of cement. She was bound for this port by
way of the Horn, but owing to a wind and heavy rain
storm, during which five men were washed overboard
and lost, and many of the sails carried away, she was
unable to round the Horn, and was forced to complete
her voyage by way of the Cape of Good Hope, in this way
covering 32,000 miles.

First Mate H.T. Reede, in telling of the voyage, said:

'We left Hamburg on February 22 with Captain Robert
Thomas in command, myself, Edward Akeman, second
mate, and thirty German sailors. We experienced strong
winds while in the Channel, and a steady blow during our
trip to the Horn. Round the Horn we ran head on into
a terrific windstorm, in which we were beaten about for
nineteen days, unable to make headway.

'On August 29 we found ourselves in the center of the
storm, which was blowing from the northwest. The sea
was running high and pounding us from all directions.
A drizzling rain was falling before the gale. Suddenly the
heart of the storm struck us. The fore topsail broke away;
then the main topsail, main topgallant sail, mizzen topsail
and the mainsail went. The sea swept over the ship, carrying five seamen with it. Those that were not carried
overboard were thrown violently to the deck and some
received serious injuries.

'When the sail blew away, the watch sang out, "Sail overboard!" Then came the sea over the rails, carrying two water casks, a hand rail, a poop ladder, and everything that was loose about the deck. After the first big wave had subsided, the watch sang out, "Men overboard!" and we could see the unfortunate sailors swimming in the sea, but it was impossible to assist them. I asked the men if they would take out a boat to try to save the others, but they said they would not. The five men lost were C. Neilson, G. Guppenberg, Charles Jesterkorn, T.H. Ryelt and August Firks.

'We were nineteen days in the storm and were forced to put back and make this port by way of the Cape of Good Hope, covering a distance of 32,000 miles in 218 days. Our supply of food just held out and no more. The cargo is damaged considerably, but just how much is not yet known. That was the worst gale that I was ever in, and I do not care to be in another like it. The ship behaved very well and is not damaged from the effects of the storm.' (*San Francisco Call*, 29 September 1902)

First Mate Reede recalled, correctly, that the men were swept overboard on 29 August, but incorrectly that it was while in the storm around the Horn that battered the *Claverdon*. Captain Thomas recorded in the ship's log, correctly, that the five men went overboard in a storm 'on Aug 29, lat. 12 N, long. 123 W'. This was just north of the equator in the eastern Pacific, over six months out from Hamburg and about a month before reaching San Francisco; the *Claverdon* had by then long since abandoned the fury of the Horn and gone about via the Cape of Good Hope towards her destination:

Président Félix Faure Loses Fifteen Men in Indian Ocean Cyclone

One vessel that lost even more men – and boys – overboard in a single lash of the sea's whip was the French barque *Président Félix Faure*, in 1898, on a voyage from South Wales to Adelaide, South Australia. In fact, she lost more than a whole watch-load of crew, quite likely unprecedented in the annals of deep-sea sailing ships:

Terrible Disaster at Sea – Fifteen Sailors Swept Overboard

It is not an infrequent occurrence for one hand to be lost from a vessel during a voyage from one side of the world to the other; but on her arrival on Monday at Port Adelaide the French barque *President Felix Faure* reported the loss of 15 men at one fell swoop. It appears that the voyage had passed without incident until February 2, when she was in [lat.] 43 deg. 10 min. south, and [long.] 67 deg. east, and was running before a strong westerly gale and heavy sea. At 3.30 p.m. a sea broke on board from each side, completely filling the decks, and for a time the vessel was staggering under the weight of the water, which caused a considerable list to port.

After a time the water cleared away, but it was found that the following members of the crew had been washed off:– Jean M. Caradec, August Le Goasduff, Ives Marie Crefell, R.A.G. Sonnett, P. Marie Palodec, Matthieu Pepperder, Jean C. Scournec, Eugene Domaldin, Francis M. Lennandais, F. Marie Marshand, Jean M. Kerboat, Louis M. Andre, and Jean M. Robert.

The suddenness of the catastrophe, together with the fact that the vessel was running before a heavy sea, prevented the lowering of a boat, even if it were possible or prudent to bring the vessel into the wind, and consequently the course was kept, and the vessel continued her trip, but with the loss of 12 able seamen, the second mate, and two apprentices.

The Faure

The vessel was built in Havre in 1896, and is a fine specimen of the French four-master. Her solid iron bulwarks are so high that a medium-sized man can just look over them comfortably, and it is evident that when a big sea was shipped it would find no speedy exit, and would run about the deck like water in a bath. Looking at her to-day, with all her yards and rigging in place and her deck gear in good order, it was hard to realise what a pandemonium she must have been on the 2nd of last February, when 15 of her crew were in an instant swept into a raging sea, and lost from sight. When asked how the calamity occurred, her master, Captain Felix Smart Frossard readily narrated all he knew.

The captain, who is fair of face, small of stature, and courteous in the extreme, had received the reporter with a sad smile of welcome, but his brow was clouded with care, for naturally he has been greatly upset by the event.

Swept By the Sea

'It was about half-past 3 in the afternoon,' he said, 'that the accident took place. All hands were on the deck, and the barque was bowling along at the rate of over a dozen knots an hour. Suddenly a sea broke on board from each side, and the vessel staggered under the shock. It took some time for the water to run off, and it was not until the deck was nearly cleared that we discovered that any of the men had disappeared, yet 15 were lost. We had not, when the water was swirling on deck, noticed them go overboard, and by the time we realised what had happened the ship must have been ten miles further on.

'When we looked astern there were, of course, no traces of those who had gone; but even if it had been of any use, and there had been any chance by going back of saving life, it would have been utterly impossible in such a gale of wind and in such a heavy sea for the vessel to round to [into the wind and stop]. All we could do was to continue on our course. We were going with a north-west wind, and there were billows running high from the south-west, which explains how the sea broke in on both sides. It took us till half-past five to get the deck ship-shape. During the voyage the water had broken on board before, but we had never had so much on deck as that.

'We had to continue our voyage with really only nine men, and had a very trying time before we got here. Two of the men who were swept about in the swirling water had a very narrow escape, and they attribute their preservation to the fact that they fought themselves free of their companions, who had grabbed at one another when the seas rushed on board. One was found in the mizzen rigging and the other on the deckhouse aft. All the victims of the disaster were young, the oldest being 34 and the youngest the cabin boy, Andre, only 16. They were all unmarried. France draws her supply of sailors almost entirely from the coast of Brittany and the shores of the Mediterranean, and 12 of the lost sailors were Bretons. Two were born in Paris, and one hailed from the south of France.' (*Poverty Bay Herald*, 16 March 1898)

Le *Président Félix-Faure* pendant un cyclone dans l'océan Indien. (*L'Illustration*, 12 March 1898)

With just nine men left to work the ship, the number lost overboard was more than an entire watch. The single loss of that many men at one time was 'one of the worst crew losses at sea known even in the Cape Horn trade' (from *The Bounty Ships of France*, by Alan Villiers and Henri Picard). The *Faure* arrived at Adelaide at the end of February 1898, two weeks after the catastrophe, a creditable 131 days passage considering how short-handed she was rendered by a single swipe of the sea's claws.

A Miraculous Resurrection

In August 1874 a young American midshipman, Harry P. De Vol, just graduated from the United States Naval School (Academy) at Annapolis, Maryland, was ordered to report for shipboard duty on the US Navy frigate *Omaha*, then at Nice, in the Mediterranean. By late September that year the *Omaha* was sailing somewhere in the Irish Sea when a violent squall struck the vessel. Midshipman De Vol was washed overboard by 'a huge sea [that] came over the side'. An officer tossed him a cork lifebuoy to do 'the little he could to save him', but his only chance of rescue, as he knew, was to be picked up by another vessel; good seamanship dictated that his own ship would never be put about to look for him 'in the violent wind and sea that were raging' at the time. He was given up for dead, presumed drowned; obituaries were published in the newspapers to that effect. The notices, however, proved premature:

Saved from the Sea – Exciting Adventure of a Young Midshipman, Lost Overboard from the Frigate Omaha

That the sea should give up its dead seems hardly a greater miracle than that in some cases it should give up its victims alive. Stories of escape from angry waves upon desolate coasts have filled chapter after chapter of works of fiction, and the power and immensity of the ocean have made it the chosen symbol of the cruelty and relentlessness of fate.

One would scarcely expect, after the exhaustion of the imagination of writers like Captain Marryat and Victor Hugo, that it was reserved for plain matter of fact to outrival the invention of the novelist; and yet there is at present stopping at the Fifth Avenue Hotel in this city a young man whose adventures and escapes pass to the very verge of the marvellous. Like so many other instances of human peril, it seems to have proved itself with its own setting of romance.

Captain De Vol père

In 1854 the gates of the Far East were first opened to Western commerce. The first vessel that ever entered a Chinese port was the *Seabird*. She was commanded by an Ohioan named P.H. De Vol. Originally of French descent, he was himself thoroughly an American in physique, nervous energy, love of adventure, and self-reliance in the moment of danger. In stature he was six and one-half feet. He had left in his home, in what was then the far West, a young wife and a boy about one year old. His own exploits in the Orient had added not a little to the credit of his countrymen in that part of the globe. Inasmuch as they relate only indirectly to the matter in hand, they should be rapidly sketched.

Attracting the attention of the then King of Siam, he was placed in command of an expedition, his son relates, against the Japanese pirates that infested the coast, and in reward for several decisive victories he was made the recipient of distinguished marks of royal favor, among them being the gift of a white elephant. Not long afterward he conducted another expedition against the pirates, and this time drove them out of Siamese waters. He was again encumbered with a gift of the same kind, and – what he deemed of much greater value – a privilege to enter the mountain region of Siam to mine for gold. On his way thither, however, he died of a jungle fever.

Midshipman De Vols fils

His strange fortunes in the East had their effect on his son. Nothing but a life of adventure would satisfy his boyish spirit, and at the earliest age possible his mother, by the aid of family friends, secured him an appointment at the United States Naval School at Annapolis. He graduated with honor, and last August, after a brief vacation, he was ordered to report for duty at Queenstown [Ireland]. Upon his arrival there he was ordered to report to Nice, where the American squadron in European waters was then lying. At Nice he was ordered on board the frigate *Omaha*, which was transferred to Queenstown.

Calamity

About the 20th of September, while less than two days' sail from Southampton, a violent squall arose, and during its continuance young De Vol was directed by the Captain to convey an order to the officer stationed on the bridge. As he was going forward a huge sea came over the side, and the frigate, with its monstrous burden, lurched heavily to leeward. The taffrail was low, and being between masts, the young midshipman was whirled with the wash over the side. The officer on the bridge saw him, and did the little he could to save him.

He seized a large circular cork life-buoy and hurled it with all his might toward the point where the young sailor was seen struggling with the waves. It was the work of scarcely more than a second. To the buoy was fixed a line of about ten yards long, and as the buoy passed over him beyond his reach, the line fell across his back. He caught the end, and while the staggering vessel drove helplessly on in the storm, he drew the buoy to him and placed it over his head. He was now safe for the moment, but he says death itself would have been a pleasing sensation compared to his feelings as he saw the *Omaha* disappear behind successive hills of angry water.

His knowledge of seamanship told him at once that no Captain would dare to put his vessel about, or attempt to lower a boat in the violent wind and sea that were raging.

'In a little while,' he relates, 'I could only see the masts and cordage [rigging] whipping against the sky, and I gave up all hope. I tried to swim toward them instinctively, though I knew it was of no use, and that my only hope was to outride the squall on my buoy, if possible, and be picked up after floating a few hours.'

The violence of the storm did not last, as he estimates, but two or three hours, although it seemed days to him, but no vessels came near enough to discover him. The water, stirred from beneath by the wind, was cold, and he began to grow numb and weak. Fortunately, the cork life-preserver, which at first was so loose that he had some difficulty in keeping it in its place under his arms, began to tighten as the cork swelled with the moisture. Subsequently it held itself well in place. It was about four o'clock when he was washed overboard. At nightfall he had grown quite weak, and his limbs were very numb.

Darkness

'As the darkness began to gather,' he narrates, 'I felt that I would have to drown. Before this I knew that my chances were desperate, but, somehow, while it was light I had hope. Then I began to pray. I don't know how long a time elapsed. At times I would pray for several minutes, and then I would find myself thinking of a thousand things about my home, and my mother, and my father, and about my past life. It seemed as if all the good things and bad things I had ever done or thought of came back to me. Occasionally I would start up as if from a revery, and strike out to swim. At such times the water and sky would look so black and pitiless that it would seem to fairly frighten me, and I would be forced to shut my eyes.

Mann über Bord!

'I can't tell how long I suffered in this way, but it seemed ages. Then, indistinctly, I remember another sensation: my limbs were numb and utterly without strength, but a pleasant, listless, dreamy sort of feeling took possession of me. My sides, which had been chafed by the movements of the life-preserver, ceased to pain me. I cannot say I was happy, or that I was entirely unconscious of my position, but I didn't seem to care. This state of dim consciousness was the last that I remember.'

Resurrection

At sunrise the next morning he was found by the United States merchant steamer *Indiana* floating in the water insensible. A great deal of salt water was found in his stomach; but he was still alive, and after careful medical treatment he was completely restored. He arrived in New York a few days ago.

On the 30th of September his mother, then stopping in Lancaster, Ohio, received a despatch from the commander of the *Omaha*, announcing the death of her son, who, it was stated, had been washed overboard in the Irish Sea. The despatch was published, and was made the occasion of many obituary notices in Ohio papers. The joy of his mother, who happened to be in this city, upon receiving the news that her son had arisen from the dead, need not be dwelt upon.

Mr. Harry P. De Vol is looking well after his exhausting adventure and almost miraculous escape. Upon one thing he is to be certainly congratulated. He has read several of his obituary notices, and confesses that he is very well satisfied with them. (*Daily Alta California*, 9 November 1874)

THE END

Also in this series

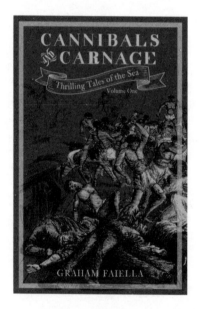

978 0 7509 9084 4